Only one man had been drinking at the bar, but as soon as that coach gun made an appearance, he downed his coffin varnish and went quickly for the back of the room, where the rest of the Blind Stud's customers were gathered. There was a card game going at one of the tables, and a few scattered inebriates besides, but nobody said a word and all eyes were on the bartender and me. I might have liked to have said this was new territory for the likes of me, but even I couldn't tell a lie that big. This was just life in a white man's world, only I never developed the kind of temperament that could accept it. I didn't really think I could change it, but I was going to go to my grave fighting it every step of the way, come hell or high water. And hungry as I was that night in Horseblood, Montana, trail weary and cold, I was for sure and for certain in a fighting mood.

HORSEBLOOD

FRONTIER AND
WEIRD WESTERN
STORIES

BY ED KURTZ

Copyright Information

CONTENTS

FRONTIER STORIES

WEIRD WESTERNS

INTRODUCTION

If this is your first opportunity to read Ed's work, I envy you. If you're returning to his work, you already know you're in for a treat.

I first became aware of Ed's talent back in 2012 when we were both featured in the third edition of the now defunct crime anthology *Thuglit*. Ed's story was called "In the Neighborhood" and it gave the reader a glimpse of the great work to come. First-person narration, such as what we have in that story, can be risky. Readers and editors tend to prefer the third person, especially those who read crime and thrillers. I suppose that's because there's always the possibility that too much of the author's personality might bleed into the story. Authors such as Chandler and Macdonald pulled it off nicely, so why shouldn't the rest of us give it a try?

Ed quickly puts any concerns of risk aside and crafts a shabby-chic narrative that pulls the reader in before they realize he's done it. His bold, dynamic storytelling was evident in this piece and, fortunately for us, it was only the beginning. He's one of those few writers who has mastered the art of both long fiction and short stories. He always finds a way to strike the stylistic balance that always serves the story and the characters first. He has a distinctive style that's present in all his work but is constantly adapted based on the tone of the tale he's telling at that particular time.

Even a cursory examination of his writing career shows a willingness to take on a variety of genres and a fearlessness about turning them on their head. Movie tie-ins (*The Ranger*), short stories (too many to list here without being obnoxious) or horror (*The Rib from Which I Remake the World*), he remains loyal to a pulpy style without allowing it to overshadow some fantastic storytelling.

He also hasn't allowed a petty thing like genre get in the way of a good story. In 2019, he decided to take on the daunting task of putting his own spin on the most American of American genres: the Western.

It's a daunting task because Westerns can not only be tricky to write, but dangerous for one's career. Stick too much to the 1950s style of storytelling and people are unlikely to read your book or watch your movie. But deviate too much from the expected norm and you risk losing the audience entirely. If a Western is deemed revisionist or too "artsy," the audience tends to stay away. Fiction history is littered with the blanched carcasses of novelists and film makers who've strayed too far from that delicate middle ground.

Westerns are also tough to write because so much of what we believe to be true is a lie. It wasn't this white-washed frontier paradise where good always wins, evil is evident and the sheriff always gets his man by the end of the episode. It was an era of complex, tough and determined people who endured a lot of suffering to build a new life for themselves and their family.

It's that complexity that Ed explores in his fantastic Western *A Wind of Knives*. The story is about "a quiet rancher in Civil War-era Texas who find his sole ranch hand and lover has been lynched, hanged by party or parties unknown. Left with nothing but his failing ranch, Daniel Hays takes it upon himself to seek out those responsible for his lover's death, experiencing puzzling new relationships along the way, including repeat encounters with a ghostly coyote that leads him to the final stop of his odyssey for revenge."

It's the kind of book that should be destined to fail and, in the hands of a lesser writer, would have failed. It seems like Ed as trying to do too many things at once. A revenge tale wrapped up in an odyssey with a coyote ghost? Oh, and the protagonist is out to avenge his male lover. That's quite a bit to take in for one novel and I'll admit I was skeptical.

But when Ed asked me to read *Knives* and to provide a blurb for the cover, I decided to take a chance. After all, it was an Ed

Kurtz book. How bad could it be? The book not only exceeded my expectations. It floored me. It manages to be revisionist while reading like a traditional Western. It not only upends expectations for that kind of book but sets its own rules along the way. Ed didn't just take an existing Western, make the characters lovers and send it out into the world. In this case, the story could not function any other way than how it was written and that is especially difficult to do in an established genre, much less do it well.

If Ed had decided to pack up his typewriter and go home after a triumph such as *Knives,* I couldn't have blamed him. But he's not that kind of writer and soon came back with a trilogy that proves his mettle. *Boon, Vengeance of Boon,* and *A Requiem for Boon* proves that a good story is a good story no matter the genre. These books span the life of Boonsri Angchuan and her companions as she rights wrongs along the vengeance trail. The result is a trilogy that no Western fan—or reader of fiction—should miss.

If you've read this far, you might be wondering why I wrote such a long introduction for a book of short stories. It's because we're not just talking about a few stories compiled to make an anthology. We're talking about the culmination of a writer's journey through a very complex and difficult genre to master. It's important for you, the reader, to understand Ed's choice of stories isn't by chance or just to be different from other Western writers working today. It's not a gimmick or a hook. Instead, it's an organic evolution of a writer who has put in the work and earned the right to tell his own kind of tales his own way.

With *Horseblood,* we see the full spectrum of Ed's talent on parade. Traditionalists will enjoy the first five stories called the Frontier Stories. Those of us who have read the *Boon* novels will enjoy a visit from the familiar Edward Splettstoesser and Boon herself. Those who prefer their Westerns with a healthy dash of the supernatural and unexplainable will enjoy the Weird Westerns section that encompasses the last five stories of the book.

Some of these stories have been published elsewhere. One was published in 2013 before A Wind of Knives hit the market. All of them show a writer at the top of his game and is only getting better. Enjoy!

Terrence McCauley

FRONTIER STORIES

DIG YOUR OWN GRAVE MY FRIEND—SPLETTSTOESSER IS COMING

A BOON STORY

1876

First time I laid eyes on Carlo and Mario, I had them figured for brothers. They didn't look much alike, but they were both jabbering in a language I couldn't make heads or tails of and they were whaling on one another with a practiced fury that put me in mind of kin. The language, I came to learn, was Italian—which was a mite like Spanish, if Spanish was French—and the two fellers talking it weren't blood at all, just fellow travelers from a faraway land. Most of my friends in those days seemed to come from someplace other than America for one reason or another, though I couldn't plainly say Carlo and Mario ever considered me a true friend, or me them. Then again, those two fools could bruise and batter one another like the sorest enemies this side of Hamilton and Burr, and to hear them tell it they were *migliori amici*, which I took to mean something like the best of pals.

Mario Girotti was as handsome a man as I ever saw, with sandy-blond hair, a square jaw like granite, and cornflower-blue eyes that sparkled when he smiled, which was most of the time. His buddy, Carlo Pedersoli, could hardly have been more different—he stood a head and a half taller than Mario, bald on top with great tufts of curly, dark hair poking out on either side, and a black beard near as long as mine. Mario was thin and cheerful, Carlo fat and peevish. And the first time I saw them, Mario was in the process of smashing a chair into splinters against the top of Carlo's head, and he was laughing like a madman while he did it.

I got to Striker's Gulch about six months after a drifter name of Shorty Lazar credited his mule with finding color in a stream it was drinking from, kicking up a gold rush in miniature and transforming an oft-avoided ravine into a teeming tent city of hopeful miners. Striker was the mule's name, or leastways it was after her owner struck it rich in that stream. Didn't make me no never mind, on account of I never came there for the diggings, anyhow. Point of fact, I wasn't anything better than a drifter my own self in those hungry days, and I was just following my nose to find some vittles and liquor. And after the gold itself, hooch and food was the foremost concern in any mining camp, no matter the size or type of ore. Seemed to me Striker's Gulch would provide, and I wasn't wrong.

Place I found had a sign staked into the mud out front that named it Ace of Diamonds, next to which was a hitching rail where a pair of bone-weary asses were having themselves a pissing contest that streamed right up to the tent saloon's front flaps. I hitched up next to them, stepped over the stream, and went inside for my supper and sauce.

The only meal on the menu was goat stew with onions, and the only spirits corn liquor they brewed in a still on the other side of the hills, in case the whole operation went up in flames, I supposed. I planted myself on a chair in front of a table made out of a flour barrel and raised two fingers to indicate I wanted one of each, stew and drink. The barman nodded that he understood, and three seconds after that, Mario smashed that chair overtop old Carlo's skull.

"*Stronzo stupido!*" Carlo bellowed.

Mario cackled, but his mirth was cut short when the barman, interrupted from his task of fetching my vittles, spun the

Italian around and clocked him on the chin. The handsome feller went down in a heap, and I reckoned that would be the end of it, but not so—Carlo roared and smashed one of his ham-sized fists down on the crown of the barman's head, laying him out flat.

Someone hollered, "Son of a bitch!" I craned my neck to see who it was, and another man was careening out from behind the bar, a bung starter in hand with an obvious intent to brain the big man with it. Carlo saw him coming, and as soon as the man raised that bung starter over his head, Carlo delivered an open-handed slap across the man's left cheek followed imme-diately by a second hard slap on the right. The barman's buddy dropped his weapon, his face red as a radish, and sat down on the floor, stunned.

Mario stood back up, rubbing his jaw, and grinned like he was having the best time of his life. He turned back to Carlo, punched him in the arm, and with a pronounced accent, he said, "Thanks, partner."

Carlo grunted in reply, then grabbed the nearest glass and drained it in one gulp. It wasn't even his drink.

I decided I liked these fellers, but there was one glaring problem, which presently I explained to them.

"That was some show, friends," I said, "but who's gonna feed me my supper now?"

"What, that slop?" said Mario, jabbing a thumb at one of the bowls at another man's barrel-table. "It's not fit for dogs to eat."

"*Probabilmente è fatto di cani*," Carlo said.

Mario laughed. "He says it's probably made from dogs."

"Jasper he knocked out said it was goat stew," I said.

"You seen any goats around this place?" Mario asked me.

He had a point. In fact, I hadn't seen a single goat, but there were plenty of stray mutts roaming all over Striker's Gulch. Of a sudden, I wasn't half as hungry anymore. I heard tell Apaches had a taste for dog meat, which was fine for them, but I chose to abstain. Hell, I'd heard the Tonkawa and Karankawa in Texas used to eat their enemies, but that sure as shit didn't mean I was going to start gnawing on every jasper done me wrong. I wasn't a picky eater, but a man needed some boundaries.

"There another drinkery in this camp?" I said.

"Two," Mario answered. "But they are even worser than this one. Come with us, we have beans and wine at our stake."

"You two have a stake together?" I was more than a little surprised, given how the first I'd seen of them, one of these men was walloping the other.

"Are you kidding?" Mario said. "We are practically brothers."

Carlo made a face and shrugged. *"Fagioli e vino."*

"Si Fratello. Vino e fagioli," Mario said, slapping Carlo on the back. "Even the angels eat beans, no?"

I didn't have any kind of clue what that was supposed to mean, but beans and wine sounded a right smart better than dog stew and shine—or nothing at all—so I followed those Italian boys right through the heart of Striker's Gulch, out of the tent city, and into the hills.

Along the way, we made our introductions, and Mario explained how it was two boys from a port town called Napolly or somesuch ended up digging holes alongside a stream with shovels, pickaxes, and a powerful shit load of optimism. Turns out it wasn't the yellow metal they were after, leastways not at the start; ol' Mario Girotti just happened to put a girl in the family way and listened to his buddy Carlo when the bigger man recommended they skedaddle for America. I didn't think it was the nicest thing I ever heard, but there were plenty of unkind doings in my own past, even if running out on a gal in foal wasn't one of them. In any event, they landed in New York City but got themselves all starry-eyed hearing stories about gold strikes and tramped their way west. Now there they were, hunched over tin plates around a pitiful camp fire, sucking down baked beans without the benefit of forks or spoons like there wasn't anything better in all the world.

Mario explained, "We never ate like this in Italy." I couldn't rightly determine if that was good or bad. To my palate, those beans were fair to middling, though the wine was mighty tasty. I said as much, and Mario responded by refilling everyone's cups to the brim. After that, he pronounced that Saint Gennaro his own self had brought us three together—two Italians and the son of German immigrants called Splettstoesser—on account of something called the *triplice alleanza* betwixt Germany and Italy and Austria-Hungary. Yet again, I was left in the lurch when it came to understanding what in the blue hell he was talking about, but I just nodded, agreed, and held out my cup for more wine.

"*Saluti*," Carlo said.

"*Prost*," I said.

And if Mario had anything to add, he was interrupted by the report of a rifle from the ponderosa pines east of the stream. The bullet struck the ground, not two feet from the toe of Carlo's right boot, and all three of us went scrambling for cover. It wasn't at all unusual to hear gunfire any time of the day or night around a booming mining camp, but it was clear as white rum that this gun was aiming for one of us—or all of us.

"Maybe it's them Austria-Hungarians," I suggested from behind a copse of boxwoods, "sore we didn't invite 'em for a snort."

"No," Mario said, laid out flat in the canebrakes along the streambank. "They are Americans."

"How can you tell?"

"Because Mack Ireland and Spanish George Armbruster are the only men who would shoot guns at us, Edward," he said, "and they are Americans."

"You coulda fooled me," I said. "Sound like an Irishman and a Spaniard."

"*Parli come un crucco*," Carlo said. I couldn't see where he'd gone, but he was close.

"He says you sound like a pighead," Mario translated. "He means German."

"I come from Arkansas," I explained.

"Arkansas *crucco*, then."

I said, "I guess," and there came two more shots from pines. Ireland and Armbruster, if that's who it was, fired at the same time, but they hadn't come any closer to killing anybody. It was going on dark and we were all three of us hid pretty good, Carlo most like the best, since even I didn't know where the hell he was.

"I know you eye-talian sons of whores is still down there," one of the shooters hollered. "You ain't getting out alive this time."

"God damn," I said. "Them boys is for certain aiming to kill you. What the hell for?"

"Still mad about a little fight in a bar back in Nebraska," Mario said.

"Christ, but you fellers like to brawl."

"Oh, they started it," he assured me. "Only Carlo hit one of them a little too hard, and now he's a little mixed up in the head. Those men out there? They're still mad about it."

"I 'spect this ain't your first run-in with them since then."

"No," Mario admitted. "They tried to kill us in Ogallala, too."

"You figure they'd quit hunting you after that?"

Mario tried to shrug laying flat, but it didn't really work, so he just grinned at me.

"Come on out and take your medicine," the other man shouted. "Dan can only eat soup now, you know that? And he babbles like a baby. You got to pay for that, and that's just the way it be!"

"They started it," Mario said.

"*Ma' va te ne a fanculo*," Carlo bellowed.

Mario didn't translate, but I figured it wasn't very nice, whatever he said. In any event, I didn't figure these fellers was like to forgive and forget any time soon, no matter who started the scuffle, which left the three of us with two choices—fight or run. And running would only delay the inevitable, which to my way of thinking left only one real option, and that was to stand our ground and fight.

"What you got for guns?" I asked Mario.

"Spencer rifle back at the camp," he said. When we'd scattered, no one thought to grab the carbine.

I had me a Colt Paterson on my person, but I didn't think I could send a ball as far as those two jaspers were. Still, they might not have known that, so I said, "Gonna cover you, so get your ass to yonder Spencer when I start to shooting."

Mario said, "You got it, partner," but he started back to the camp before I even drew the revolver. One of the boys on the ridge cracked off a shot at him, the round striking the dirt mere inches from his heel, and I yanked my Colt Paterson free to start triggering off balls at them. That put a stop to their fire, and it gave Mario the time and relative safety he needed to reach that repeater. It was a good thing he was as fast as he was, too, because I fired my pistol empty about the same time he got that long gun in his hands by the fire. I lit a shuck over to where he stood by the fire, and Mario levered a cartridge into the breech before taking careful aim at something I couldn't see and firing at it.

One of the men on the ridge cried out, "God damn it, I am killed."

"Ireland," Mario said, and he jacked a fresh round into the breech. "Now Armbruster."

Armbruster roared like a mean old bear and came sprinting down the rise and out of the gloom, firing his Henry rifle indiscriminately as he screamed. One round flew high over our heads, while another splashed into the stream far to the left of us. Mario drew a bead on him, the barrel rising and falling as he got used to the pattern of Armbruster's movement, and then he shot the man right between the eyes. The man's head drooped, his eyes wide and glassy like marbles, but his legs kept pumping for a few more strides before they kicked out from underneath him and he collapsed into a pile of limbs in the shortgrass.

"Hot damn, son," I said, "that was some shooting."

"Shame I had to do that," Mario said, shaking his head sadly.

Behind him, Carlo emerged from the gathering dark and went calmly to the same spot he'd occupied before, where he sat his great bulk down and dug back into his bean supper like nothing at all had happened.

"There's a man loves him some beans," I said.

"Shame I had to do that," Mario said again. He laid the Spencer back down and crouched across the fire from Carlo, his face in his hands.

I said to Carlo, "What's stuck in his craw?"

Carlo shrugged and shoveled another spoonful of beans into his mouth. I didn't know if that meant he didn't understand what I'd said, or if he was just too invested in his beans to care.

Later, when there were no more beans or wine, I helped the men collect the bodies of Ireland and Armbruster, and with one shovel between the three of us, we all took turns digging a fresh hole in a vale that was full of holes, only this one was for putting in instead of taking out. We buried the Kansans, packed the dirt back down on top of them, and added their rifles to Mario's Spencer by the campfire. Carlo was snoring almost as soon as he was prone on the ground, but Mario stayed awake, sipping hot coffee from a pewter cup and staring blindly at the dying embers.

"First killing?" I said.

"No," he said, shaking his head. "No. First time I killed a marshal's son, though."

"Marshal's son," I said, surprised. "Which one?"

"Ireland," said Mario. "Been anybody else, just some nobody like us, we would not have let them chase us so long. But him I did not want to kill. He forced my hand, Edward. He left me no choice, but the law will not see it that way."

"Damn," I said. "Maybe it's done. Seemed a real hard case to me, that boy. Could be his daddy knows it, and the business is done now."

"Not a chance. Remember the man Carlo hit back in Nebraska?"

"Sure, Dan who can only eat soup now."

"Dan Ireland," he said. "That same marshal's other son."

"Double damn," I said. "What're you gonna do now?"

"Run. There's no gold left in the gulch, anyhow."

I knew about running, and I knew about lawmen who didn't give up even when they were in the wrong. It wasn't any kind of life I'd recommend, but it looked plain to me that Mario and Carlo were already in that particular fraternity with me. And near as I could tell, there wasn't any getting back out of it once a man was initiated. These boys were outlaws, now.

In the morning, I expected to wake up alone, but to my

surprise the Italians were still there, packing up their possibles along with the two newly acquired rifles. I helped myself to the tepid remains of the morning's coffee in the pot, and Carlo dumped the dregs. He packed that, too, without bothering to rinse it out in the stream. Seeing he was in an all-fired hurry to light a shuck out of Striker's Gulch, I gulped the coffee down and tossed him the cup.

"*Grazie,*" he said.

"Where next for y'all?" I asked.

"Who can say?" Mario answered. "We maybe let San Gennaro decide for us. And maybe our brother Edward will say a prayer for us, no?"

"Not really a praying man, friend."

He smiled, his cornflower eyes sparkling in the morning light. "Then a prayer from you will carry even greater weight, *amico.*"

"I see what you mean," I said.

And when I made camp that night, some twenty-five or thirty miles to the south of that dried up old mining camp, I sure enough did say a prayer for Mario and Carlo. I asked that mean old man upstairs to do right by somebody for once and let those boys off the hook. I told him I was a Doubting Thomas at best, an out-and-out heretic at worst, so my even bringing a thing like this to him at all had to be worth something. It was the first time I prayed in a passel of years, and the last time I ever would. Of course, when everything was said and done, it didn't do one damn lick of good—but I didn't know that for sure and for certain for another five years gone.

1881

"Well, I'll be go to hell," I croaked, my throat caked with trail dust and hands gone to shaking from too long spent sober. I had located a lonesome adobe saloon in a sand-blown desert town much the same way a divining rod finds water and I walked into the place with a powerful thirst. The town called itself Little Miracle and the cantina was ingeniously named Cantina. The sparse crowd inside was mostly comprised of Mexicans in wide-brimmed sombreros, strangers to me, but two faces at the bar stuck out to me like a pair of sore thumbs. "Mario and Carlo."

Carlo hissed at me to be quiet. Mario chuckled affably and patted the barstool to his left.

"You must be mistaken, friend," he said with a wink. "Our names are Denver Dave Hill—" He indicated himself. "—and Big Bill Spencer." He pointed a thumb at Carlo, who was even bigger than the last time I saw him.

"God damn, but you're right," I said, taking the stool. "Too much sun in my eyes in this godawful place and I can't hardly see a man's face right. I'm Edward Splettstoesser, and I reckon I'll buy you boys a round by way of apology."

The bartender responded by way of setting up three almost clean glasses and pouring a few inches of Taos Lightning into each of them. We toasted—*saluti, prost*—and slammed down our drinks at the same time. With that pleasant warmth in our bellies and burn in our throats, and I said, "So, what is it brings you boys to the desert?"

"Silver!" Mario replied. "The hills around here are lousy with deposits, I can feel it."

"Lord loves a drunk and an optimist," I said, and I signaled the barman for another round. It'd been some time since I enjoyed the company of friends like that, so I was feeling generous. Generous and still thirsty.

The second round went down smoother than the first, and then so did the conversation. In a quiet voice, I asked Mario whatever happened with that marshal they'd been worrying about all those years back, but I regretted broaching the subject when I watched all the mirth drain out of his face.

"Still we run, Edward," he said. "Still we hide."

"Seen him?"

"Twice. Once in Leavenworth, Kansas. That was about a year after Striker's Gulch. Then in seventy-nine, in Virginia City, Nevada. That time he saw us, too. There was some shooting, but we got away."

"Why don't you hie on out of the country?" I wondered aloud. "Try old Mexico? Hell, your Italian can't be all that different from the Spanish they talk down there."

"*La prossima volta sarà l'ultima volta,*" Carlo said.

"He says the next time must be the last," Mario said. "Truth is, I thought about Mexico, myself. But Car—*Bill* is right. A man cannot run forever."

"Been two years," I said. "Might could be Ireland done gave it up by now. Might could be he died."

"Ireland is not dead," Mario said with a bitter laugh. "He is here, in Little Miracle. This time, *we* followed *him.*"

I pert near choked on my second whiskey when I heard that. If it had been anything other than whiskey, I just might have. Instead, I threw the forty-rod back, savored the burn for a second or two, and then said, "Now, why on God's Jesus-green earth would you do something like that?"

Seemed like an instance of the fox chasing the hound, but I wasn't one to tell a man how to go about his business. I reckoned these fellers had grown so tired of looking over their shoulders that they figured on just turning themselves in. Course, that meant hanging for sure, which mayhap they didn't quite understand. For all I knew, they didn't hang killers in Italy, though I supposed they must do. Wasn't nothing but people anyplace you went, and people were either killers or they killed killers.

But before I could warn them about the ropes in their immediate future, Mario said, "Either Marshal Ireland listens to reason, or he listens to our guns." He sounded powerfully sad when he said it.

"I can appreciate that," I said, "but don't you 'spect killing a United States Marshal'll just put more law dogs on your back trail?"

"*Cos'altro possiamo fare?*" Carlo said, staring straight ahead at his own reflection in the mirror behind the bar.

Mario said, "He says what else can we do?"

"Well," I drawled, lengthening the word to an unnatural sound while I tried to talk myself out of what I was about to say. "Could be maybe I'll go talk to him for you."

Mario's eyes widened and he showed his white teeth to me

in a huge, open-mouthed smile. "Do you mean it, Edward? You would do this for us?"

"Might could," I said, "if'n it'd help."

Mario grinned to hell and back. Even Carlo smiled. The barman asked if we wanted another round and I said, "Why not?" For all I knew, it might very well have been my last, so this time, I sipped slow.

United States Marshal Ireland sat at a table in the back of the Rimrock Restaurant, his back to the wall and one hand curled around a mug of coffee. He was a wiry, rawboned man with deep-set black eyes that peered out of a lined and leathery face, taking in every detail of his surroundings in a careful and methodical way I supposed he couldn't even help anymore. His star was pinned to his shirt so as to leave no room for questions about who he was or why he was in Little Miracle. I knew him right away, and though he watched me walk into the place, after one good look the lawman turned his attention elsewhere. He evidently saw nothing threatening about me, to which I took some small offense, though I wasn't really sure why. I reckoned my old friend Boon would've said it had something to do with my sex and how we menfolk were always trying to prove ourselves out in the worst ways, but she wasn't there and I had me a job of work to do.

"Marshal Ireland?" I said as soon as I was within polite talking distance.

"Who's asking?" His eyes went back to the door, so he wasn't looking at me while we spoke. So much for politeness.

"My name is Edward Splettstoesser, and I come to talk to you 'bout them Italian boys you been tracking."

Now I had his attention. Those dark crow eyes of his snapped back to my face and he sat up straighter in his chair, working his jaw like he was trying to chew a stubborn chunk of gristle.

"Ain't any reward," he said.

That made sense to me. Ireland didn't want every manhunter in the territories out to take the kills he wanted to do more than anything in the world. Girotti and Pedersoli were his to cut down, and he wasn't fixing to lose that satisfaction.

Course, that made what I'd come to do just that much harder. The old dog was even more focused on killing my pals than I'd accounted for.

I cleared my throat and said, "You mind if I sit?"

"Yes, I do," Ireland said. "State your business or get on your way. You stink like a hog farmer and it's putting me off my coffee."

"It has been a lot of years since I worked with hogs," I said. "But mayhap it gets inside a man, he does it long enough."

"Why don't you just tell me where they are and go back to your wallow?"

It took a right smart of grit to keep myself from smashing that smug son of a bitch's coffee cup against the side of his head for talking down to me that way. I knew it wouldn't do any good. Way things stood, he was only after Mario and Carlo. Wasn't any percentage in putting myself on the list when I was only trying to help.

"Listen, Ireland," I said, taking a seat across the table from him anyway. "I understand vengeance, and I understand riding that kind of trail with nothing else on your mind. I ain't really done it my own self, but I've rode drag on it to another's point. But you gotta see how it is."

The marshal curled his upper lip into a sneer that revealed big, yellow teeth underneath. "How is it, hog farmer?"

"What done happened to your first boy was an accident, just a fight gone bad. And the other'un? Shit, he's the one harried them. That was self-defense, plain and simple. I was there, Marshal, and I will vouch for it."

"You were there." He said it not like a question, but just repeating the statement of fact as he rolled it around in his skull and narrowed his beady eyes until they were practically closed. "I expect that makes you an accessory to murder, don't it?"

"Can't say as I see it like that," I said.

"Don't matter what you do or don't see, son," Ireland said. "Law's the law, and the law says you're an accessory to murdering my boy."

I hadn't noticed when the hand he'd been holding that cup with ducked under the table, but I realized the sly old bastard had a gun in it now. He'd have been stupid not to, and I didn't think Marshal Ireland was a stupid man. No, stupid was walking right into a tight like this of my own free will like I'd done.

"I'm gonna want you to place both hands on top of the table," said the lawman. "Slow and easy." I did as he instructed. "Now, I seen your rig when you walked in here. Crossdraw, on your left, which means you're right-handed. I want you to use your left hand—and your left hand only—to take out that shooting iron and put in in front of me. You're gonna do it slow, and you're not going to touch anything but the grip. Any part of you grazes the hammer or the trigger, I will blow you out of that chair and straight to the Devil, understand?"

"Sure," I said. "I understand."

I stalled a couple of seconds, trying to gauge the man across from me, and whether or not he'd be fast enough to shoot me before I could throw some lead his way. I reckoned he might be, and I didn't much feel like gambling with my life, so I did exactly as he said and laid that revolver down right next to his coffee cup.

"Got yourself a belly gun?" he asked.

"I do not."

"How's about a pig-sticker, hog farmer?"

"I do not," I said again, this time through my teeth.

"This Remington I got pointed at your balls is chambered for .44-40 cartridges," Ireland said. "You'll bleed out, but not before suffering a mighty lot with your manful equipment blown to pieces. It's got a hair trigger and I never think twice once I've made up my mind to shoot a man. Don't put me in that position, son."

"I will try not to," I said. "I like my manful equipment the way it is."

"I am sure you do. Follow my instructions, don't do anything stupid, and your cock and balls will stay the way the good Lord made 'em."

"Be my d'ruthers."

He smiled cruelly and said, "Stand up."

I stood up, keeping my hands out in front of me.

"Good," he said. "Now, let's us go see your eye-talian friends and have us a little chin-wag. Then you can dig their graves for them, savvy?"

"Dig your own grave, amigo," came an impish voice I recognized from the doorway. I squinted at the backlit figure until Mario walked into the light of the restaurant, a pair of mismatched Colts in his hands. He nodded at me, I nodded back, and he tossed the iron in his left hand to me. "Splettstoesser is coming for *you*, and he's got friends."

I caught that Colt by the grip and held on tight as I scrambled to get on top of the table before Marshal Ireland sent me to hell, walnuts first. The lawman did indeed touch that hair trigger, and his Remington barked beneath the table in the half-second before I was above it, whereupon my not-unsubstantial weight collapsed the whole thing right onto Ireland's lap. His shooting arm was pinned beneath me and the wreckage of the table, so I took the opportunity to smack him hard across the face with the barrel of the gun Mario gave me the borrow of.

The front sight at the end of the barrel carved a deep gash from the marshal's right earlobe to his nose. The wound spilled a curtain of dark blood down his face and the man roared, spittle and blood flying, as he lifted both the table and me off of him. I went tumbling backward and crashed into the chair I'd been sitting on. The chair was reduced to splinters and wouldn't ever be sat upon again. And, looking up at the lawman with the Remington pointed directly at my face, I wasn't completely convinced I'd ever sit another chair again, either.

I closed my eyes, knowing damn well I wouldn't have the time to try for a shot of my own before his ball sailed through my brain, and when I heard the loud crash I mostly figured that was what it sounded like when a man took a bullet in the head. But then the more I thought about it, the more I doubted I'd still be thinking about anything at all if I had been shot dead, so I opened my eyes again to see if I could determine whether I was alive or not. Turned out that crash wasn't the sound of my death, but the straight-backed chair Carlo had taken from another table and thrown at Ireland. That chair wasn't quite as decimated as the one I'd fallen on, but it broke up a bit when the back collided with the marshal's head and shoulder.

Ireland hollered angrily, spun away, and smacked the other side of his head against the wall he'd had his back to when I first came in. He was disoriented then, but all the same he lifted that Remington and brandished it madly even though he was probably seeing double. Only a few folks had been inside the restaurant when I arrived, and most of them lit a shuck out of there once the trouble started. But the few who remained finally decided to get shed of the place lest they catch a stray bullet fired by a rage-maddened marshal. It was a good choice, and one I would have made my own self if I wasn't already in the thick of it. This was partly my fight, after all, and I owed those Napolly boys for saving my bacon with that chair.

"*La sua pistola!*" Carlo boomed.

"His gun, Edward," Mario said. "Get his gun!"

I said, "Right," and as Ireland swung his pistol like he'd drunk a gallon of rotgut whiskey, I slammed the palm of my free hand against his shooting arm. The marshal dropped the Remington, and right before he could stoop to pick it back up again, Carlo rushed him. The big man jammed his large belly against the marshal, who flew back against the wall again, and when Ireland rebounded to respond with his fists Carlo slapped him with one hand and punched him in the breadbasket with the other.

"God damn you," the marshal wheezed as he doubled over, "I am an officer of the law."

"Sorry, officer," Mario said with a shrug. "But we just don't cotton to letting you kill us without a fair trial."

"*Non saremmo mai stati processati,*" Carlo said while he bodily lifted Ireland by the back of his pants.

"No, you're right, Carlo," Mario admitted. "We wouldn't let you take us in to be tried, either. Fact is, your son was a killer and a mean son of a bitch if I ever saw one."

"Sounds like they both was," I put in.

"One started that fight, true," said Mario. "And the other? Well, a man's got a right to defend himself, hasn't he?"

"Then you had best kill me right here and now," the marshal growled, dangling like a newborn kitten from its mother's jowls, "or I will not fail to take you out the next time. All God damn three of you no-account bastards."

"In cold blood? While you can't even defend yourself?" Mario looked genuinely shocked at the idea of it. "Why, Marshal—how could you even dream up such a thing?"

"I'd do it," I said.

Carlo looked at me, then down at the man he had hanging from his belt, and then over to Mario, at whom he nodded. Seemed like Carlo was all for snuffing the lawman out, too. But ol' Mario Girotti was starting to look like he had a different idea altogether.

We rode south, Mario and me astride a pair of matching duns that flanked the Studebaker wagon Carlo drove from the box behind the mules. The horses were theirs; the wagon and mules we traded my mount for, though none of us bothered to inform the hostler about the transaction. By the time he found out, we'd have been well on our way to the border.

In the back of the wagon, behind drawn flaps, Marshal Ireland was trussed with ropes and gagged with a handkerchief—our captive. First time we stopped to rest the mules and horseflesh, I offered him water, but he hollered soon as the gag came out, so right back in it went without a drop to refresh the ornery jasper. We didn't stop again 'til round about midnight, by which time I reckoned the old boy was thirsty enough not to make noise again. All the same, after I watered him, I gagged him again.

That night we made a cold camp in an arroyo encircled by towering cacti and scrubby ironwoods, with one man on watch in four-hour shifts. Come morning, none of us was well-rested, blinking in the bright desert sun and wishing for just one more hour of sleep. Mario accepted the unpleasant duty of supervising the marshal's morning constitutional behind a mess of scrub brush, and we all of us chewed on leathery deer jerky and called it breakfast.

"A desert grave," Ireland said after swallowing his first

mouthful. Mario was hand feeding him, like he was a pup. "You'll want them mules of your'n to walk over it a time or two, or it might still get found."

"Shut up and eat your jerky," I said.

The marshal grinned and turned his head to Mario. "You really planning on making me dig my own grave, dago? I can't hardly feel my hands, you know."

"Keep insulting me like that, Marshal Ireland, and you won't get the rest of your breakfast."

"Shove it up your ass," Ireland grunted.

Mario shrugged and popped the remainder of the marshal's portion into his own mouth.

Carlo said, "*Stupido idiota.*" I didn't need Mario's translation for that one.

Most of the rest of the day we spent riding in backbreaking silence, the terrain hard and dry, the sun high and hot. As much as old Ireland bitched and complained about his lot, I envied the old boy; he got to ride under the shade of the Studebaker's bonnet without a horse between his legs, shaking his spine to splinters. Course, what Mario had in mind for him next was no cause for jealousy, and that was coming up in an all-fired hurry. We'd reach the border about halfway into Cowskull Canyon, and we entered the northern mouth of it before nightfall. And that was where we expected to come across Mario's friends.

He'd telegraphed from Little Miracle to some place south of the border, near to the gulf. Mario's message was in Italian; the response he received came *en español*.

Cañón del cráneo de vaca. Tomará el flete.

"Cowskull Canyon," Mario told me then. "They'll take the freight."

The freight, of course, was Marshal Ireland. The friends, such as they were, turned out to be not only outlaws, but *piratas*—pirates. And the plan was simple enough: we were shanghaiing the old son.

"I cannot kill a man when it is avoidable," Mario explained, almost apologetically. "But this way, he lives, just far away from us, yes?"

How far was anyone's guess, but in short time I expected

Ireland would be bundled aboard some clipper or sloop awaiting him in the Gulf of California and bound for distant shores. The lawman would either work or get keelhauled, at which point his fate was in his own hands and out of ours. Judging from the warm reception he received from his new captors in the canyon—a rowdy bunch of half a dozen desperados— Ireland was just the sort of man they were looking for, so my guess was he'd work. Mayhap, someday, he'd make his way back to American soil and resume his search for Mario, Carlo, and perhaps even me, but I knew it would take him a long, long time to manage that. And who knew? Ireland might just as likely find an affinity for the sea, or some comely celestial gal on the other side of the world. Stranger things had indeed happened.

The desperados tied Ireland to the mule he'd be riding for the rest of his journey to the sea, and after a few words and a pull or two from an unmarked jug of clear liquor that kicked like chain lightning, we turned around and headed back north.

It was a hell of a lot of work to get rid of a man who was plaguing them just to keep from finishing him off, but it never was my call to make. Hell, might could have been the weeks and months and years ahead of that man would make him wish we'd shot him dead and buried him in the desert. I'd never know, because I never saw or even heard tell of U. S. Marshal Ireland again. If he ever made it back to the States, he never found me, and I seriously doubted he ever got a hold of those Napolly fellers, either.

Point of fact, I never did see them again, my own self, to my everlasting regret. I parted ways with them just south of Little Miracle, where I asked whether or not they intended to keep digging for silver in those parts.

"I am tired of digging," Mario told me. "Carlo wants to see Denver, try cheating at cards for a little while—at least until we get caught."

He gave me another one of his impish smiles, this one clearly indicating that neither one of them had learned their lesson. I was a man hard to change, too, so I reckoned I understood. To my tremendous surprise, Carlo stepped down from the wagon and pulled me into a tight embrace that damn near popped my head clean off.

"*Addio,* Edward," he said.

"So long, big feller," I said. "And good luck with them cards."

He smiled like he understood, and I figured he did. I reckoned Carlo Pedersoli understood every single word I had ever said to him.

Mario shook my hand with two of his and said, "*Grazie. E ciao.*"

I nodded. They went east with the wagon and one of the duns. I went north with the remaining dun. And after dark, when I sat by a small fire I'd built with cow shit and dried creosote, I felt a cold, harsh loneliness in me that I hadn't known since my old friend Boon hied out on me in California. Worst part of having friends was leaving them—or getting left behind. Though I supposed a man couldn't rightly have one without the other, the warmth without the pain.

Sleep came to me while I thought of Mario and Carlo, and it overtook me while I dreamt of Boon and, strangely, Marshal Ireland. In my dream, the old boy was toiling hard on the decks of a three-masted schooner, pulling ropes and climbing nets and timbers with the best of them, his arms like wiry bundles of ropes and a sailor's beard down to his chest. He answered every captain's command by following through, and his companions among the crew both liked and respected him. The old lawman had found a place where he fit right in like a key in its lock, and unlike me in my lonesome camp, Ireland would never want for friends again.

Then again, for all I knew, the irritable bastard refused a single command and got himself thrown into the sea, his arms and legs still bound, for his trouble. Alone in his impudence, ever sinking to the cold, black depths of the bottomless ocean. Seemed just as likely, if not more so, considering the man's single-mindedness in tracking the Italians halfway across the country.

But it was nice dream. Nice enough while it lasted.

TANGLEFOOT

Jez wasn't allowed in the Tanglefoot—Surprise Township's sole tavern—on account of having kicked the living shit out that preacher one Saturday in April. The sonofabitch hadn't been drinking, of course; just standing all straight and righteous by the bar with the good book in his hand but no drink in the other, hollering about gloom and doom and the nasty end folks was setting themselves to, mayhap Jez especial. He said the good lord wanted white folks to have the western territories, that the red man wasn't nothing but an ignorant savage wouldn't know salvation if it upped and bit him on the henry. Jez didn't give a toss about any of that. He'd heard it all before, and he usually figured he agreed with it so long as he wasn't expected to give it much thought. Assuming there was an Old Man in the clouds pulling the strings—and he only half-believed that, anyhow— Jez reckoned if the old codger didn't want men like him traipsing over every goddamned acre of land west of the Mississippi, then that preacher's good lord would damn well do something about it. But he didn't, so that was that.

"Red Indian drinks and carouses and carries on 'cause he don't know better," was what the preacher man said. Tom Foley guffawed at that because he was sitting next to Tall John Running Bear, who was scowling fair hard by then. "Jesus wants you to inherit this country, but not rollin' 'round drunk and balls-deep in syphilitic whores every other night."

Jane Preston shouted: "Who you callin' a whore?" and there was more laughter. She stomped up the stairs to the landing, cursing a blue streak that lingered in the smoky air even after she'd slammed her door shut.

"This fucking pissant," Tall John growled.

"Aw, don't pay him no mind," was Tom Foley's advice.

"Shoot, you ever been to Saint Louie? You cain't get one drop down your throat without the Salvation Army crawling half-ways up your asshole about it. Only way they's know how to let off steam. Let him have his fun."

"I'm great on religion and all," John replied, but he trailed off, shaking his head.

Across from him, leaning over the table but long out of the game—he wasn't ever too lucky at cards—Jez nodded and tipped his glass up to his mouth. "Betcha Jane don't open her legs for nobody tonight, though," said Tom. Jez nodded at that, too.

"Then that's the real crime," said Billy Shooter, showing his teeth, which were half of them capped in gold.

Jez belched and teetered away from the table to lean back in his chair. He rolled around Billy's words in his own mind for a moment, considering whether or not the preacher taking Jane out of the game for one night was worth getting his fur up; he decided it wasn't. Not after three full glasses and a pair of shots of Christ-knew-what with the German or Swede or whatever the hell he was buying drinks for whoever sauntered past his end of the bar. His peter wouldn't be up for it, not all liquored up like he was, and all he'd get for trying is ashamed and angry. Besides, the night was still young. It was a Saturday night and most of the fellows were flush. Preacher wouldn't have picked then and there to cast brimstone and hellfire any otherwise.

He shook it off and, unsteadily, rose to his feet. His hip caught the edge of the table and a stack of chips came crashing down. Tall John turned his scowl from the preacher to Jez, who grinned and said, "Sorry. Gotta piss."

On the way out, past the batwing doors and into the muddy street, it occurred to Jez he'd never seen the Indian except sitting at that same table—he had no idea if the man was really tall or not. The thought got him to chuckling, and he chuckled all the way off the porch to the street, and around to the narrow alley where he untied the front of his trousers and set a loud stream splashing against the side of the Tanglefoot. And while he swayed and urinated, Jez reckoned he was maybe a bit drunker than he'd set out to get and he realized just how tasty a ribeye from the kitchen would taste if his purse still had coin enough to cover it. The girl who worked the kitchen most nights was a mousy-haired, wide-eyed thing from back East, a Tennessee child in a grown woman's body who threw meat on the griddle whenever the barman hollered at her to do so. The barman was her uncle. All he ever did was holler at that child, but a greasy slab of beef from her little kitchen went a long way toward settling a stomach soured on whiskey. Jez licked his lips as he tucked himself away, almost tasting the damn thing already, when a man's shadow filled the mouth of the alley.

"Brother Jeremy," said the preacher.

"Shit's sake, pastor," Jez drawled, feeling a dribble on his thigh. "Get out the way. I'm goin' back in to put that girl to work on some victuals."

"A man cain't live on bread alone, brother."

"Ain't bread I'm after. Come on, preacher. Move aside."

"Now you wouldn't be thinkin' 'bout sticking your peter in that child, would you, Brother Jeremy?"

"Goddamnit, all I'm thinkin' 'bout is a rare-cooked ribeye and a short beer," Jez said, his voice rising—though now that the idea of that Tennessee girl as something other than just the Tanglefoot cook was in his head, it was hard to push it back out again. There were better looking women in Surprise—not a passel of them, but a good few—and there was no getting around the girl's odd demeanor and deep anxiety when face to face with any one of her uncle's clientele. But the young woman was built big and she was strong as an ox, and though it never quite seemed to register when he'd seen it in the past, Jez knew now there was something awful nice about the way a big woman's shape moved underneath homespun when she was in a hurry to get a meal together.

It was as though the preacher man had put the very thought into Jez's head he claimed he'd come to take away. Even stone dry that'd have been one to puzzle over, but as things stood Jez was more than a little agitated about the whole situation. He wrinkled his nose at the preacher and studied his face closely, for the first time: sunken, pitted cheeks, small black eyes, a nose that seemed to crumble off to the left like falling rock. Everybody else in the Tanglefoot had had about enough of this pious, sanctimonious little sonofabitch, everybody apart from Jez his own self, who really couldn't have cared one way or another what he did or said. But now? Now...

"You best get on home, Brother Jeremy, or wherever you aim to make your pallet tonight. You got the devil in your eyes, plain as day."

Jez blinked, a few time in rapid succession, as though trying to blink that devil away. As though he could feel it.

"All's I want," he said, his voice even but forced, "is my steak and beer, preacher. Now you get on out my way, like I said."

The liquor seemed to burn hot in his veins now, rushing its way around his system, through his thumping heart and up into his brain, buzzing, then roaring like whitewater. Sitting still all that time inside, most of it staring lazily at his glass, or at the other men at the table still in the game, the firewater only swam along at a comfortable, leisurely pace. A slow summer crick, winding its way anyplace, wherever, didn't matter. Moving about though, getting his blood moving again, and now this brazen clergyman shoving deviltry into his skull like cartridges into a breech chamber...

Jez's blood was up.

"Now look here, Jeremy—" And that was all the preacher managed to say before his nose collapsed, flattened flush with his craggy cheeks. The cartilage crunched all papery, a wasp's nest, except instead of an angry swarm all it spouted was red-black blood and tiny white shards. To Jez it almost seemed like he was watching some other man pummel the preacher man, as though he was completely apart from it, observing with disinterest. But there was no denying it was his own fist, clenched so tight the knuckles went white right before they got painted red.

The pastor's hands went up too late, palms out, pleading silently for peace. His lips quivered, sputtering. The blood spattered out from the nucleus of his face like a tomato dropped to the street from a roof.

"Guhn," he said.

Jez could hardly believe the man was still standing. He'd never been much of a scrapper, Jez, but like anyone he'd been in a few tussles now and again, and usually when a fellow took a hard, well-aimed haymaker like that he went down on his ass. Not so the preacher. He just stood there, stunned, looking like Jesus himself was in that piss-reeking alley along with them. Jez came close to telling him he ought to fall down, but instead backed the sentiment up with an uppercut to the chin. The preacher's teeth clacked together and he whined before winding round, twisting his legs up, and finally going down into the mud the way he should have in the first place. He dropped into the slop with a dull, wet smack.

Blood bubbled past the preacher's lips, mixing with the stuff already erupted from his compacted snout. His black frock coat spattered with the brown mire in which he lay, the man moaned pitifully and peeled his eyes wide at Jez, who loomed over him, panting and baring his teeth.

"Nuh," said the preacher.

Jez said, "I *told* you to get on, goddamnit."

The preacher closed his eyes and, weakly, raised his hands again. This time it was not a plea for peace, but to protect his face from further damage. But Jez couldn't hardly see the man's face, anyhow; his field of vision was obscured by the liquor and his rage, and by the persistent images of the kitchen girl in her swishing homespun, great wide hips and jutting bosom, freckles like little brown stars on her face and pale neck. His groin stirred, his henry swelling and pushing up against the front of his piss-damp trousers. He couldn't tell if it was for the girl or the thrill of the violence, the unmitigated pleasure of putting a big-mouthed bastard in his place. *You won't be going to no meeting tomorrow*, Jez thought, and he reckoned it was a mighty good lesson not only for the preacher but all those pompous folks in his flock as well, who'd be left to gawp at one another in a silent meeting hall come Sunday morning before turning back to home. *Serves 'em right.* And he decided what came next served the preacher man right, too: a hard, sound kick to the ribs, the crunching collapse of a rib satisfactorily evident at the tip of Jez's boot.

He licked his lips but found his tongue too dry; the job was done, and there was still the matter of that steak and short beer.

Jez delivered one more kick for good measure, straight to the kidney, and grinned as the fabric of the preacher's left trouser leg darkened. He then rolled his neck, let his fists uncurl back into hands, and stepped over the mewling man in the mud to find a small group of onlookers across the way, in front of the haberdashery, glaring at him with something like horror in their eyes. *Christ*, Jez thought, and he said, loud enough to be heard from across the street, "Had to be done—man wouldn't let me by."

This he punctuated with a shrug, and he made his way back to the Tanglefoot's porch to knock the muck off his boots before heading back inside. Between him and the batwings stood the big barman, Tennessee Jim, his thick arms crossed over his chest and bald head gleaming with sweat, like usual. Jim's look was none too friendly. Jez sighed.

"Hell, Jim. You know that addle-headed Bunko artist was askin' for it."

"That may be," said Jim, "but you cain't go round killin' pastors for doin' they job, Jez."

Jez laughed. "He ain't dead. Shit. I just licked him a little, that's all."

"Still and all."

"Like that, Jim?"

"It's like that."

Jez drew a long, humid breath into his lungs and shot a glance to his right, where some of the erstwhile onlookers were gingerly crossing the sludgy street, making a bee-line for the preacher. His face now almost entirely smeared red and black, the preacher was sitting up but swaying, dazed. Half a dozen folks, mostly women, circled round him and hauled him to his feet. A fresh spout of blood pulsed from his smashed nose.

"Get you on home, Jez," Jim said. "I 'spect the marshal will be round if that pastor wants to put a charge agin you."

Finally he let the breath out: a long exhale that whistled through the spaces between his clenched teeth. He looked over the barman's shoulder, past the batwings and into the Tanglefoot, where the pinochle was interrupted because Tom and Tall John and all the rest of them were staring at him with their hands on the table, their faces masks of disapproval or resentment or maybe both. And just some fifteen feet away from them, in the open entryway to the kitchen, stood Tennessee Jim's niece, the cook, drying her chapped hands on her filthy apron, her cheeks flushed pink and mouse-brown hair damp with sweat. It was only at that moment that Jez realized he hadn't the slightest clue what she was called, what her name was. He'd never even spoken to her. Not once.

The people assisting the preacher broke into a commotion when they realized the man couldn't walk properly at all, so some went to collect a litter to carry him away while others stayed at his side, cooing, and wringing their hands and praying.

To no one in particular, Jez said, "He'll live." With that, he turned with a grin for the barman, then pivoted on his heel to start the short walk home.

———————————

"Pastor Bill," the marshal informed Jez come morning, "is set on turning the other cheek."

Jez sat on a straight-back chair in the dog-run between the main house and the guest quarters, where he stayed at his sister and brother-in-law's inconvenience, rolling a cigarette. The tobacco was too dry and crumbly, but it'd smoke. He was naked to the waist and in his stocking feet, his yellow hair spiked up all over like a prickly pear.

"I don't reckon on following up on any of it without Bill's say-so," the marshal continued, "but you ought to know I'm of a mind to change his. That's one damn hell of a beating you gave him, Jeremy Rawlins. I guess his nose is ruined and he can't take a breath without he pains them broken ribs."

Despite the lawman's age—fifty or thereabouts was Jez's estimation—he had boyish dimples and an untamable cowlick that did no favors for his pretense to authority. Jez struck a match and lighted the smoke, from which he drew deeply, his lips puckered tight around the open end of the paper.

"He paid the piper," Jez said, the words tailed by a plume of blue-white smoke. "Three times I told him to get out my way."

"Bill's a hard-nosed man," the marshal said, and he was wincing before he was done saying it. Jez erupted into a peal of throaty laughter, the rest of the tobacco smoke in his lungs punched out in pulses. "Shit, Jez—I don't hardly think this is funny. You know you're not to go back inside the Tanglefoot ever again, don't you?"

"Cain't see why. I only did what every other man in there wanted to do his own self. And I never would've hadn't he come up on me pissin' in the alley. A fella cain't even make water without that holy roller yammerin' on about lakes of fire and a God who don't abide drinkin' and cards. I 'spect I reckoned already if that's heaven, I don't aim to go."

"Your theology ain't my business," the marshal said.

"It sure as shit ain't."

"But the matter ain't sewed up just yet. You might've killed him, Jez."

"Might've."

"And folks don't much cotton to nobody whalin' on a preacher."

"Ain't up to folks."

"No, it ain't. It's up to Pastor Bill. I'm to see him again this morning, check up on him, like. We'll see how he sees the thing in the fresh light of morning."

"We'll see," said Jez.

He cast a squinty glance up at the sun lifting up over the Sunday morning horizon, the sky white as snow.

He washed in the basin he kept in his room and rooted around for his cleanest shirt, ignoring the mild throb in his temples. The knuckles on his right hand smarted from where he'd pounded the preacher's chin and there was a crick in his neck from sleeping drunk and crooked on his pallet all night. Buttoning up the shirt, he rolled his neck hoping to dislodge whatever knot had poked its way into the muscles there. It didn't do much good.

Jez did not expect anything to come of the marshal's minor threat—if Pastor Bill was set on Christian forgiveness the day before, he'd be just as set on the same today and tomorrow and for the rest of his life. There never was a more obstinate son of a bitch in Jez's acquaintance, which in this case suited him just fine. And it was with no little pleasure that Jez started to consider, as he stepped into his boots and made his way back out into the hot morning sun, that forgiveness might not have been the preacher's sole impetus for refusing to put the marshal against him. An even better reason, he decided, was something closer to fear.

Or, at least he hoped so.

His sister's property sat in the crook of a slight hill and the rise of another, between which a winding footpath curved round before meeting up with the road into Surprise, just spitting distance away. Jez intended to pick up some rock candy and a new shirt, one he'd had an eye on for a few days, at the general store, where he also hoped to find his friend Turk Jansen. Turk wouldn't fuss about heading into the Tanglefoot for a bottle on Jez's behalf, rendering Tennessee Jim's ban effectively meaningless. Maybe he'd even share the whisky with the old lush, get Turk to collect his rifles and go out to the meadows to pick off some rabbits or squirrels. He had to admit: his blood was still up from the day before, and it would be mighty satisfying to feel the buck of a Springfield against his shoulder, smell the acrid gunsmoke and see some critter spin off into its death throes. Anything to get that goddamned preacher out of his skull; him and the sin he put in Jez's head.

The store was open but Turk wasn't there. Often he sat sipping his coffee on the bench in front, its oak smoothed by the rear ends that had occupied it over the years, but it stood vacant. *Too early*, Jez reckoned. Inside only a few folks milled about, three or four, picking through catalogues from back East or comparing hats in a silvered-glass mirror with a gilded frame. None of them noticed Jez when he entered the store, his boot heels clopping against the floorboards, until a woman raised her eyes from a two-year-old Sears Roebuck and emitted a small gasp.

Meeting her gaze, he recognized her as one of the women fussing and tending to the preacher while he was turtled up in the mud. He smiled and offered a curt nod.

"Ma'am."

She slammed the catalogue down on the counter with a sharp hiss and marched out of the store, her skirts swishing crazily around her legs. Jez laughed.

He collected a handful of rock candy but put the shirt off for another day, paying the man in the bowtie with what remained in his purse—money he'd hoped to spend on steak the night before. The girl's steak. Again he wondered what her name was, and how come he never thought to ask anyone before. The clerk took his money and Jez poked a jagged nugget of the candy into his mouth as he sauntered back out into the street. The mud was beginning to dry up in the heat of the morning sun. The crystalized sugar started to dissolve in the heat of Jez's mouth.

Yes, we'll gather at the river—

He tested the cracked surface of the street before stepping onto it, afraid that it might still be soft underneath, a trick. It held his weight. Jez turned right and wandered westward with the sun at his back.

—the beautiful, the beautiful river—

The air was warm but not overpoweringly so, and the birdsong from the copse of junipers back of the blacksmith's was pleasant enough, but as Jez walked on, his heart picked up to an uncomfortable pace. The main thoroughfare was unusually vacant; eerily so.

—gather with the saints at the river—

"Who the damn hell—?"

—that flows by the throne of God.

The church was a whitewashed clapboard affair, boxy except for the squat steeple at the north end of the flat roof, a wooden cross on top. Jez stopped cattycorner from the front door, diagonally across the street from him, and tried to remember the last time he set foot inside the place. Couldn't have been even once since his Ma died, and that was six winters past and he hadn't wanted to go even then. Holy rollers and liars and false-facers, *your ma was a grand old lady, yes she was,* when they couldn't have

walked ten damn minutes to bring a pie or a smile when she
was laid out and dying slow all those long, cold days. Oh, Pastor
Bill made his appearance, all right—his mouth full of scripture
and eyes agleam with a preacher's love of death, how they loved
it when a body fell away, how that sanctimonious sonofabitch
reveled in a soul passed any which way, heaven or hell, what
did he care? Either way it gave him cause to rant and rave and
he didn't love anything as much as that, spewing that rot even
when a man only wanted a piss in the alley by his lonesome.

Jez's hands collapsed into fists and his heart beat faster still.
He didn't realize he'd dropped the candy to the hard, dried
mud at his feet. The church was filled up—

(*Here's the church, and here's the steeple*
Open the door and see all the people.
Here's the parson going upstairs,
And here he is saying his prayers.)

—only the parson was laid out at home with a smashed face
and a broken rib—less than he deserved!—so what in the blue
fuck were these bible-bumping bastards doing raising up their
voices in there?

Jez wanted a drink. He wanted to lick that preacher man
again. And he wanted to kick the walls of the church down
until there wasn't anything left but rubble and broken bodies
trapped underneath. Cords stood out on either side of his neck
and his hairline moistened with hot sweat. He worked his jaw a
little, and then he crossed the street directly for the church door.

Let 'em gather at the goddamn river, he thought as he reached
for the handle to pull the door open. *But they sure as shit won't
gather here.*

———————

It was as he vaguely remembered it. Two rows of straight-
backed wooden pews, four to a row, painted brilliantly white;
the door at the back, behind them; a slightly raised rostrum,
a cross on the wall behind that, plain oak and unadorned in
the Protestant fashion. There stood nobody on the rostrum, of

course—but the pews were full, or at least peopled with standing congregants, some of them with tattered hymnals resting gently, reverently in their open palms, others singing from rote memory. Each voice struggling to outclass the others, raising their song to high heaven, irrespective of key. In the time it took for Jez to cross the street and yank the open the door, Surprise's Sunday faithful had gone from gathering at the river to bringing in the sheaves.

We shall come rejoicing! Bringing in the sheaves!

Jez stepped through the doorway, out of the sun, and narrowed his eyes, running them over the backs of the two dozen or so heads, the women's bonneted, the men's bare before the Lord. At the front of the church, a glossy black head raised higher than most others swayed mildly from side to side, emitting a froggy, baritone voice Jez recognized as John Running Bear's. Two facts were now evident to Jez: that Tall John really was mighty tall—six foot three, if he had to guess—and that the old boy was a Praying Indian. Who knew? He had to laugh.

Going forth with weeping...

Sowing for the Master...

But his laughter was drowned out plenteously by the hymn. This didn't sit too terribly well with Jez, so he reached back and seized the door handle and he slammed that door shut so hard that the clapboard walls juddered all around. The voices petered out then, in stages, a few at a time until only Tall John could be heard, croaking up at God. His song so loud and self-righteous he didn't even notice he was the only one left singing.

"For shit's sake John, quit your goddamn hollerin', will you?"

That was Jez, punctuated by a grin that was all teeth. The Indian fell silent mid-syllable and, slowly, dropped his head and turned where he stood to look Jez in the eye. Every eye in the place was on Jez now, some of them burning with loathing, some blinking with something he hoped to Christ was fear. Tall John only stared, his face a queer mask defying interpretation. Jez met his gaze in kind, letting his own face relax and doing his damnedest to ignore all the others for the moment.

"Ain't no pastor here," he said to the Praying Indian. "Sunday's cancelled."

"You get on home, Jez," said John.

"I said there ain't no meeting this week," Jez came back, straightening his spine and tipping his chin back. "I won't have it, John. All of ya'll. I won't."

"Brother, please," came a voice, small and timid. Jez heaved a sigh, exasperated, and deigned to see who was talking. A woman stepped out from where she'd been standing among the congregants, second from last row, and he recognized her as another one who'd rushed to help Pastor Bill in the mud and the blood in the alley beside the Tanglefoot. "Have a set with us. It's good you ain't to go in that saloon no more. You're always welcome here, don't you know that?"

Jez knitted his eyebrows and he thought, *I wish I'd kilt that preacher man. Yes I do.*

To the woman, he said, "You don't follow me, woman. It's you ain't welcome here. Any of you. I whipped that preacher and I'll whip any of ya'll with a mind to sing one more fuckin' word out that hymnal. That's the truth, now, and I mean it. So go on and get. Everybody. Right now."

He sidestepped to the edge of the aisle between the rows and pointed a shaking index finger at the door he'd slammed shut. His jaw twitched and his scalp tingled. Tall John Running Bear scowled. The woman, her cheeks flushed pink, wove her fingers together beneath her bosom and dragged a deep breath into her lungs before pushing it back out in a lilting song:

Onward, Christian soldiers,
Marching as to war—
With the cross of Jee-sus
Going on before.

Jez's mouth turned down at the corners, and before the woman was quite finished bellowing the last of the stanza he hauled back and drove a powerful open-handed slap across her left cheek. The cheek went from pink to an angry red, a welt rising up right away, and she fell backward in shock against the stocky smithy with his bright yellow beard. The smithy caught her up in his arms and the woman got to caterwauling, and Jez threw back his head and howled with laughter.

"I *told* you," he said. "I goddamn well done told you."

The smithy embraced the wailing woman, tears streaming down her face, cooed into her ear: "It's all right now, Beth, it's all right."

Jez rolled his shoulders and breathed deeply through flared nostrils, his eyes getting wild as he surveyed the penitent.

"No more of this," he said through clenched teeth, his voice strained with barely restrained anger. "No more."

Tall John pressed past his nearest fellows into the aisle, his narrow frame seeming to swim through the arms and legs, his dark, shiny head bobbing as though at sea. Jez saw Tom Foley among them, nearly knocked over by the Indian and sitting down on the pew in a sort of defeat. Jez opened his palm again, a little pink still from striking the woman, Beth, and held it up to John.

"No more," he repeated. And with that, he pivoted and went back to the door, which he opened, passed through, and shut gently behind him. The sun seemed infinitely brighter and hotter now, though it had been fewer than fifteen minutes since he'd gone into the church. He shielded his eyes with the flat of his hand and glared, narrow-eyed, down the street. There were more people milling about now, though none of them took notice of him. And a few of them were coming or going from the Tanglefoot, finishing or beginning breakfast or luncheon, or having an early nip to get them through the morning, or possibly dropping by shamelessly for a poke with good old Jane Preston, of whom battered and broken Pastor Bill so volubly disapproved.

Jez dropped his hand and walked purposefully toward the saloon.

The mud, all but completely dry now, kicked up in dusty clouds at his feet.

The church door creaked open behind him.

Jez paid it no mind, walked on.

From the batwings appeared Billy Shooter, a stub of a cigar clamped between his gold-capped teeth. When Billy saw Jez, he cocked his head to one side like a puzzled coon dog and popped right back into the Tanglefoot. Jez snorted. The floorboards of the saloon's front porch were in spitting distance. A

passel of shuffling, stamping, tramping steps sounded in the
street. Then: Tall John Running Bear's froggy voice...

At the sign of triumph Satan's host doth flee—

Others joined; only a few at first, mostly women. But then
the men, too. Then, everyone.

—on then, Christian soldiers, on to victory!

A procession, Jez knew. Trailing him to the Tanglefoot. *Let
'em.*

Beth's voice rose for a moment above the others, even John's,
bellowing:

Hell's foundations quiver at the shout of praise,
Brothers, lift your voices, loud your anthems raise!

It was if she expected the foundations of Hell were to be
found beneath the Tanglefoot, or perhaps underneath wherever
Jeremy Rawlins happened to stand. He shook his head, stepped
up onto the porch. He could see the barman's head just above
the batwing doors, his eyes fixed on Jez already. Nearby stood
Billy Shooter, and Turk Jansen, too. Jez paused at the swinging
doors and gave Turk a nod. Turk moved his eyes to the floor and
sighed. Jez pushed his way inside, the Christian Soldiers not far
behind.

Like a mighty army moves the church of God,
Brothers, we are treading where the saints have trod.

The batwings swung open, then the other way before coming quickly to a stop, closed again. Jez's boot heels thumped on
his way to the bar. He shot a crooked smile at Tennessee Jim,
who grimaced. Turk took his glass in hand and walked away,
passing Jez by, avoiding his glance. *Traitor,* Jez thought. *Goddamn
turncoat.* He watched the back of Turk's head as it grew smaller,
moving quickly across the room before stopping at a small table
near the piano, under the staircase, where he sat and stared,
unblinking, at the amber liquid in the glass.

"Fucking coward," was what Jez said about that.

The procession reached the porch about then, all singing
voice and clomping boots and shoes, whereupon Jez turned
back to the barman and planted both palms firmly on the pol-
ished oaken bar top.

"I want a whisky," he said, and as he spoke, his eyes flitted

past the barman's forbidding look, past the glasses and bottles behind him, clear over to the entryway to the hot, steamy
kitchen in back, where the girl stood gawping right back at him.
She didn't look any too pretty to Jez just then, in the painfully
sober light of day; all bug-eyed and red-faced, her brow dripping cloudy sweat and her mousy hair a rat's nest. He frowned.

Jim said, "I won't serve you, Jez. I said so, and I won't."

"I'll have that whisky now," Jez said, as though he hadn't
heard a word the barman said. The batwings creaked apart. Tall
John Running Bear was the first one through, though his brothers and sisters were close at his tail.

Gates of hell can never 'gainst that church prevail (he roared),
We have Christ's own promise, and that cannot fail.

Jez tilted his head back and groaned. He hadn't yet realized
that not once since he'd left the church had he looked back at
the church folk at his heels, but he did when he looked now
and saw the enormous wooden cross gripped tight in John's big
hands. It was the cross from the wall, behind the rostrum. That
solemn, somber, unembellished, thoroughly Protestant cross
that the big Praying Indian must have taken down to lead the
pageant. Jez opened his mouth but forgot straight away what he
was going to say. So he closed it again.

John proceeded into the Tanglefoot until he stood no more
than a couple of feet from Jez. All of his brethren gathered all
around him, their hands clasped to their breasts, their chins
wagging up and down as they completed the hymn, only to start
it right over again. The barman scooted away to the kitchen,
wrapped his arms around his (not terribly pretty, unnamed)
niece. Jez cleared his throat, noisily and disgustingly, and spat a
thick yellow wad on the floor between Tall John's feet.

The Indian's brown eyes burned like fire.

"Onward, Christian soldiers," he shouted, rather than sang.
"Marching as to *war.*"

And he hefted up the cross like a sword and smashed the
outermost crossbeam hard against Jeremy Rawlins's temple.

—with the cross of Jesus going on before—

Jez went stock-still for a moment, his eyeballs bulging
almost comically, as a thin trickle of blood worked its way out

of his greasy hair and down the length of his jaw.

—*Christ, the royal Master, leads against the foe*—

"Juh—John," Jez sputtered. "I play cards wit' you."

His bulging eyes rolled and his jaw flapped open, and he grasped the edge of the bar to keep himself from toppling over. He decided he was afraid. The blood was spilling down his face more liberally now. It was all the color to be found there; his cheeks and brow had gone nearly stark white.

—*forward into battle, see his banners go!*

"You whoreson, you sonofabitch."

Jez got both elbows up on the bar and bobbed there, as though adrift and hanging on to a bit of shipwreck for dear life. His blood had spattered the bar and made purchase difficult, slick.

Tall John, towering above him, shook his head sadly; the gesture of a disappointed parent. The second verse kicked up on the heels of the first and the Indian raised the cross up high again, let it hover for too long a moment, brought it smashing down again, this time against the crown of Jez's skull. Jez dropped like a sack of grain, moaning, "*Nuhhhh.*"

He landed on his backside, his legs splayed out in front of him, and swayed from side to side with an imbecilic expression until at last he fell backward with a dull thud. John stepped over him, straddled him, and drove the base of the cross into the felled man's face again and again and—

—*we are not divided, all one body we,*

One in hope and doctrine, one in charity—

—and again until his own sister couldn't recognize him, maybe not even God. Bone and cartilage crunched; the nose was flattened and cheeks caved in. But even those who elected to shut their eyes or look away kept on singing, kept their hands tight to their breasts, their hearts lifted up to heaven. Before long there wasn't anything left of Jez's face, not even eyes (or not so anybody would notice), and though no one made a point of announcing it there was no doubt that he was stone dead. And that was that.

"Onward, Christian Soldiers" melted back into "Shall We Gather at the River," and the procession gradually backed its way out of the Tanglefoot, back out into the bright afternoon sun, and sang its way all the way back to Pastor Bill's little white clapboard church. This time no one was leading the charge. Tall John melted into the throng, the cross dragging in the dust.

Soon our happy hearts will quiver
With the melody of peace…

The cook-girl wept. Her uncle patted her red cheek.

Someone coughed.

Billy Shooter said, "I'll go fetch the marshal."

No one said anything about that.

WOLVES

I.

Nelda lit out in November, just before the snows came, about as soon as she cottoned to the fact that the crops weren't ever going to yield and there wasn't ever going to be a penny in the cabin Amos built for her. Both of Amos's men were gone by then, Arkansas Aubrey and Little Nick Sanchez, both of them hoping to prove up when the Homestead Act was passed, but disappointed into disappearing when they learned that Amos would never be able to live up to the act's terms to maintain a whole quarter section. He was going to lose the land he'd worked so hard to keep fruitful, so he lost his wife and his farmhands and his crops, and most of the meager half-dozen cows he let free graze the meadow grass to starvation and disease and Arapaho raiders. Now all Amos had left to him was the cabin he built with Nolan, his boy with Nelda, whom he had, too.

But the snows were coming, and the word from Denver said winter was going to be fierce. The larder was spare and the outlook bleak. Amos slaughtered the two cows he could find on the meadow and hung their gaunt carcasses in the dugout, where he salted some of the meat and left the rest to chill in the increasingly cold nights and days. He rationed the meat between him and Nolan, supplemented it with lumpy cakes made from low-quality flour and thin coffee cut with barley that barely tasted like more than dirty water. And in the first week of December, when the first flakes came down lazily from the gathering clouds in the late evening, Amos knew without a doubt in his mind they would not have enough. He uncorked a bottle of rye he rarely touched and sat on the cabin's front porch, the home's finishing flourish, and sipping from the neck he watched his ruin float gently and beautifully from the darkening sky.

By morning the shortgrass was blanketed with brilliant white, undisturbed and unspoiled, and the snow still fell. It came now in fat, chunky flakes, hard and heavy like a frog-strangler in springtime. Amos awoke on the porch, near frozen solid beneath a quilt Nelda made back in Arkansas, before Colorado and before the war, when Nolan was swelling her belly up big. She hadn't taken much with her when she went.

Amos moved his legs, stiff and achy, and shifted to an upright sitting position. He could hear the snow peppering the naked poplars that spotted the range. In the far distance, the mountains were completely obscured by the misty gray curtain that filled the frigid air. It was going to get worse before it got better. This much Amos knew.

With no small difficulty, he rose to his feet as the quilt sloughed off of him like a snakeskin. From inside the cabin he heard the clanging of ironware, and for a short moment he was disoriented enough to think his wife was in there, cooking. Couldn't be. He reached for the leather strap in the door and pulled it open to find Nolan at the pot-bellied stove, boiling strips of beef and dropping dollops of greasy flour balls over the flame.

"Chrissakes, boy," Amos rasped, the words accompanied by wisps of white steam. "Don't use up all the victuals. Winter's only just started."

"You been on the porch all night," said the boy, not looking away from his work. "You was like to freeze out there, Papa. Gonna need something hot to warm up your insides."

Amos pulled the door shut and tightened the strap, shivering against the cold deep in his bones.

"From here on out," he said, shuffling to the table, "you ask permission before you touch them rations, hear?"

"I understand, Papa," Nolan said, reddening. He set the lid on top of the pot, swinging slightly over the fire, and turned contritely toward his father. "I'm sorry."

The aroma of baking flour went into Amos's nose like ambrosia. His mouth watered even as his anxiety heightened, quickening his heartbeat and bringing a cool sweat to his brow. He seated himself at the table and awaited breakfast. And he wondered how many more breakfasts there were going to be.

II.

Two weeks before Christmas, Nolan came tramping and gasping through the snow, back to the cabin, with a wooden shovel grasped by the haft in one hand. Amos came to the door and watched him approach, winding through the pathway they had both worked on digging through the waist-high drifts, the boy's face bright pink and glistening with ice.

"Andersons are gone," Nolan called out as he drew near. "Their cabin's plumb empty, expect for some chairs and a dog carcass. Guess the dog went in to die where it's not as cold."

"Probably a wolf," Amos said, shaking his head.

"It was all rotted up. Hard to tell."

"Heard some yowling some nights back. They're better suited for this shit that we are."

"Nothing to eat for 'em," the boy surmised. "I didn't see nothing out there, Papa. Not even a bird. Never mind no cows."

"Any of 'em was left is dead now. Eaten, or buried under all the snow and ice. Damn it. *God* damn it."

"Papa—"

"Come on, now—get inside."

With a prolonged sigh, the boy leaned the shovel up against the front of the cabin and followed his father into the relative warmth. He noted right away that the coals in the stove were barely smoldering, but it was nonetheless a damn sight better than outside. Amos lowered himself into a straight-backed chair, directly beside the black iron stove, and closed his eyes.

"What's for supper tonight, then?" Nolan asked sheepishly.

"No supper," his father barked, wrinkling his nose. *"Maybe tomorrow."*

III.

The howls returned a few nights later, low and gravid with lament and hunger. Amos lay awake in the dark with only the almost imperceptible glow of the dying embers in the stove to see by, listening. The one horse in the corral, a paint the boy called Little Rock for the best memory of his life, when the three of them went into town to buy Nelda a new blue dress, whinnied as the howls came closer, louder. Amos rose from his pallet, pushed two shells into his shotgun, and went in his stocking feet to the porch. He had reckoned before that Little Rock would end up on the supper table before the New Year, and he'd be damned now to let some hunger-mad wolf beat him to it.

His eyes narrowed to slits, Amos peered into the unkind darkness, the barrels jutted out, and waited. The snow came on and on, the clouds from which they fell dark and slate-gray, swallowing the moon. The paint snorted. The howls did not resume.

He listened to his own breath, and he watched it spew out in plumes. He waited for the clouds to shift, for the moon to shine, but it never did. If the wolves were close now, they were stalking silent. Maybe splitting up: some for the horse, some for the beef in the dugout. And one for Amos.

Softly, he went down the three icy steps from the porch to the snow hard-packed on the earth below, his every step crunching just slightly. The double percussion twelve-gauge jammed tight to the meat of his shoulder, his eyes sighted straight down the barrels. The snow continued to stipple the crystalline landscape before him, needling into itself, coating the shotgun and Amos's thinning black hair. The soles of his feet seemed to burn from the cold through the thin wool of his old stockings, but he pushed it far from his mind. Listening. Watching.

So little food. Such a long winter.

He stopped a few paces from the bottom of the steps and waited.

Then: crunching, weight on frozen snow and ice. Steps in middle distance, almost directly in front of him, somewhere in the pitch. Amos held his breath, held fast to the shotgun. He hadn't fired it in ages. Hadn't needed to. The back of his neck flushed hot and, almost giddily, it occurred to him that he might do more than merely save Little Rock for himself and Nolan. He might very well add wolf meat to the meager menu as well.

Amos blinked twice in rapid succession and, with the next set of steps breaking the crisp surface of the snow, he swung slightly left, trusting his ears and his instincts, and fired both barrels at once. The shotgun bucked like a spooked mare and he staggered two or three steps back, unprepared for the kick. The flash burned into his eyes, and his ears developed a high, almost imperceptible whine from the noise of the blast. Gradually, it all came back: the darkness, his balance, the whispery sound of the snow. The gun slowly lowered, almost of its own volition. Amos gazed into the night. Thought about how he hadn't the presence of mind to bring more shells with him when he went outside. Now he was essentially unarmed. Defenseless.

"You best get on out of here," he barked. He wanted a reaction, a howl or whine or anything at all. Something to let him know he'd made his point, maybe taken down one or two of the bloodthirsty bastards. But there was nothing. He exhaled long and loudly, and cradling the gun over his forearm he went forth in the direction he had fired. It was then that the clouds finally thinned as the wind picked up, pushing them to the south and opening up a hole in the night sky for the moon to shine through. Silvery light bounced off the snow in a shower of glittering points, and the dark red smear on the path he and Nolan dug gleamed, too. Amos spotted it, furrowed his brow. Already the snow was endeavoring to cover it up, like a buried secret. He picked up his pace, hurrying to follow the blood before the moonlight quit on him.

Little Rock let out a high whine and snorted some more. Amos jumped a little, but kept his focus. The path bent sharply to the right, the white shelf that angled off there dotted with blood and buckshot. He round the corner and, at last, found his quarry.

She was, remarkably, still alive—though only barely. Her boar suede coat hung open, spread out on either side of her like stunted black wings. The blue blouse underneath, riding up to expose a finger's breadth of fish-white belly, was stippled with shot, each tiny hole fringed black and seeping red. Her right cheek too was freckled, the flesh welting up where the buckshot pierced, torn open where a cluster struck all at once. Neck and hands smeared with blood. Icy blue eyes streaming tears. She kicked her legs languidly, as though trying to run away. Her bosom rose and fell, her wide-open mouth gasping for air.

Amos gasped, too.

"Nelda," he said. "My God. Nelda."

IV.

Nolan kept constant vigil, refilling the lamp with oil when the flame grew weak and repeating every prayer he could remember from the short time he'd spent in Sunday school back in Arkansas. His mother didn't seem to hear, nor see, nor do much of anything apart from moan pitiably and pour sweat. Her face was pallid and clammy, the bandages Amos affixed to her face and breast and ribs sticky and dark. When the boy asked his father how it happened, Amos remained silent. And when Nolan wanted to know whether or not his mother would live, all the man could do was squeeze his eyes shut and try not to breathe.

He wanted to know things, too. Things like why his wife had come back, and how she'd made it through the blizzard, clear across the frozen prairie to her erstwhile home. He would have waited to ask; he would have waited months and years to find out. But on the third night after Amos shot his estranged bride in the dark with his percussion twelve-gauge, Nelda released a small, wispy mewl and died.

Nolan wept silently for a full day. Amos didn't say a word, and he barely moved a muscle apart from gently pulling his dead wife's quilt up and over her still, white face. The day after that, he set to carrying the body out of the cabin, first wrapping it carefully in the quilt that was now a burial shroud. Nolan helped, taking his mother by the feet. Together, they transported her to the dugout, where she would have to remain until the blizzard let up and the snows melted sufficiently enough to send for an undertaker, and maybe a pastor. Until then, she would have to wait with the beef.

V.

The wolves returned on Christmas Eve.

There were no songs in the cabin, and no stories, and no laughter. The coals, as always, smoldered in the stove. Instead of goose, Amos and Nolan chewed slowly and quietly on strips of beef cut thin and distributed sparingly. Rather than waste oil, Amos extinguished the lamp an hour after dusk, sent his boy to his pallet, and retired to the front porch, where he sat and gazed at the faint, faraway stars blinking down at him.

Occasionally, his eyes drifted to the southeast, in the direction of the dugout. At night he couldn't see it, but he knew precisely where it was. And so—he soon learned—did the wolves.

They came back in a pack of half a dozen, prowling quick and quiet through the drifts, the moonlight occasionally throwing a glint off their mysterious, staring eyes. Thick coats of gray and white, they looked like wraiths more than animals, and their intent was clear when Amos observed them circling the dugout like a military detachment or Indian raiding party. None of them made a sound; their steps didn't even seem to crack the surface of the snow. But when the hinges on the low-slung entryway to the dugout squeaked, Amos knew they had returned. He bolted into the cabin for the shotgun, biting back the rising nausea that accompanied his inevitable memory of the last time he'd fired it.

"What's happening, Papa?" Nolan muttered from his pallet.

"Stay inside," Amos snapped. "I'm fixing to take care of it."

He loaded the shells as he sped back out into the frost and the snow, snapping the breech shut and drawing a bead at the dugout. Now the beasts, emboldened by their find, quit any semblance of furtiveness and growled at one another, tearing at the beef with their slavering jaws. Amos could count four of them right off, playing tug-of-war with a massive, frozen slab of pink cow meat, the heat of their muzzles thawing the flesh they were so crazed to devour. And though this theft of his stores would mean the end of him and his son, it was the remains of his wife that concerned him most. He wouldn't have these devils desecrating Nelda, even if it did mean starvation. He'd slaughter every last one of the wolves and eat them raw, right down to the marrow, before their filthy fangs could touch a hair on her head.

So where, Amos wondered with mounting anxiety, were the other two wolves?

The beef split apart with a cracking rip, throwing two pairs of the animals apart from one another, only to resume their battles over the meat. Amos trudged through the thigh-high snow as quickly as he could and unloaded with a hard squeeze on both triggers at the nearest couple, showering them with shot and disrupting the feast with the blast and the wolves' agonized yelps.

The other two in his view dropped their respective sides of the slab and backed away several paces, snarling, their white lips curling menacingly over exposed fangs. Amos wasted no time reloading, having stuffed as many shells into the pocket of his coat as he could when he got the gun. The wolves he shot thrashed wildly, crying out and reddening the snow. Amos kept sight of them in the corner of his eye as he took aim and fired at the remaining two. One went down, dead on impact, whilst the other shrieked in an eerily human-like manner, kicked up its back legs, and then fell into a lope directly for Amos. With no time to reload again, he flipped the shotgun so that he gripped it by the still-hot barrels and swung the stock hard at the charging beast's head, cracking its skull and dropping the animal to the ground. No sooner had it collapsed did he pound the butt of the stock against the crown of the wolf's head again and again, pulping its brains. He only stopped when a low, rumbling growl sounded behind him, signaling the appearance of the missing two.

They emerged from the dugout, backs arched like cats with the fur standing up, their long yellowish teeth bared and ready. Amos pivoted, turning the shotgun the right way round with one hand and thrusting the other into his pocket for more shells.

He snagged a handful, too harried to be specific, and instantly dropped all but one of them to his feet when he pulled them out of the pocket. Armed with only one, he loaded it, closed the breech, and fired in the time it took the nearest of the wolves to reach him. The close-range shot tore into the animal's neck and jaw, blowing it apart in a red mist through which the second wolf leapt into the air, paws stretched forward and face wild. Both chambers empty, Amos finally froze with fear. He had put up a tremendous fight, all things considered, but he really hadn't expected to lose it. One small mistake was apt to cost not only his own life, but Nolan's as well. The wolves would make quick work of Amos, and be away with the beef before the boy could know a thing about it. And when all Amos wanted in the first place was to protect Nelda's body, the impending loss stung greater still. He wasn't too sure he cared if the damned beasts gnawed the meat from his bones or not, but not her. Not his beloved Nelda.

"Go to hell," he rasped when the gigantic paws collided with his chest and pushed him hard into the snow. A fraction of a second later the wolf whined miserably and tumbled away from Amos, rolling over the powder before scrambling to its feet again. Blood matted the fur at its right flank. The beast half-yelped, half-growled, and then loped a wide half-circle for the nearest section of beef, which it bit into and carried off into the night.

Amos blinked rapidly and held his breath, waiting for pain that never came. He was all right. He was safe. He sat up, jerkily, and squinted into the darkness. A sliver of light shone over the area where the first two wolves were felled. One lay dead, but the other was gone, a trail of red spots left in its wake. Four dead, then. Four dead and two survived, though he reckoned they would likely die of their wounds somewhere out there on the frozen prairie. He certainly hoped so.

"Papa—Papa, are you all right?"

The boy stood in his dressing gown and boots, both hands grasping the splintery handle of a pitchfork. The tines all but glowed from the blood and fur on their points.

Taking him in, the lamplight backlighting him, Amos marveled. He grinned, but when he turned his head back to the carnage in the snow and realized the entirety of their beef stores was gone, the smile melted and his lungs deflated in his chest.

"We're ruined, son," he said. "We're finished."

He shut his eyes and leaned into his knees, feeling the cold radiating throughout his body for the first time since he came outside that night. Why did the damned fool boy save him from release? Why did this suffering have to continue?

Amos fought back the tears he felt welling hot behind his eyes and rose to his feet.

"I'm going to see to your mama," he said, avoiding Nolan's gaze. "Get them carcasses up to the porch. I'll cut 'em up come morning."

VI.

"It's nasty."

Nolan wrinkled his nose and grimaced, working his jaw with his mouth open.

"Eat it," his father commanded. He too chewed on the gamey meat. January was half gone and the wolf flesh was dwindling. Still, the boy never failed to complain about having to eat it.

"Wish we still had that beef."

"Well, we don't. And wolves eat rotten stuff, dead things. That's how come they smell so bad."

"And taste bad," Nolan added.

"That, too. But it's what you got, so quit your bellyachin' and finish your supper."

The boy crumpled his eyebrows and chewed faster, harder, concentrating on the process even as he swallowed. Amos had tried cooking the meat every way he knew, from boiling it to frying it up in the cast iron pan. He cooked it until it hardly had any flavor to it, which was how they both preferred it, but the taste still rankled. It was tough and tangy, and it carried the faint scent of death about it. But soon it would run out, and Amos figured the day was just around the corner when both he and his son would wish for just one more bite of the fetid meat.

What neither of them talked about was how the animals ravaged the corpse in the dugout before they got killed or chased off. Already ripped up by the buckshot that killed her—and going gray and leathery from time and putrefaction, despite the cold conditions of her temporary resting place—the wolves that got to her nearly tore her left arm clean out of the socket and chewed up her side until the ribs showed. The sight of it come the next morning hit Amos like a hammer to the forehead, stunning him into horrified silence until Nolan crawled down after him and let loose a wild scream. Shaken back to a likeness of stability, Amos turned and pushed his son out into the daylight. The boy sobbed awhile after that, and neither of them spoke of it at all. Even now, at the supper table, while both of their minds were so clearly fixated on that terrible sight and what it meant for their stores, nothing about it was said aloud. And what it meant was that at least one of the wolves got a taste of Nelda's flesh, and there simply wasn't any way of knowing whether it was one Amos and Nolan ate or not.

The upshot was that the beasts didn't return. Night after night, after the meager and unpleasant repast, Amos sat on the porch in his coat and hat and listened to the incessant snowfall, but he heard nothing more. After the first few nights, he didn't bring the gun; just his rye whisky, which was nearing empty. This he parceled out as sparsely as the wolf meat, but nothing short of total abstinence would keep either from disappearing completely before winter was over.

That day came when the snow finally let up, a week before the end of the month, giving a clear, bright sky to illumine the mounting panic and hunger that beset Amos and his son. Nolan slept until noon, whereupon he rose and went to the table, sat down, and stared vacantly at the roughly-hewn wood, unburdened by plate, bowl, or cup. Amos, on the other hand, rose at sunrise and spent the whole of the morning traipsing around the waist-high snow, searching for signs of melting, or tracks on the distant, invisible road. Anything that might signal an end to the isolation. He found nothing. In the afternoon he repeated the process, but this time with the twelve-gauge in tow. Anything that moved was apt to be shot, but nothing moved apart from a bank of clouds, huge and imperious, drifting in from the north. Another snowstorm was coming.

Dusk fell early, as it always did in the dead of winter. Nolan remained at the table, sitting still and quiet in the gathering dark as the temperature once again plummeted outside, where Amos stood in the vanishing path. He leaned on the shotgun like a walking staff and stared with restless purpose at the dugout.

VII.

It was worse than the wolf meat, though he couldn't be sure if the overwhelming grief and guilt had anything to do with that. Tears streamed down his cheeks, scoring furrows through the dirt that accumulated on his face from lack of washing, and he moaned with the first swallow. The small fire he'd made choked the dugout with gray-black smoke, spilling out through the open entryway, spreading the foul odor of seared, rotted meat into the snowfall. He could only barely breathe after a while, huddled up in the stinking heat. He burned the tips of his fingers plucking the pieces from the flames to poke into his mouth. Unbearably, his own body betrayed him: the stomach rumbled, the mouth watered. The wobbly feebleness from days on end of swelling hunger seemed to settle straight away.

He ate until little remained of Nelda's right arm but the bones and tough tendons. When he was done, when he had his fill, he scooped dirt over the little fire and crept back out, on hands and knees, and shoved snow into his mouth by the handful. It melted immediately and washed cold and clean down his throat, but he knew all the snow in Colorado couldn't undo what had been done.

VIII.

Though he was certain it was only a dream at first, the cry of a magpie, met in reply by yet another in kind, made Amos bolt up ramrod straight and reach for the gun. He felt a slimy patina on his face and neck, having sweated profusely in his sleep, and his head seemed to spin around from weakness and fatigue. His hand grasped at the air while the other hurried to rub the sleep from his eyes so he could see where he'd last laid the shotgun.

Once the fogginess faded from his vision, he could see quite clearly that the gun wasn't there at all.

Racing to step into his boots and get outside, Amos shot wild glances at the stark white sky in search of the birds. He spotted them looping circles to the west, cawing at one another, three in total. Tiny coal-black blurs in the heavens, swooping freely around one another as though at play.

"My gun," he muttered through chattering teeth. "The hell is my goddamn gun?"

He bit his lower lip and trembled. A dull heat rose from his core, spreading out through his limbs, his fingers and toes. *The boy*, he thought. *The boy took it.*

"Nolan!" Amos roared, spinning round to survey the boundless pallor of the dead world surrounding him. "Damn your eyes, boy—*Nolan!*"

His voice carried up and out over the frozen lowland, echoing in waves that reached the magpies, inspiring them to silence and flight. In an instant they were gone, and the sky was again empty. Amos glared at the hollow air where they frolicked moments before, and he whimpered.

"They are gaunt from want and famine," he whispered, the words of Holy Writ escaping white from his lips and rising up to the vacant firmament, from which no bird was provided to him, where no god watched while his creation suffered and starved. "Fleeing late to the wilderness, desolate and waste…"

His eyes went up from the snow to the horizon, stretching on infinitely in all directions, and he wondered how far he would get if he started walking, how long before he collapsed and how long before spring burned up the winter and revealed his bones to the next man to happen along. The thought brought a perverse smile to his face, though he wasn't at all sure why. Something about release, he reckoned. Escape.

"Want and famine," Amos said. "Want and famine."

Swallowing dry, he turned back for the cabin when he caught sight of the dugout from the corner of his eye, and the thin gray pillar billowing out from the entryway, half-hidden by the previous night's snow. He paused, puzzled and somewhat afraid, trying to work it out in his addled mind. *It's burning.* But how? Why?

"Nolan?"

The wind pushed the smoke in a southerly direction, toward Amos. The scent of a wood fire filled his nostrils, and something else, too. Something vaguely vile.

He sniffed at the air and gagged a bit. It smelled a little like the wolf meat—rotten, unpalatable—but different, too. His stomach lurched and he grunted at it, at the lack of control he had over his own body. With a deep breath he craned his neck to get one last look at the sky, to see if the magpies maybe came back round. They hadn't. Amos heaved a sigh and started for the dugout.

The smoke came thicker now, blacker. It had a greasy quality to it that seemed to cling to Amos's skin and buckskin coat. The smell was worse, too: sickly-sweet, with an unmistakable undercurrent of decay, like the smell of rotting carcasses dotting the plain after a summer buffalo hunt. Amos pinched his nostrils shut and ducked into the dugout. The air stung his eyes so that he had to squint them to slits. He could only barely make out the shadowy form hunched ape-like over the building flames until the firelight lit up the face, the oily skin and mouth dripping with grease. The boy was crying, shaking all over as he sobbed, as his tongue curled out past his lips to pull a gray wad into his mouth. Beside him, in the dirt, lay the shotgun. Behind him, the outrageously mutilated remains of Nelda. Of Amos's wife. Of Nolan's mother.

"No," Amos wheezed, his throat burning. "Jesus Christ, no."

Nolan thrust his face up, his glassy eyes rolling around the dimness enveloping the fire until they focused on his father. Once he recognized Amos he shriveled up into himself, chewing faster and edging closer to the gun.

Again the words of scripture came to Amos—*and ye shall eat the flesh of your sons, and the flesh of your daughters shall ye eat*—and he said aloud, "What of mothers?"

And he laughed.

And Nolan seized the double percussion shotgun that might otherwise have brought down magpies from the dead winter sky, and he shot his father in the chest from three feet away.

"She left 'cause of you," the boy whispered, hardly audible

over the crackle of the flames, after Amos crumpled to the dirt and the din of the blast quieted in his ears. "She won't never leave me, Papa. But Mama never did want no part of you."

IX.

They hanged him in the spring, in Denver, on a wet afternoon with fewer spectators than generally expected. Arkansas Aubrey was the one to find him first, just a week and a half earlier, before the marshal and Deputy Jensen and the Morrell brothers, who weren't so much invited as just insinuated themselves into the situation. Aubrey came upon the boy whittling a stob on the porch while the last of the snows melted to brown slush on the yellow shortgrass. He'd come to see about hiring back on until he could make his way down to Texas, but his heart sank when he saw how poorly the plot looked and no cattle anywhere in sight. The cabin didn't look much better: the roof was sagging in the middle, and the snow had left mud and debris all over the façade. There were gray-white rabbits hung up from the eaves, their fur matted dark with blood, waiting to be cut up and cooked. The shotgun rested comfortably against the door jamb. They talked a while, though the boy was short with his words and never once looked the old hand in the eye. When Aubrey asked to go inside to see Amos, Nolan merely gestured with his head, as if to say, "Help yourself."

The bones were laid out on the pallet to the eastside of the cabin, blade-scarred and blackened by fire, atop the quilt Nelda made, the colors of which were starting to fade. They had been carefully arranged to affect some semblance of their original organization that was not precise, though clear enough in intent. Two near complete skeletons, side by side, carved clean of anything that wasn't bone. Upon seeing the grisly tableau, Arkansas Aubrey let out a high squeal and went stumbling back to the porch, his breath short and eyes wide.

Nolan just shook his head, never once pausing the whittling he was doing with the only knife he ever used, and he said with practiced tranquility: "Wolves."

HORSEBLOOD

A BOON STORY

The night before I killed Grady Thurston, I wasn't looking for anything more than a hot meal. Horseblood, Montana didn't have the friendliest name of any town I'd been in lately, but it was going on night when I came within shouting distance of the place and I wasn't keen on riding on in the dark. Besides, my stomach was growling loud enough that it was starting to spook the nag I'd stolen outside Bozeman. It was a small enough settlement but on the main roads, so that strangers wouldn't be out of the ordinary among them. I hadn't ever earned any warrants against me in that territory, but I still wasn't altogether sure that there weren't one or two federal papers on me, which might dog me anyplace I went. Still, I was hungrier than a tick on a dead man, and if anyplace was risky, then Horseblood was good enough for me to rest my mount and fill my complaining belly.

It was just my damn luck that the café was closed and shuttered for the night, which meant supper was coming from the saloon next to it or nowhere at all. Horseblood's principal public house was called the Blind Stud, and judging by the hitching rails to either side of it, the joint was having a quiet night, which suited me just fine. I hitched the nag far enough away from the aggravated paint at the far end the rail to keep from further irritating the animal, and I went inside to see about a little grub.

"No Indians," was the greeting I received from the bartender, before I'd completely cleared the swinging doors. I was not unaccustomed to this particular type of greeting, and yet somehow I never quite got used to it. As a matter of fact, it seemed to get my blood up more and more each time some jasper tried it on me.

"I ain't Indian," I told him through clenched teeth, and I let my hand drift near to the Colt .44 I had holstered in my belt. That was my preference of manufacturer and caliber. Used to be a .44 conversion Army percussion Colt, but I was carrying a Frontier model rechambered for the .44 by the time I entered Montana. Double-action, and I'd tied the leather to my leg after dismounting outside, just in case I needed it in my hand in hurry. "I'm Siamese."

"I don't give two wet shits what tribe you are," the barman said, doubling down. "This here is a white man's establishment and I ain't having you stinking the place up. Now hie on back to your papoose and your teepee before I make you."

In one swift movement, he swept a double-barreled coach gun from beneath the bar and into both hands. It was a practiced maneuver, the sort of thing he'd done a hundred times or more when he was all by his lonesome, just hoping for moments like this. I could kind of appreciate that.

Only one man had been drinking at the bar, but as soon as that coach gun made an appearance, he downed his coffin varnish and went quickly for the back of the room, where the rest of the Blind Stud's customers were gathered. There was a card game going at one of the tables, and few scattered inebriates besides, but nobody said a word and all eyes were on the bartender and me. I might have liked to have said this was new territory for the likes of me, but even I couldn't tell a lie that big. This was just life in a white man's world, only I never developed the kind of temperament that could accept it. I didn't really think I could *change* it, but I was going to go to my grave fighting it every step of the way, come hell or high water. And hungry as I was that night in Horseblood, Montana, trail weary and cold, I was for sure and for certain in a fighting mood.

"Mister," I said, "I am just tired enough that I could see myself walking out of here to go find somewhere else to eat my supper, but I'm hungrier than I am tired, and you are right on the edge of making me madder than I am hungry. And I'm *real* God damn hungry."

The shotgun wasn't quite aimed at me, not yet, but it wasn't exactly pointed at the floor, either. It was somewhere in between, and whichever direction the bartender chose to move it was going to determine the rest of his life, whether he knew it or not. Likely he imagined he could raise it up another ten inches and pull its twin triggers before I could get my iron out of the leather, but if so, he'd have imagined wrong. I practiced, too, and probably a hell of a lot more than he ever did.

"Ain't my place," he said at some length. "Ain't my rule."

"The Indian rule," I said.

"That's right."

"Well, I ain't Indian."

"You ain't white."

"That so? Shit, I almost forgot."

"Jesus Katie Christ, Artie," hollered a man from the card table in the back. "Put that scattergun up and give the woman a bowl of stew. Ain't hardly fit for a pig to eat, anyhow."

Most of the other men at the table laughed a little at that, and Artie's round face reddened from his neck to his forehead.

"Mr. Parker said…" he began.

"Jess Parker's in Missoula and won't be back for weeks," the card player cut in. "Quit being such a pain in the ass and spoon up some of that damn stew, you fool."

Artie's mouth curled into an ugly sneer, his eyes shooting to the card table and then back to me. He then pushed a sigh out through his nostrils and put the coach gun back under the bar. Next, he brisky marched the length of the bar to a door in the back, through which he vanished. When he returned, he held a steaming bowl with a wooden spoon sticking out of it, which he deposited on the top of the bar. The man looked fit to burst, and I had to admit to myself that I was enjoying the spectacle quite a good bit.

"How about a beer to wash it down, Artie?"

He looked like he'd been slapped, but the scrape of a chair against the floor in the back stopped him for any further protest. Artie was seething, but he poured that beer for me, and I sat down to my supper with no more horse shit from him.

The stew was awful, and I didn't dare guess the source of

the meat, but it was hot and it cured my hunger. The beer wasn't bad, and as soon as I finished it, I prepared to pay for my meal when the card player sidled up to the bar beside me and said, "Allow me."

He dropped a handful of coins on the bar.

"I think you done enough," I said. "And I thank you for it."

"No thanks needed. Truth is, Jess Parker wouldn't have batted an eye at you, but he said one time he didn't want Indians in his place, and it took root in Artie's mind to never let in anybody who isn't white."

"Wager it don't come up too often out here."

"No, it doesn't," he said, smiling. "Name's Grady Thurston. I'm the only sheriff's deputy in Horseblood."

He stuck out his hand, and I shook it reluctantly. I didn't tend to enjoy the company of lawmen any better than I did the company of bigots, but the man had done me a favor. He'd done Artie a much bigger favor when it came right down to it, but I was grateful all the same.

"Boon," I said.

"Like Daniel Boone?"

"Like Boonsri Angchuan."

"I don't think I'll try that one," Thurston said. "But I'm proud to know you."

"Obliged," I said, and I rose to make my way outside.

Grady Thurston followed me.

"What brings you to Horseblood, anyhow?"

"Just passing through."

I went to my nag, which I'd planned on stabling for the night, but now that I'd caught the attention of the local law, I figured on moving along. It didn't seem to me that Thurston was playing some kind of long game to take me in, but I just didn't like being that visible. So much for the comfort of a feather bed in a hotel room; it was another cold camp for me.

"We get a lot of that," the deputy said, "but not a lot of you."

"No, Deputy Thurston," I said, untying the string on my mount, "I am a God damn anomaly."

"I will take your word for that," he said. "And you can take my word that the Horseblood Arms is the best hotel in town, on account of it's the only one we have got so far. It's just one street over, if you take your left up yonder on Rolling Street and then right on Second. Can't miss it."

"I believe I'll just move on, deputy, but thanks all the same."

I stepped up into the saddle. Thurston stepped aside to let me wheel the nag around to the street, but he wasn't quite through with me yet.

"Would you really have drawn on Artie in there?" he asked me. "With that shotgun already in his hands and all?"

"Good night, Deputy Thurston," I said, and I rode away in a lope for the eastern hills on the far side of Horseblood, away from any more complications.

The last time I got cozy with a lawman, things went sideways in a hurry. I had no interest in getting to know anyone else in that profession, no matter what they did for me, though I still reckoned Thurston had done more to help the barman than me. There was no question in my mind that I could have gotten a shot off on him before he had the chance to aim and pull those triggers, though of course if I had, then I would have gone hungry for the rest of the night. Still, that stew was wretched.

I struck camp in the foothills of the mountains looming over Horseblood in the east, where I found a steep bluff to keep my back against while I faced the darkness under the sheepskin saddle blanket that came with the nag. I propped my head up on the saddle itself, and I kept that Colt Frontier under the blanket where I could get to it. It sure as shit wasn't the Horseblood Arms, but I'd been camping this way most nights for a large part of my adult life. It was the life I chose, because of how I felt about the choices that had been made for me. The world hadn't been very nice to me, so I wasn't altogether too friendly to the world, and that unfriendliness of mine meant I had to keep moving most of the time if I didn't want to end up dead or jailed. It was just the ways things were, and there wasn't any turning back now.

Though I'd kept a keen eye on my back trail on my way to that spot and hadn't built a fire to alert anyone or anything to my presence there, I was soon aware that me and the nag were not alone in the foothills. I knew straightaway that it wasn't Blackfeet or Crow lurking about shadows close by; they wouldn't have been so clumsy in such a laughable attempt at stealth. Twice my stalker slipped on the scree, sending miniature avalanches of pebbles scattering down the lower end of the bluff where he skulked. The idiot might as well have carried a flaming torch in each hand and screamed at the top of his lungs.

Annoyed, I sat up from my blanket, laid the pistol on my lap, and said, "Come on out, Deputy Thurston. You're about as quiet as a Gatling gun in a thunderstorm."

The sheriff's deputy chuckled softly and walked down to the bottom of the bluff before doubling back to where I sat against it. I could make out the shape of him, backlit by the half moon and a clear sky full of stars. He stopped about ten feet away from me and said, "Hello, the camp."

"I believe I am out of your jurisdiction now," I said.

"Not really here on official business."

"Then you had best get your ass back to town, because you got the wrong woman for what's in your mind, Thurston."

Again, my hand flitted closer to the .44. But Grady Thurston just laughed.

"Oh, no," he said. "Nothing like that, either."

That was a relief, but I wasn't getting any more patient.

"What the hell do you want, then?"

"To be brief," he said, "I want you to kill me."

I wasn't any kind of gun for hire, and I'd never gone in for mercenary work no matter how empty my purse or hungry my belly. I'd hunted a bounty or two when I couldn't rightly see any way around doing it, but plain and simple murder for money wasn't something Pimchan Angchuan's girl ever done, whatever the price—and even if the target was also the one doing the hiring.

"You're crazy," I told the deputy.

"I assure you I am not."

"Then why don't you put a bullet in your own brain, you want to die so bad? Just don't do it here next to me."

Thurston grinned, and the grin turned into a laugh. I didn't join him.

"You misunderstand me," he said. "What I want is for every-body in Horseblood to *believe* you have killed me. I want to be dead in every sense apart from—"

"Actually sucking grave dirt," I finished for him.

"Exactly," said Grady Thurston. "I want no question in any-one's mind on the matter. I want an obituary in *The Horseblood Examiner* and articles in *The Helena Independent* and *The Pioneer*. I want a funeral and a pine box buried in the cemetery with witnesses. And I want folks to see you, ma'am, gun me down in broad daylight right in the middle of Front Street."

He'd spoken so quickly and manically that he had to catch his breath, squatted on the rock he'd chosen for his seat at my camp and mostly ignoring the quirley smoking in one hand. The deputy had rolled it himself and managed to get more tobacco spilled on the ground that inside the damn thing.

"Why me?" I asked him.

"Because I know what you are," he said. "The sheriff hasn't any dodgers on you that I know of, so don't worry about that. It's just experience. I saw how you carried yourself with that shit-for-brains bartender back at the Blind Stud and there just wasn't any question. You're a gunhand."

"Mayhap I am," I half-admitted. "But that don't hardly mean I invite murder charges against me."

"You telling me you don't already have a passel of them?"

"Didn't say that."

"That's what I thought," said Grady. "You're a gunhand, all right, and one more killing in some no-account town like Horseblood isn't going to change much for you. What's more, I'm willing to pay. I don't expect any favors from anybody, much less a stranger. You do this for me and pull it off right, and I'll pay you five hundred in cash money."

"That's a lot of money, deputy."

"I need this done, ma'am."

"Quit that ma'am shit," I told him. "Name's Boon."

"I need this done, Boon."

"Why?"

"Because if you don't convince that God damned town you have murdered me," Grady said, "Sheriff Burnham is going to do it for real."

It wasn't until the following morning that I made the acquaintance of Sheriff Quint Burnham, and I made that meeting happen more or less how Thurston asked me to do it—I made a scene the law couldn't ignore. "It would be best," the deputy told me the night before, "if Quint knew you're a gunhand, too."

He didn't have to explain. I understood perfectly. By formally introducing myself to the town of Horseblood as a gunny and a troublemaker, my apparent killing of its sole deputy wouldn't be questioned. Leastways, it wouldn't be so long as the dead man didn't get caught walking around after he was killed. We were both of us going to have to get shed of that place and in an all-fired hurry once the deed was done, and that was where the plan got a mite sticky. Not only did Grady Thurston have to stay dead in the minds of everybody but him and me, but there had to be something to put in that pine box when it was all said and done.

Something—or somebody. If the body went missing as soon as the man was "dead," the whole plan would go to shit. In that case, Sheriff Burnham would still want to kill his deputy, and I'd be out five hundred dollars, and I could really use that five hundred dollars. That, and ol' Quint would be like to kill me, too. Or at least he'd try, and even if and when he failed to do that, I'd just have that many more sons of bitches looking to end me.

In other words, what me and Grady had us was half a plan. But according to the man I was supposed to kill, time was short and it was essential we get started straightaway. I told him it was his money, and by sunup I was looking for a fight to start in town. I didn't have to look long.

———————————

Artie was meandering down Rolling Street with his hand over his eyes to keep the sun out. I guessed Jess Parker didn't pay the dumb bastard enough to buy himself a hat, or else Artie was just too stupid to think of it. Whichever the case, he paused when he got to Second and lingered a moment in front of a hardware shop with a selection of new rifles on display in the front window. He seemed especially taken with the Sharps-Borchardt falling-block carbine right in the center of the display, licking his lips and peering so close to it that his breath fogged the glass. Other than the café I couldn't get into the previous night, it was the glass window I'd seen in Horseblood, so I doubted the owner much cared for the likes of Artie clouding it all up with his rank breath.

"Hey, Artie," I shouted at him from across the street. "With breath that bad, you're like to bust that glass."

The Blind Stud barman stiffened, startled at first but then just angry, and he pivoted to locate me on the boardwalk some five yards away.

"The hell you just say to me?"

"I was just wondering," I called back, "how much shit a man's gotta eat to end up with breath like that? Come to think of it, that your own shit you been eating, or somebody else's?"

I hiked my gun hip out and cocked my head in the other direction, watching him close and waiting for him to react. Even across the grubby street, I could see how red his face was getting, and I could see his fists clench into fists on either side of him. Artie wasn't carrying any obvious weapons, no gun belt or belly shooter sticking out of his pants, but it wasn't a gunfight I was looking for. I just wanted to kick up a little dust was all.

Then again, I hadn't counted on just how mad I was like to make the man, and I surely didn't account for him smashing the glass window with his elbow to get at that carbine. The glass covered the boardwalk at his feet like ice breaking up on a river in spring, and he rushed to get at a box of cartridge as soon as he had the coveted Sharps-Borchardt in hand. I'd wanted a little fisticuffs just to make an impression, but here Artie was turning up the heat a hell of a lot more than the situation called for. Truth was, I never got one whiff of the man's breath and couldn't judge it one way or another. Either I accidentally landed on a sore spot with him, or he was still mad about the business in the Blind Stud when he'd tried to toss me out. Whatever was stuck in his craw, I sure wasn't about to let him throw a shot at me, and definitely not with a .45-.70 round that could take half my head off at that range. It wasn't at all what I wanted, but I didn't have any other choice but to draw down on the dumb bastard.

"Don't do it, Artie," I warned him. I had him covered, dead to rights, before he ever got that round loaded into the breech-block. "I was only raggin' you. This ain't any kind of shooting matter."

"I am tired of you," he said, and by God, he jacked that cartridge down into the breech and took his aim with the pilfered carbine.

Mayhap I pushed a little too hard. Oftentimes, I forgot that men tended to be more sensitive than a newborn foal. Trouble was, this foal had a buffalo-killer with a 24-inch barrel pointed at me now, so I did the only thing I could do. I squeezed off a shot, and I struck the stock which exploded in a shower of splinters that needled Artie like shrapnel. He pulled his own trigger, but the big round slammed straight down into the street before he dropped the ruined rifle and got to hollering about all the jagged shards jutted out of his hand, shoulder, and neck. To my way of thinking, the son of a bitch ought to have been thanking me for not putting that bullet in his brain where it rightfully belonged, but I didn't reckon he was the grateful kind.

Of course, any other time, and I wouldn't have thought twice about ending Artie's life right where he stood, but these were unusual circumstances. If I found myself locked up or on the run, I wasn't ever going to see the plan through with Thurston, which meant I'd never see that half a grand, either. And now that the shooting was done and a curious, if cautious, crowd was starting to gather, I still wasn't convinced I wouldn't have to run. What was supposed to be a minor scrape turned into gunplay, and that just wasn't something Quint Burnham could possibly ignore.

"Leather that iron, honeybun," the sheriff said when he arrived on the scene. "And drop that belt to the ground."

He was a pot-bellied man of maybe fifty, though I never could rightly tell how old a white man was, on account of how poorly they always seemed to age, especially out west. I had me a dear friend in a white man out of Arkansas, name of Edward Splettstoesser, who was roundabout the same age as me but looked some ten or fifteen years older. They had just about everything that mattered sewed up tight for themselves, white men, but at least there was one small curse to plague them for it. For all I knew, Quint Burnham was only thirty-five.

Whatever his age, the lawman had a Peacemaker drawn on me and a pair of pale blue eyes trained hard on my hands. I shrugged and dropped my .44 back in its holster, then unbuckled my gun belt, just as he commanded. Artie sure wasn't going to be any more trouble, and the only other person in sight with a gun was Burnham.

I said, "How do, Sheriff."

"Let's see them hands, girly."

"Name's Boon," I said. "Not honeybun, and not girly."

"What's your Christian name?"

"Ain't a Christian. But Boon's my given name, if that's what you mean."

"Figures you ain't," Burnham said with a sneer. He advanced several steps and narrowed his eyes, examining me closely. "Indian?"

"Nope."

"Mex."

"Siamese."

"The hell is that?"

"It's what I am, damn it."

I had my hands up, palms out, but the sheriff kept that Peacemaker on me all the same. He grunted, then shot his eyes across to where Artie was sitting on the broken glass with his back against the front of the hardware store. Someone was helping him pluck splinters out of his flesh while another man stood haranguing him about the window and the carbine, presumably the shopkeeper.

"He have a reason to smash yonder window to get at that gun?" Burnham asked me, returning his harsh gaze to my face

"Reckon he meant to kill me," I answered.

"Never did nothing like that before," he said. "Can't say as Artie's a man anyone much cottons to, but he never did nothing like *that*."

"He did today."

"Looks that way. Just as soon as you come into my town."

"Looks that way," I said. "You fixing to arrest me for defending myself?"

Burnham's brow knitted into a severe knot at the bridge of his nose and he sighed. "No, don't reckon I will," he said, like he was disappointed about it. "But I don't want the sun to set on you in Horseblood, *Boon*. You can either hie on out of here right this minute, or hand over that Colt to me and come get it back on your way out. Either way, make sure it's before dusk, or I *will* lock you up."

"On what charge, exactly?" I asked. "The self-defense, or just not being white enough to your taste?"

"You're not wanted here," a gruff voice boomed suddenly from the crowd. I swiveled to seek it out, and from the throng of nosy townies emerged Deputy Grady Thurston. He had one hand resting on the grip of his revolver. "Put this town on your back trail like the sheriff said, or it'll be your own damn fault what happens to you."

"Stand down there, Grady," Burnham said, waving one hand at his deputy and holstering his sidearm with the other. "It's all in hand now."

I raised an eyebrow at Thurston, maybe marveling a little at his theatrics. Seemed like he missed his calling and ought to have been on stage someplace like Chicago or New York rather than the deputy of a ramshackle settlement nobody ever heard of like Horseblood. Still, the performance got the job done; now it was Burnham trying to keep Thurston on a leash from attacking me. I didn't expect it was going to come as much of a surprise to the older man when he came to believe I'd shot the younger one, and to seal the deal, I made a gun with my fingers and fired one off at Grady with a sideways grin.

"Be seeing you, Deputy," I said, and I walked away from him, the sheriff, and all the rest of the crowd, with my gun and belt lying on the ground behind me.

Acquiring a new weapon was as easy as waiting for Grady to get clear of prying eyes and over to where I was whiling away the afternoon back in the foothills and rimrocks. It wasn't my own .44 he brought me, since that would be much too suspicious, but a double-action Adams revolver chambered for .36 cartridges.

"That's what I carried in the war," Thurston explained. "I keep it clean and oiled, but I haven't fired that gun since the last Johnny Reb it killed at Rappahannock Station back in sixty-three."

"Didn't see the rest of the war through?" I asked, accepting the revolver from him.

The deputy lifted his shirt up to reveal the bumpy crater in the skin over his ribs on the left side.

"Took a bullet from the same man I killed that day," he said. "Sawbones at the camp hospital didn't figure on me living through the night. I did, but they mustered me out of it."

I nodded. He dropped the shirt back down and looked aggrieved I wasn't more impressed. Fact was I had plenty of scars of my own, including bullet holes, but I wasn't fixing to strip for him to get a look-see at them. Instead, I changed the subject.

"This what you want me to shoot you with?"

"That's right."

"With what, blank cartridges? Like one of them Bill Cody foofaraws?"

"Nope," Grady said, "real cartridges. Blanks are too obvious. Wouldn't nobody believe that up close."

"Well, I hate to break your heart, hoss," I said, "but real bullets kill people when they hit vital parts, and they can sure make you wish you was dead otherwise. I can put a round in your shoulder or something like that, but it could still kill you."

"Not my shoulder," said Grady. "Right here, dead center."

He pounded himself on the middle of his chest with a closed fist.

"Armor, then," I said.

"Steel plate, bound in silk. Bought it off an Indian trader last summer 'round Deer Lodge. Cost me a small fortune, but I sort of figured I might could find a use for it."

"This'd be it."

"You just make sure you strike me dead center, like I said, and I'll go down like I was killed. The steel will take the bullet, and the silk will make it sound like it hit me and not the plate. I'm even gonna fix a little leather pouch with pig's blood in it so I bleed when I'm shot, too. Real believable like."

"You got everything figured out," I said. "How about your 'body?' And the grave?"

"Leave that to me," the deputy said. "All's you got to do is aim true and squeeze that trigger. After that, get the hell out of Horseblood and wait for me at Devil's Fork, like we said."

Devil's Fork was a spot between Horseblood and Miles City where the trail split off, one side through a narrow, rocky canyon and the other across a wide and deep spot in the Yellowstone River. Neither choice was ideal, hence the name.

"Wait," I said, "and hope you show up with what you owe me."

"I'll show."

"So you said."

"I'll show," he said.

I would have preferred some kind of guarantee, but I knew I wasn't going to get one. The deeper I got into the deputy's plan to turn himself into a ghost, the less I wanted to be a part of it. Still, though I was many things that weren't very nice, I liked to think I was a woman of my word when it counted. That, and being on the lam, riding the outlaw trail I rode, was hungry going when a body tried not to rob most folks. I needed the money, so I was going to take my chances with Grady Thurston.

The gun delivered, he made to sneak back into town before

pausing at his blood bay mare with one hand on her mane. "You know," he said, "you haven't asked me why Burnham wants me dead."

"Dozens of men want me dead," I told him. Truth was, I didn't particularly care why the sheriff had it out for his deputy. What went on betwixt law dogs and white men was no concern of mine, as I didn't trust any one of them as far as I could throw a Conestoga wagon.

"Thinks I killed his wife," Grady offered.

"Still didn't ask," I said to his back. "But did you?"

"Not on purpose," he said. "There was a robbery in town. Couple of jaspers from Missouri thinking they'd be the next best thing to the James-Younger bunch, raising hell across the territories and like that. Stuck their shooters in a bank teller's face and tried to make off with what they stole. I happened upon them, and we traded some fire there in the street.

"Shot one in the head, the other caught lead in the gut but he managed to get up in the saddle, anyway. I was afoot, but I gave chase and emptied my revolver at him. Should've known better than to shoot while I was running like that—couldn't never hit the side of a barn when I was running." Grady snorted a bitter laugh at his folly. "The boy died eventually, but he was far from Horseblood when that happened. The only body I shot when I went after him was Alice Burnham."

"An accident," I said.

"The boy whipped his mount around the corner of Front and Severin, riding hard for these same hills," Grady said. "I come 'round that corner, two shots left, and fired both of them off one right after the other. Kid galloped off, and when the dust settled, somebody screamed. That was Mrs. Parker, the saloon owner's wife. She was the one first saw Alice laid out in the street like she was, my last bullet gone right through one eye and out the back of her head. I reckon she was dead before she knew she got shot, which I expect is a blessing."

"Beats suffering," I agreed.

"Sure," said the deputy, and he half-turned to look at me behind him, his face blank. I hadn't exactly expected he'd be crying or anything, but his expression was just flat, like a death mask. "Thing is, if it was me? I'd want the son of a bitch who shot my wife dead, too, whether it was accidental or not. I don't blame Burnham one bit, Boon. I just don't want to die just yet."

"Then let's get you killed so you don't have to die just yet," I told him.

———————————

The pretense was simple enough, handed to me as it was by the sheriff himself a few hours earlier. I was commanded to leave town by sundown, so at dusk I moseyed back into the Blind Stud and bellied right up to the bar where Artie stood with wide-eyed shock at my appearance.

"Whiskey," I said. "And leave that scattergun be."

His right hand was wrapped up in bandages from the damage he'd sustained in our brief scuffle, but the fingers were still free and usable.

"You ain't supposed to be here," Artie said. To his credit, he kept his voice level and his hands where I could see them.

"I'm here, and I'm a mite thirsty. Whiskey."

Artie froze, his eyes flitting from me to the back of the saloon, where I knew Grady was seated at a table with some of his poker pals. I didn't turn around. My eyes never left Artie's face, which was fast draining blood.

"Listen," he said, "I gotta work mornings at the hardware store 'til I pay off that window I busted, and I'm on thin God damn ice with the sheriff. Now, Deputy Thurston's setting just yonder behind you, and he's looking hard this way, so I can't serve you without we're both in a mess of trouble, you understand?"

"I didn't make you bust that window," I said, "and I ain't getting less thirsty sitting here listening to you whine and jabber. You make me ask for that drink again, I'm gonna hop over this bar, crack your skull like an egg, and get my own fuckin' whiskey. What's it gonna be, Artie?"

Artie said, "Why me, Lord?" But he poured the forty-rod into a glass and set it down in front of me like a good boy.

I threw the drink back in one go and slammed the glass down with an exaggerated sigh of contentment.

"Another."

"That's enough," I heard Grady boom from across the saloon. "Artie, she's done here."

The bartender put his hands up and walked away from me, quickly, like he was afraid I might back-shoot him. And while Artie got away from me, Grady Thurston closed the distance between us in a few long strides. I kept my back to him, and he laid a hand on my shoulder from behind. What happened next wasn't part of the act; it was sheer instinct. I kicked the barstool away, pivoted to shake his hand off, and shoved Grady hard with both hands on his chest. He staggered back, pinwheeling his arms, caught completely off guard. I never much took to being touched by men, and especially not when my back was to them. That was just Grady's poor luck.

I imagined the hand of his that went dropping for the Colt leathered in his belt was something like instinct, too. My gun hand swept down for the Adams he'd given me, but I gave him a second or two to make sure he drew first. That wasn't scripted, either. About all that was concerned the idea that Grady was going to try to take me in, and I was going to shoot him for his trouble. How it happened exactly was just going to be a matter of chance, more or less.

And as chance had it, he *did* draw on me first.

"I tried like hell to give you the benefit of the doubt when you first came in here," he said. "But you have done run out of chances with me, lady. You are gonna drop that iron just like you dropped the other'un for Sheriff Burnham, then you and me are gonna take a little stroll down to the jail together, nice and peaceable."

I said, "Nope."

That Adams .36 was in my hand as fast as I ever drew, but for the first time in my life, I hesitated before squeezing the trigger. My reluctance was plenty long enough for Grady to fire at me, to my tremendous shock and surprise. Little of the little dance we were doing was planned down to the details, but I was damned sure this wasn't part of the scheme. As soon as his finger curled around the trigger, I dove for the floor, so the shot slammed into a bottle behind the bar instead of my head. Up to then, Artie had been watching with the rest of the men at the back of the place, but when the ball went up like that, he went to scrambling for the back door, along with most of the others.

"Jesus Christ, Grady," I spat at the floor. There weren't but two men left in the Blind Stud, so I knew I had to act fast if there was going to be any point to any of this. Without witnesses, the whole deal was soured, and those two fellers were spooked and ready to bolt. The time to put our charade to an end had come. "Guess that's that, then."

I rose up to my knees, and as Grady brought the barrel of his Colt down on me, I fired off two quick shots right in the middle of his chest. His eyes popped wide and made a perfect O with his mouth. The Peacemaker fired one more shot, from reflex more than anything, that smashed into the side of the bar.

"My God," Grady said, and with that, he dropped to the floor like a sack of flour falling off a wagon. Blood spread out from the two holes in him, no more than an inch and a half apart, soaking his shirt.

That blood trick worked, I thought, but that was before I realized it was leaking out his back, too. A claret pool was forming underneath him, and the more of it there was on the floor, the whiter Grady's face became in contrast.

There wasn't any blood trick. The man was dead.

"Oh, God damn it," I said.

At last, the two remaining witnesses ran for the swinging doors in front, falling into the street and hollering over one another for the sheriff. And why the hell not? A crazy woman every man jack in town knew had a beef with Deputy Thurston just murdered him in plain view. "Grady, you damn fool."

Gingerly, I touched his bloody chest with two fingers, just to verify that he wasn't wearing that steel plate he was supposed to have on. All I felt was flesh. I even lifted the checkered shirt to triple-check, as though I really needed to, and he didn't have so much as an undershirt on underneath. Just two ragged holes, one of which went straight through his heart, because the damn fool hadn't followed through with his own plan and gotten himself killed for it—for real.

But why?

I wasn't fixing to linger around Horseblood to figure out what went wrong. If there hadn't been a price on my head in the Montana Territory before, there sure as shooting was one now, so I mounted my nag and gigged her into a hard lope for anyplace but there.

I stayed clear of the foothills where Grady Thurston and I hatched our ill-fated plan, unsure if he'd told anybody about me hiding out there. For all I knew, he'd been setting me up from the start, though I could hardly see why a man would get his own self killed just to get at me. I thought it more likely he thought he'd get the drop on me back at the Blind Stud, plug me before I could get off a shot at him. A man who played poker as often as he did was already a man fond of taking his chances, but that was one gamble that didn't pay off—and the last bet he'd ever place. Still, there was a powerful lot of hullabaloo with all the planning and the history with Burnham for him to have just wanted to gun me down from the beginning. None of it stood to reason, and the more I studied on it, the more puzzling it became.

And that was the main trouble for me now, the puzzle of it. Common sense commanded I get shed of Montana altogether, but I knew damn well this whole thing would plague me to no end if I never sussed out why everything went so sideways. That was just the way my damnable brain worked; once a thing like this found purchase up there, there was no getting the roots out 'til I saw it through to the bitter end. For that reason, I didn't hie on out of the territory like I ought to've. No, I rode directly for Devil's Fork, and there I waited to see if anybody showed to shine a light on the dead man I left back in Horseblood.

I saw the lights after midnight, tiny pin-pricks like blinking stars in the middle distance that slowly grew into torches as they neared Devil's Fork. Four, by my count, which wasn't the biggest posse anybody ever sent after me. It wasn't the posse its own self that interested me, anyhow; leastways, not half as much as how they knew where to find me. That was something I'd been giving a lot of thought to while I waited in the rimrocks at the mouth of the canyon there, watching my back trail for the men I knew were coming.

Oh, I didn't know at first, not at all. When I got there, I hobbled my nag and hunkered down, and I reckoned I'd wait for a few hours but move along after that. From there, it was only a matter of picking one of the two unpleasant paths out of there, or doubling back to find myself a different road to someplace else. I didn't expect it was going to much matter, so long as it was away from Horseblood, but after a short spell of studying on that, none of it mattered to me—out of no place and all of a sudden, I fathomed what happened when I killed Grady Thurston in the Blind Stud Saloon. It came to me like an arrow into my brain, and I couldn't help but laugh a little at how dumb I felt for not seeing it sooner.

And that was when the lights came.

"All right, boys," I said, "let's see who y'all brought to see me."

The first face I could make out with any certainty was Quint Burnham. He looked tired and aggrieved, maybe even a little guilty that he hadn't locked me up the first chance he got. Part of me almost wished he had, too, just so I wouldn't have killed poor old Grady.

After Quint came an unexpected member of the posse: Artie from the saloon. His hand was still wrapped up, but he could carry that scattergun of his just fine. I doubted he was anybody's first choice for a last-minute round-up of men to go combing the hills for me. Probably the old boy was the first to volunteer, and I supposed he was going to be the one to really watch out for. That son of a bitch had himself a grudge.

The last two members of Burnham's posse were strangers to me, just townsmen who either volunteered or got pressed into service for one reason or another. Neither of them looked particularly invested in the job, which suited me right down to the ground. The fewer wild cards I had to deal with, the better.

Burnham, raised a hand to quiet the men and slow their approach when he wasn't much more than fifty yards out from where I crouched, watching. The other three crowded up behind him, the four mounts nickering some and stamping their hoofs in the trail dust at the fork. It would have been easy work to pick them all off, one by one, but that wasn't something I wanted to do if I could avoid it. Way I saw it, there was only one man responsible for what happened that night, and he wasn't there.

"Hello, boys," I called out.

"That you, Boon?" the sheriff called back.

"It's me."

"You turning yourself in?"

"I am not."

"Doing this the hard way, then?"

"We gonna flap our mouths all night, Sheriff?" Artie cut in. "Or we here to put that bitch down?"

"Shut the hell up, Artie," one of the other men said.

"Why don't you make me, Roy?"

"God damn it, Artie," Quint Burnham said, pinching the bridge of his nose like his head was starting to ache. "Just be quiet, will you?"

"She kilt Grady in cold blood, and you wanna palaver with her," Artie whined.

"Wasn't cold blood," I countered. "I was fooled into it, Burnham. And I'd wager if you study on it a minute, you can sort out who it was that done that."

"What the hell are you talking about?" the sheriff said.

"Grady hired me to make it look like I shot him," I explained. "A false killing to keep you from killing him for real."

"That's preposterous. Why on earth would I want to kill Grady Thurston?"

"Told me you blame him for the death of your wife, Sheriff."

A couple of the men snorted and snickered at that, and I didn't have to wonder why.

"That's some tale, missy," Quint said, "accounting for the fact that I ain't ever been married."

"I figured," I said.

"Even if that were true—and I wouldn't bet a wooden nickel that it was—how do you come to turn a false killing into a real one, then?"

"He was supposed to have him a steel plate underneath that shirt," I said. "Of course, he didn't. I even double-checked, I was so shocked by it, and wouldn't you know there was something other than that steel plate he didn't have under that shirt, either?"

"Which was what?"

"A scar from the bullet he caught at Rappahannock during the war. He showed it to me, but when I looked after he lay dead on the floor, it wasn't there no more. Hell of a thing, Sheriff Burnham, an old war scar up and disappearing like that."

"This bitch is either drunk or crazy," Artie scoffed. "Whichever way, she ain't making a lick of sense, Quint. Now, are you gonna go get her, or do I got to?"

"You can sure as shit try," I shouted to Artie. "Mayhap you'll do better than the last time you tried, but I doubt it. And this time, I won't aim for the stock."

The little bastard failed to respond that that.

Quint Burnham said, "Grady Thurston didn't serve in the war, Boon."

"Figured that out for myself. Bet his brother did, though. Known me a lot of liars in this life, and a good one knows to sprinkle in some true facts here and there to keep it credible. When he told me about that scar, I reckon the other Thurston boy was telling me his own truth instead of a lie about Grady."

There was a spell of quiet then, the posse men rolling what I'd had to say around in their skulls to try and get a handle on it. First one to speak was one of the two men I didn't know, who said, "Ol' Grady had a brother, Quint?"

"Jeezum Crow," Quint said, "ain't any one of you sons of

bitches going to call me Sheriff Burnham while we're on law business?"

"How's about it, Sheriff Burnham?" I said. "Did ol' Grady have himself a brother?"

"Guess you know he did," Burnham said, a hint of disappointment in his tone. "Dix was in the calaboose down Missouri way, last Grady told me. Armed robbery. There was a killing in Indian Territory they couldn't never pin on him. God damnedest thing, two twin boys as different as Cain and Abel."

"Except Cain done his own killing work," I said. "Didn't trick somebody else into doing it for him, way I recall."

"Christ on Calvary," Artie spat then. "You're not buying any of this horse shit, are you, Sheriff Burnham?"

"Artie," Burnham said, "you are a pure-dee pain in the ass and I never have cared for you. Boon, I am inclined to bring you in under protective custody until we can get to the bottom of this here mess. It ain't arrest, but it ain't optional, neither."

Artie sputtered a bit, but he couldn't come up with anything to say. I didn't have as much trouble with it.

"I appreciate the offer, but I think I'll decline," I said.

Burnham lightly gigged his mount, a chestnut gelding with white socks, and loped up closer to the rimrocks where I stooped.

"Now, you listen here, damn it," he boomed. "That's a good man you shot to death in my town, and I'm not hardly fixing to let you off that easy, girl. I am willing to hear you out, which is more than damn nigh any other white man would give you, but you try and run from me and I will fire on you, hear?"

"You wouldn't be the first," I told him. I edged back a little, just to get in range of my nag's hobble to untie her legs. I expected Burnham was a man of his word, and that as soon as I got shed of those rimrocks there was going to be gunfire. It wasn't something I wanted, mostly on account of not wanting to spill any of these men's blood—except for maybe Artie, the little shit. But I sure as hell wasn't going to surrender to any lawman's jail cell. If Quint Burnham wanted me in it, he was going to have to make me, and I knew damn well that wasn't happening.

No part of it was a good thing, any way I looked at it. Mayhap some men might have let me go, but I could tell Quint was as by-the-book as they came. I could try the old Apache hideaway trick, hang off the saddle behind the nag's body, but I wasn't getting any younger and thought it might could be safer if I was to just face the lead those boys threw my way. That I had some experience with, at least, whereas I'd never actually tried the Apache trick.

I also had experience with getting shot at well before it was any kind of fair, so when the first couple of rounds were squeezed off, I ducked back behind the rocks and ground my teeth. Artie, if I had to guess. But if it'd been a bet, I'd have lost.

The posse's horses whinnied and hoofs got to kicking up a fuss while the men shouted over one another and jangled their tack.

"God damn it, who goes there?" Sheriff Burnham hollered.

A latecomer to our little powwow. I poked my head up to see if I could get a look. Sure enough, a new man was riding hard from the narrow canyon bluffs. He was astride a sixteen-hand stallion black as coal and firing potshots at the posse with a repeating rifle. The lawmen scattered in all directions, most of them firing their irons wildly in response, but not a one of them was like to hit the broad side of a barn that way. The newcomer wasn't in a terribly better position, hard as it is to aim from the saddle of a galloping mount, but he had surprise on his side.

"Ain't that some shit?" I said, and since the shooter wasn't aiming any of those rounds at me, I rose back to my full height, stepped up into my saddle, and drew the Adams revolver given to me by the very same man attacking Burnham and his men.

Leastways, so I presumed, and my presumption was rewarded when the sheriff shouted, "Dix Thurston, that you, son?"

"You was 'sposed to kill her, you dumb son of a bitch," was Dix's response to that. "Ain't you ever heard about eye for an eye, Sheriff?"

That said, Dix jacked a fresh cartridge into his rifle's breech, took careful aim, and fired the round that killed Sheriff Quint Burnham. The bullet didn't take the man's eye, but it did slam right into his chest and knock him clean out of the saddle. Burnham struck the ground in a cloud of dust and moved no more.

Artie screamed, wheeled his mount around, and charged Dix, squeezing off shot after shot from a double-action revolver until the hammer fell on a spent shell and Dix shot him in the throat. I was surprised to see he even had that little shooter, but not half as surprised as Artie was to catch lead with his Adam's apple. He dropped the gun and clamped both hands around the wound, looking for all the world like he was trying to choke himself instead of stanch the blood flow. It wasn't long after that before he, too, slid off his saddle and fell in a heap to the ground.

I wasn't going to mourn him. But I felt powerful sorry about Sheriff Burnham. I didn't have a lot of love in my heart for lawmen, but the man hadn't deserved to get cut down like that. And if I was going to be forced to pick sides, I certainly wasn't siding with Dix God Damn Thurston. In point of fact, the remaining two men in Quint's posse fell into hard gallops back to Horseblood, leaving me alone to face the man who set me up to murder his own kin, so the only sides left were his and mine.

"Okay, then," I said, and I let my nag pick her way through the rimrocks, down to the fork in the trail where two men lay dead and a third turned his stallion to watch and wait.

———————

"Gotta say," Dix said, "I did not account for that man to be so understanding."

He crossed his hands over the saddle horn, his repeater on the saddle just behind it. On closer inspection, I saw it was a Spencer calvary carbine, probably magazine-fed and chambered for the .56-56 rimfire cartridge, if I was to guess. Made sense, given how crack a shot he was on that big bit of horse-flesh between his legs.

"It was some surprise to me, too," I said. "Most times they shoot before asking any questions."

"If he had," Dix said, "he'd still be alive, the poor fool."

"But I might not be."

"Was my plan."

"Didn't work."

"Nope," he said. "Didn't."

I said, "Why Grady? Seemed an all right jasper to me."

"Don't rightly recall asking your thoughts on him," Dix said. "But what the hell? Truth is, I dreamed it up one night as the one killing I was certain to get away with. I stabbed a half-breed Army scout in the heart down in the Cherokee Strip and don't you know they sent five United States Marshals after my ass. Five! For a fucking *half-breed*. Got to thinking a man can't hardly get away with anything anymore, and there it was, like God his own self put it right into my mind for me."

He tapped himself on the forehead with two fingers and grinned ear to ear. It was some kind of self-satisfaction for a man who schemed the murder of his twin brother.

"Just to see if you'd get away with it," I said.

"That's it," he agreed.

"You didn't," I said, and I fired three quick shots, one right after the other, at his face. The rounds pierced both eyes and drove a dark hole through his upper lip. Blinded and spitting bloody bits of tooth and tongue, Dix Thurston looked like he wanted to say something, but instead he toppled off the left side of that beautiful black, his boot stuck in the stirrup. "Eye for an eye."

He never went for that Spencer. Not with me. It just stayed where he'd laid it, across the saddle lengthwise in front of him, while I had his Adams in my hand all the time. Dix must have known I'd use it; he wouldn't have chosen me for his damned scheme if he didn't think I was a hand with a gun. But the old boy just sat there and waited for it, like it was his time, carved in stone and irreversible.

I reckoned those marshals were likely still after him, and now that his one last horrible hurrah had gone sideways, Dix preferred picking how he went rather than getting cut down by whoever they sent out of Fort Smith. He chose me over them, not that it really made any difference. Either way, he was dead.

And as far as I was concerned, that made the world a mite nicer to be in, without him in it.

All the same, he'd gone and used me again, forced my hand and made me kill the remaining Thurston brother. That was why, when I loaded up the bodies of Quint Burnham and Artie to take back to town for a proper burial, I left Dix to the buzzards and bugs. It was more than a man like him deserved, a killer who killed because he could.

———————

Autumn came to the Montana Territory like a slap to the face that year, and the winter that came after that was one of the worst in memory, with snow blizzards that ruined entire ranches and killed hundreds of thousands of cattle across the Great Plains. I hied out before that, but not before the territorial government concluded that I'd murdered not only the Thurston brothers, but Sheriff Quint Burnham and Arthur "Artie" Hochstetler, to boot. Nobody bothered to put the pieces of the puzzle together, to look at the differences in the rounds between the bodies and match them up to the guns each participant likely used. I expected it was just easier that way, pinning the whole bloody affair on me, and in the end, I didn't reckon it much mattered. Even without the two murder charges I hadn't earned, there was enough on me to hang me twenty-five times over, so I figured if they wanted to blame me it was their prerogative.

It wasn't as though the real killer got away with it. But I was going to—at least for a while. Nobody got away with anything forever, because in the end everyone had their turn in the dirt. Mine turn was coming, but not yet.

Not quite yet.

THE LAST WILL AND TESTAMENT OF JACKSON WARD

I.

The foolscap was torn, water damaged, and the ink was washed out in several places, but between the three of them, they were able to piece it together and make out the words and intent of the document. Emma Hanlon bent over the table, spectacles perched on her hawkish nose, and studied the will carefully by the light of the oil lamp as though it was the first time she had ever seen it. In fact, Emma had read the will so many times already that she had mostly memorized it.

Lawyer Reed lounged nearby in his wingback chair, working on a Spanish cigar that filled the office with acrid, blueblack smoke, and absently tapping two fingers on the arm of the chair. Robert Hanlon paused his incessant pacing long enough to watch the smoke gather in the lamplight, looking for all the world like the very spirit of Jackson Ward was rising out of the greasy glass chimney among them. Shaking this off, he resumed his trek to the back of the office, where he turned on a heel and stalked back to the front again.

The lawyer coughed and sat forward, heaving a sigh.

"I daresay the damned thing is not going to change, no matter how many times you read it," he said.

Emma Hanlon grunted without taking her eyes off the foolscap.

Robert said, "But my God, Reed, just who in the blue hell *is* Audrey Jo White?"

"His *beloved*," Reed said. "You read it, too."

"Ward never married," Hanlon protested, maintaining his nervous pacing. "I'd stake everything I have on it. He's having his fun with us from the grave. That's all this is."

Reed drew in a mouthful from the cigar and held it, his cheeks puffed out, until the smoke started to drift from his nostrils.

"He was not a respectful man," the lawyer said at length. He added, "Sorry, Emma."

Emma Hanlon pursed her mouth and narrowed her eyes. Her face looked red as a strawberry in the glow from the lamp and she closed her eyes for a moment, composing herself.

"You need not apologize to me, Mr. Reed," she said. "My brother was a lot of things, but respectful was not one of them. Nor responsible, honest, pious, or any other quality one may wish to find in a kinsman." She removed the spectacles and set them gingerly on the table, beside the will, before raising her eyes to meet the lawyer's gaze. "If we hadn't shared the same mother, I would tell you he was a son of a bitch."

Reed coughed again. Hanlon stopped pacing in the center of the room and cleared his throat. Emma almost looked like she was suppressing a smile at the men's discomfort.

"Do you plan to honor it?" the lawyer said.

Hanlon scoffed. "Certainly not."

"It's legal," Reed countered. "Assuming there is any such person as this White woman."

"Then where was she when we buried the old rascal?" Hanlon said. "I say if she wants the inheritance, she can come plead her case for it. But since none of us has ever heard of her, and I doubt very much that she's anyplace to be found in town, never mind the county, I say…"

"I'll find her," Emma said, cutting her husband short.

"You'll what?" said Reed, rising to his feet.

"You will do no such thing," Hanlon said.

"I will, Robert. I can and I will. Jackson was what he was but he was blood and he's dead. It's one last thing to honor kin, and then it's nothing more ever again. I am going to find this woman and really put my brother to rest."

Hanlon and Reed regarded one another cagily. Emma folded her spectacles, returned them to their case, and left the room.

II.

Outside an unpainted tavern with a false front and a sign designating the place as The Irish Rose, Jackson Ward paused in the street to finish his smoke and wonder about the never-ending road that brought him there. He'd ridden into Ten Trees on the far side of town, where he quickly resolved to stick around for at least one night. Accordingly, he boarded his dapple gray and the pack mule he'd won over a game of five card stud back in the Indian territory, which he kept ever since but did not need. And although he had stake enough to look for a hotel or rooming house rather than spend another night sleeping rough, the saloon caught his eye first, before he ever had a chance to look for digs.

Sleep could wait; *The Irish Rose* presented the solution to a more pressing need.

Inside, a scattering of men drank, smoked, played faro, and flirted with doxies beneath the haze of a wagon wheel chandelier. At one end of the room, a sleepy-faced man in a plug hat with his sleeves pulled up to the garters played a mellow tune on an out-of-tune piano. At the other end, a bartender cleaned glassed with a rag behind an ornate bar that Ward figured to have been imported from someplace back east, if not Europe. The dark, shiny wood was intricately carved with curlicues, vines, and what looked like the wooden women that served as mastheads on tall ships at the corners. The whole rig seemed almost ridiculously out of place in a watering hole like that, but Jackson Ward did not resent it so long as the liquor behind it was for sale. He sidled up to the nearest masthead, a bare-chested mermaid grasping at curlicues with both hands, and made a noise in his throat to signal the bar man.

"Rye," he said when the man looked his way.

"Any kind in particular?"

"Cheap."

The bartender half-shrugged, set down the glass he was cleaning, and squatted until he was out of view to go in search of his cheapest rye whiskey. A moment later, he brought a glass with three fingers of dark brown liquid to where Ward stood between two stools, leaning on the mermaid.

"Two bits."

"That's your cheapest?"

"Take it or leave it, buster."

Shrugging his aching shoulders, Ward dug a pair of a coins from the right front pocket of his Levi's and dropped them on the bar. The bartender scooped them up, grinned crookedly, and returned to that glass he'd been cleaning. Ward followed the bar man with his eyes as he made his way back down to the middle of the bar, and that was when he first saw her.

She was slight of frame, milky pale, her hair pinned up, the color of straw. She wore calico, a cameo at her throat that caught his eye. Ward thought her eyes were golden at first, but realized quickly that they were only reflecting the setting sunlight coming in through the windows as her eyes glossed over with tears. One tear broke free, sliding down her high-boned face while she reached for the gin sling in front of her. The heels of her black leather ankle boots hooked a low crossbar on the stool she occupied, her dress sloughing all the way down to the floor, and she drank deeply, nearly emptying the glass before setting it back down to wipe her eyes with the back of her hand.

Green, Ward could see at last. Her eyes were green.

She flashed them at him, and he turned away, reddening with shame for having stared so long.

Jackson Ward finished his drink and signaled the bartender for another. When the drink came, the bar man frowned and leaned in close, conspiratorially. He said, "Don't you go thinking she's some damsel in distress, now. She works the cribs out back, you know."

"Doxie," Ward said.

The bartender nodded solemnly and said, "Special kind, too. Maybe not for you, pal."

"Maybe not." Ward sipped the rye and cast his gaze away

from the bartender, back to the woman. Her gin sling was gone, glass and all, and she had turned her attention to the swinging doors that led back out into the gathering twilight. He'd known prettier women by the score, but there was something there, something he had not come looking for but couldn't quit gawking at. "Maybe not."

He'd paid for it before, like most any other man he ever knew, though that had been some years back. He was a younger man then, with different needs. Anymore, all Jackson Ward cared to think about was where he was headed next, whether or not he had the poke for a hot meal or if he had to start thinking about riding the grub line looking for handouts. Once a rowdy, now a roustabout. And he was tired. He was just so tired.

"I'll be wanting one more after this'un," he said without taking his eyes from the girl in calico. "And her next gin sling is on my coin, too."

"Fine," said the bartender.

She got her drink before he finished his second. The bar man gestured at Ward and she turned her slender neck to look at him. Her eyes were still wet, the one hand on the bar trembling almost imperceptibly. A moment later, she was seated beside him, both hands on the gin sling, and she said, "Can you take me out of here?"

And, without giving it a second thought, Jackson Ward nodded his head and said, "Yes, I can."

III.

Emma Hanlon visited the detective at regular weekly intervals, always on a Wednesday. It was a four-hour journey one way to Abilene by stage and she never stayed the night, opting instead to make the same long trip back, arriving home under the cover of night. The man she conferred with was called Oscar Smith and claimed to have served both as a policeman in Philadelphia as well as a Pinkerton agent for a combined total of thirteen years before striking out on his own. Whether or not this was true was moot to Emma, who judged the man to be shrewd and experienced based solely on the way with which he comported himself. All the same, some seven weeks had passed since first she hired him, and he had yet to find hide or hair of her dead brother's mysterious beneficiary.

Emma was growing impatient, both with the delay and with her dwindling savings.

"There must be a thousand Whites in Texas alone," she said, her legs crossed and one foot bouncing anxiously as she spoke. She faced Smith, who sat behind an ostentatiously large desk and peered back at her over steepled fingers. "How many have you investigated so far?"

"None," he said, to Emma Hanlon's tremendous chagrin. She began to retort, but the detective cut her off. "As I doubt very much that is her real name. I believe what we are dealing with here is a confidence woman, Mrs. Hanlon. A low sort who bewitched your brother and tricked him into signing over his inheritance to her—and indeed, most likely killed him himself. Such a woman would not be so sloppy that she would conduct her grim business under her own Christian and family names."

"My God." She began to sweat, the horror of it crawling over her like flames.

"So, no, Mrs. Hanlon, I am not investigating Whites. I am investigating the sort of trash to which this woman undoubtedly belongs until such a time that I hear an eyewitness account of one who has used this name or something close to it. Then I will be on the correct path."

Emma said, "I never imagined," and sniffed loudly.

"It is not yours to imagine, Mrs. Hanlon. A considerable portion of my job is to deal with these dreadful aspects of our society so that fine ladies like you needn't. Come Saturday, I will take the morning stage west to follow up on some intelligence I have acquired regarding a dusty little hole in the ground called Ten Trees. I am told there are people there who might offer a substantial break in my case, after which time I will finally be able to provide you with some answers, should things go well. I trust that satisfies your troubled mind some?"

"A confidence woman," said Emma, shaking her head and fidgeting with a handkerchief she couldn't remember holding before. "Jackson Ward, you damned fool."

"I will find her," Smith declared, his chair whining beneath the weight of him. "And you will have your words with her before I turn her over to the U.S. Marshal's office."

"And she won't get one penny more from this family, the monster."

"Nothing more," agreed the detective, "but a rope around her neck."

IV.

They rode in silence for more than an hour, he leading on the dapple gray with her close in tow astride the mule. She rode sidesaddle for a considerable distance, intent on maintaining her decorum, but as night fell fully on the stony flatland she spoke up at last, requesting they stop so that she might change into something more appropriate to the circumstances of travel.

"We'll camp here," Ward said, wheeling the gray about and dismounting with some discomfort. He was no longer able to ride long distances without chafing and pain, something he'd been trying to ignore for the better part of a year. "No sense in keeping on in the dark when one or both of these animals is like to stumble and break a leg."

"Sleep rough?"

"I don't see any hotels around."

The woman chuckled, a small and sweet sound that brought a smile to Jackson Ward's face in spite of himself. Ever since they'd ridden out of Ten Trees he had been trying to determine what, exactly, had been his motivation to accept the woman's proposal without so much as asking why. He had his suspicions that it had everything to do with her line of work there, something worth escaping, Ward imagined, especially the way the bartender talked about her and her services. Still, all she had to do was ask and Ward leapt right into the part of white knight and savior, eager to whisk her away to wherever it was she wanted to go. Yet until she raised her voice about stopping, that request had been the only words she'd ever said to him. He figured he was getting soft and hoped it wouldn't be something he'd live to regret.

"Clear night," he said, helping her down from the mule. "Warm, too. We can have a little fire, though I'm sorry I have no victuals to suffice for supper. If you think you can make it, I'm sure we'll make do with something or other tomorrow."

"I'll make it," the woman said.

Ward nodded, unsure if she could see him in the near-total dark, and then went about the business of collecting kindling and firewood to build the fire. His eyes gradually adjusted to the night and the appearance of the moon from behind of bank of slate-colored clouds helped, so while he stacked cords of mesquite over a bed of sagebrush, he watched her. And once the brush crackled with pulsing flames that licked at the bottom of the mesquite, he watched her still more closely, strangely unable to take his eyes away from her.

Had he been alone, Ward would have preferred a cold camp, and for a moment he wondered if the only reason he built the fire was to make the woman more comfortable, or if he just wanted to keep studying the line of her neck, gracefully arcing up from one exposed shoulder like a snow drift, or the way one thick lock of her golden hair had come loose of the bun and now fluttered like woodsmoke over one downcast eye. It was a lot of years since he last felt so utterly bewitched in this way, and as he continued to stare, he tried to determine if he liked it or not.

"Do you always gawp at a lady so?" she said at some length, raising her chin just enough to meet his gaze over the campfire.

"Not much," said Ward. "What are you running from?"

She turned her head to glance back over her shoulder, back in the direction of Ten Trees. "Them. Myself. Everything."

"Can't be an easy life."

"Life is never easy."

"No, I don't guess it ever is." His stomach rumbled, empty apart from the rye he'd had back at the tavern. "I'm Jackson Ward."

"Hello, Mr. Ward," she said softly. "Audrey Jo White."

"I'm proud to know you, Ms. White."

"We'll see, Mr. Ward," said Audrey Jo. "We'll see."

V.

Emma Hanlon took two days to reach her decision, and on the morning of the third day, she boarded the stage for Ten Trees. She retained Mr. Smith's services for the time being but did not inform him of her intentions—there was always the possibility that she, an untried amateur at the game of ratiocination, would come up empty-handed. All the same, armed with the new information imparted to her in last meeting with the detective, Emma could not let it go. Maybe Smith would get to the woman before she did, but if there was a chance she might get ahead of the detective, she was going to take it.

Her first stop was the city marshal's office, just beside the post and telegraph office where she disembarked from the stage. Once inside, a trio of men went from throaty laughter to embarrassed silence, shuffling their boots on the floor and mostly avoiding eye contact. Emma could guess at the kind of jokes the men were swapping, but waved it off and said, "Which one of you men is the marshal?"

The eldest of them, a gray-haired curly wolf who stood over six feet tall but couldn't have weighed more than one hundred fifty pounds soaking wet, stepped forward and said, "That'd be me, miss. Charlie Hillborough."

"Then I will come directly to my business, Marshal Hillborough. I am looking for a woman who goes by the name of Audrey Jo White."

One of the other two men, burly and short, cleared his throat and traded a disconcerted look with the last man, the youngest, whose thin mustache twitched as he shot a glance back at the marshal.

Hillborough said, "Gents, if you don't mind."

The two friends of the marshal nodded and, without a word, made their way out of the office. The young man shut the door behind him, substantially dimming the close, windowless room.

"Why don't you take a seat, miss?"

"Missus," Emma corrected him. "Hanlon."

"Mrs. Hanlon, then. Coffee?"

"No, thank you."

"Just me, then. Wife says I drink too much, but I don't see how I could operate without it. Older I get, more I need in a day."

Emma clasped her hands at her middle and lowered herself into a chair facing Hillborough's desk. There, she waited in silence, watching him closely as he went about the business of pouring black coffee from a tin pot atop a small iron stove in the corner. She noted the lack of steam rising from his dented metal cup and wondered, idly, if the marshal always took his coffee cold.

"I will be happy to answer any questions you have, Mrs. Hanlon," he said once he returned to sit behind the desk. "But first, might I ask why it is you have come looking for Ms. White?"

"My younger brother has recently died."

"I am sorry."

"And he has willed his portion of our family inheritance to this woman, about whom none of us know a thing."

"I see."

Absentmindedly, he blew on the surface of the murky coffee. Catching himself, he half-smiled and downed half of it in one gulp.

"Used to be she was in the employ of Catherine Mullaney, just a five-minute walk up Center Street here at The Irish Rose. Working girl, after a fashion."

"A whore, you mean."

"Lady in waiting," the marshal said with a wink. Emma was unmoved by his wit. "Normally, I would not know the names of these women, being a Christian man my own self, but Ms. White was peculiar. I suspect she still is."

"How is that, Marshal Hillborough?"

The marshal finished the rest of his cold coffee, set the cup on his desk, and drew a long breath in through his nostrils. While Emma awaited his answer, Hillborough collected his thoughts and sorted out how he was going to convey them to her.

"Fact is, Mrs. Hanlon," he said at some length, "nobody ever was altogether sure whether Audrey Jo was a woman or a man."

With that, the marshal finished off the rest of his coffee and watched for his visitor's reaction. None came for several long seconds, but gradually her brows gathered into a bunch at the bridge of her nose. She shot up to her feet and she emitted a harsh, brief snort.

Marshal Hillborough leaned back in his chair and waited for it to come together in his visitor's mind. When it did, Emma finally sat back down, speechless.

VI.

The winter previous was a mild one, leading into a dry spring. Jackson Ward walked the length of the creek bed abutting the five acres he'd been trying to prove up over the course of the past year, kicking at loose rocks, peering at the scratchy saltcedar and blackbrush. Beyond this, where the land sloped down into bowl, sat a spattering of neighboring homesteads on the periphery of the vast Bar-T. Ward could see clearly from where he paced that the grass was greener, the ponds wet, the animals robust and crops colorful. The country there was not quite facing drought, at least not officially, but the topography was against him; water flowed down, away from everything he had that needed it. What started as a squat was fast becoming a failure. Inwardly, he damned himself for ever thinking he had the sand to pull it off. Outwardly, he strained against the moisture welling up in his eyes.

Love had done a job of work domesticizing Jackson Ward. He did not much mind it, preferring quiet nights with his woman to lonely ones wandering the middle border with no thought to tomorrow. She kept his faith and he kept her secrets. They shared a warm meal every evening, an even warmer bed every night. And in the mornings, he rose to walk the boundary of a small parcel of God's green earth that would belong to the government of the United States until he could sufficiently establish his acumen at tending it and making something useful of his labor. His doubts grew day by day.

But not about Audrey Jo. Never about her.

Should everything fall apart, he decided, he would just have to find something else to do. Anything to hold onto what he had.

They took in a light breakfast after he returned the cabin, a shambles when they found it but much better appointed, homey even, since A.J.'s ongoing project of overhauling it had begun. Ward fixed the stove-in roof, but everything inside, from the hand-sewn curtains on the structure's sole window to the lace draped over the rough-hewn table at which they sat and ate, was done by her hands. So, too, she helped to feed and range their four sheep and never so much as winced when the time came to take and kill a chicken from the coop—she would twist the bird's neck with her bare hands until it snapped and have the fowl defeathered in less time than it took to roast it.

He set his fork down beside an unfinished plate of fried potatoes and regarded her with something near to a smile playing on his lips.

She said, "What is it?"

"We are going to make it."

"I know," said A.J. "I've always known."

Her eyes crinkled at the corners, evincing lines that had only begun to develop in the months since settling on the cabin, but they widened again as she cast her gaze away from him, to the open window.

Before she could announce what she saw, Jackson turned in his chair to find a man riding a gaunt palomino, unhurriedly approaching by way of the Bar-T.

"Who is that?" he said then, his voice weak in his throat.

A.J. said nothing. Only watching.

A few minutes passed, the two of them seated, facing the window, until the rider came at last into clear view. The rounded, flat-brimmed padre hat bounced on his gray head as the reverend, donned entirely in black, neared the cabin. Straight-backed, his gnarled hands curled over the reins in front of him, the reverend pulled into a stop some fifteen feet from the window and stalled a moment, staring back at them.

Jackson heaved a sigh. "Suppose I'll go see what he wants."

A.J. nodded, keeping her gaze on the window and the man beyond it.

Outside, Jackson ran his fingers through his mop of brown-gray hair, long overdue for a cut, and waved the other hand at the horseman.

"Morning, reverend," he said.

Dismounting with some obvious discomfort, the bony man said, "Haven't seen you in a lot of Sundays, Mr. Ward."

"Just me and the wife," said Ward. "No one to work if I'm not here."

"The wife," the revered parroted. "She here, too?"

"What can we do for you, Reverend?"

"Folks talk, Mr. Ward," he said, patting himself down to knock away the dust and burrs as best he could. "Starts off the same, among they selves, but it always comes on back to me in time."

A.J. had appeared in the doorway by then, one hand on the frame as she watched and listened. Jackson looked back to her, then returned his attention to the preacher.

"Reverend," he said.

"How is it," the preacher interrupted, "that you are married to Audrey Jo but she has not taken your name?"

"We have no children. Never saw the point."

"No children, indeed. And why is that, Mr. Ward?"

"God's will," Ward said through clenched teeth. He was growing agitated and tried to rein it in. The old temper. The old Jackson Ward. It just wouldn't do anymore. "Not for me to know about things like that."

"Just so," agreed the reverend. He rocked, slightly, on his heels. "There's just no limit to the mysteries of the cross. And it sure does seem like there's something of a mystery here, too."

"No mystery a'tall," said Jackson, narrowing his eyes at the clergyman. "Just a man with no business being here, keeping me from my work."

The two men regarded one another silently for a full minute until the reverend broke away, turning his eyes to the woman in the cabin's doorway.

"Good day to you, Mrs. White," he said with a tight-lipped smile, and with that, he walked back to his mount and with some difficulty climbed back onto the saddle. Ward watched him carefully, every step of the way. "And to you, Mr. Ward. Be seeing you."

Jackson did not move an inch until the reverend was nearly out of view, vanishing back into the distance of the Bar-T and the settlement beyond, on the other side of the sprawling ranch. It was only then that he returned to his bride, who worried the hem of her dress while shaking her head.

"It's nothing," he said. "Busybodies. You know."

"I know," A.J. said.

"It's nothing."

"It'll be something."

Ward reached for her hand, held it in his. He looked down on her with loving, sympathetic eyes, but inside him a red rage was beginning to boil.

VII.

Years had come and gone since anybody in Ten Trees had seen or heard of Audrey Jo White or the nameless drifter who up and took her away one day, without a word to anyone. Emma was disappointed, expecting it to have been weeks or months, a trail she might could follow, but these tracks were long blown away by time. She spoke to the barkeep at the saloon, a dingy and sinful place that made her skin crawl, as well as a farrier, the hotelier, and a one-eyed man who kept the livery stable and spoke mostly in grunts and single syllables. All of them knew or had heard tell of the White woman. None of them knew what ever became of her.

And to a man, they all broke eye contact and grew visibly uncomfortable when Emma Hanlon said the woman's name. She did not ask why. The sheriff had already told her that much. There was something terribly queer about her late brother's inheritor, something wrong and unconceivable, an affront to the natural order of the Good Lord above. It should not have surprised her that Jackson had gotten himself mixed up with something like that, yet it did, all the same. He was feckless and dishonest, lazy and impious. A lost sheep if ever there was one.

Fact is, Mrs. Hanlon, nobody ever was altogether sure whether

Audrey Jo was a woman or a man.

The statement seemed, on the face of it, so simple and concise. Yet Emma could make no sense of it, heads nor tails. It violated her core understanding of the world in which she lived—God's world—as though she had been told the woman was, possibly, some unthinkable creature from pagan mythology, half-horse and half-bird. A monster. Some nightmarish denizen of hell. Her head spun at the thought of it. Her heart palpitated and the skin on her face and neck felt hot, clammy.

And then there was the old woman, bent and shriveled, watching anxiously over her dining room in the only restaurant in Ten Trees, the Alhambra. She introduced herself to Emma when the younger woman came in, her throat dry from the heat and stomach uneasy from a full, long day with nothing to eat. Mrs. Early, which Emma found amusingly appropriate for anyone serving breakfast, though nothing was at all amusing about what the older woman had to say about Audrey Jo White when Emma answered honestly about her business in town.

"Ran off with a bandit, she did. Killed a man up near to Arkansas some time back."

What on earth have you done, Jackson? What have you done?

VIII.

The trouble began with some drovers up in Kansas, and it took months to trickle back down to the Bar-T. Cowhands. Rowdies. Their chits paid out, work done. Looking to blow off steam and getting to know the only women in town they were allowed to cavort with, per the agreement made between a city marshal and the trail boss. Booze flowed, secrets whispered. And a story was told, somewhere, by someone, about a special kind of doxie you sometimes see in places like that, for a different sort of hunger. One of them used to work a crib back down in Texas, it was said, Ten Trees, and she went largely unmolested because there always came along some odd duck who'd heard the same strange secrets, too.

A.J., they called her. Audrey Jo.

Summer stayed dry for the most part and what little rain

they had did what it always did, which was to follow the land down, down, away from the crops and animals on the hill and onto the Bar-T, where it pooled and became somebody else's good fortune. Jackson Ward walked the dry creek bed, morning after intolerably hot morning, squinting at the sparkle of the twin creeks below, where it forked and flowed for another man's use, damning a god in whom he never much believed and cursing himself for failing his wife so miserably.

"What'll we do?" she asked him, the lantern light pulsing like little lightning as the flame guttered out, the oil burned away.

"Move on," he said. They sat together at the little table, but there had been no supper. There had been no meals of any kind that day, or the day before. Just grazing on flour biscuits and seeds, like the drifter he used to be but that she never was. "It's over. I'll never prove up now. It was a gamble and a bad one."

"Jack."

"Only thing I was ever any good at was doing nothing at all."

"You're the only good man I ever met," she said. He shook his head but she reached for his chin, fingers gently turning his face toward hers, and he saw the tears in her eyes. "The only one, goddamnit."

"I been a lot of things weren't much good, A.J."

"Another life. Before you were you and I was me."

Now Jackson nodded, understanding. She'd spoken like this before, once while observing a black witch moth squeeze itself out of its obsidian cocoon beneath a joist in the cabin's shabby roof. Before he was him and she was her. She smiled, and Jackson did, too.

"A.J.," he said, softly, but a shout from outside cut him off before he could say more.

"Jackson Ward," came the voice, loud and urgent. "You at home, son?"

Audrey Jo stiffened. Her husband twisted in his chair to peer at the door, as though he could see through it to identify the source of the voice on the other side.

"Ward?"

"Who's that?"

"It's Blake Stiles, son," shouted the visitor. "Up from Bar-T. I have Doc Brandt with me, Ward. We'd like to speak with you."

Ward looked back to his wife and they shared a brief, uneasy gaze. It was late, going on dark. Neither of them had ever met the doctor from town, and they had only briefly spoken with the rancher here and there in all the months since Ward first laid his hopeless claim to the spread.

Some weeks had come and gone since the reverend's visit, but Ward knew this had to do with that. And maybe more, besides.

"Who comes at night like this?" A.J. said, her voice a near whisper.

Her husband said nothing to that, because they both knew already. Little that was good ever went on after sundown.

"I'll go see him," Ward said after a long, silent moment. A.J. touched his hand and shook her head. He tried to force a crooked, comforting smile, but it turned out a grimace so he relaxed his mouth and went to the door.

There in the dooryard sat two men on horses, backlit by the setting sun so that they looked like living shadows. Jackson Ward squinted at them as if trying to determine if they were who they said they were. Stiles removed his hat then and, fidgeting idly with the string, nodded perfunctorily to Ward.

"Long time, Ward."

"Long time," Jackson agreed.

"Looking a bit peaked up here, you don't mind my saying."

"Water's hard to come by. Most of it comes down to you."

The rancher nodded again.

"True enough," he said. "Maybe we could work something out about that. Have you haul some barrelfuls up the hill from my pond. Something like that."

"Maybe we could."

"I'd be obliged to lend a hand."

"Right smart Christian of you," Ward said.

"I try to be white to my friends," said Stiles.

The man beside the rancher said nothing in all that time, nor did he remove his hat. He just sat his mount, gloved hands on the bridle and head bobbing almost imperceptibly as though he might be sleeping or drunk. Ward sniffed, scratched the back of his neck, and then gestured with his chin to the doc.

"Somebody sick?"

"It's a delicate matter, Ward," Stiles said. "Uncomfortable as hell, tell you the gospel truth."

"Nobody forcing you to stay."

"Wouldn't you rather me than the marshal?"

"Marshal," Ward repeated, quiet and slow. "You're starting to sound purely serious, Blake Stiles."

"Serious thing," Stiles said.

"Best come out with it, then."

"Reckon I best."

With that, the rancher dismounted, and having done that he swatted the doc on the leg to shake him awake. Doc grunted and shook his jowls. Ward thought he looked for all the world like a wet dog, the old sot.

"I don't mean to sound inhospitable," Ward said, "but I don't recall inviting you men inside. How about telling me what you want before climbing down from those mounts?"

"Come on, Ward," Stiles said. "You know damn well what this is about. You already done chased the reverend off, and you know how folks' tongues wag. Doc's just here to settle everything up with a quick examination. Real medical-like, nothing he ain't done a hundred times before."

"Examination?" Ward said, backing up a few steps, closer to the door. "Examination of what, Stiles?"

"Why, your wife, Jackson. You got to know by now what people are saying. What they're thinking."

Jackson Ward narrowed his eyes, held his breath. From behind him, he could hear the leather hinges on the front door creak. She was back there, his Audrey Jo, listening through the crack in the door. He let the breath out and drew another in, long and deep.

"Was a time," he said at some length, "I never went anyplace without some iron strapped to my hip. Felt naked without it."

"I expect folks talk about that, too," said Stiles. "Everyone knows you raised some fair piece of Hell in your day."

"Always kept a portion of it inside, Blake. Let's not let it out now."

For some reason, that startled the doc to full wakefulness. He sat up straight in his saddle and looked to Ward as though he had no idea how he'd gotten there.

Stiles said, "You have normal relations with your wife, Ward?"

Jackson's sun-browned face reddened. He took another step back and said, "That's some kind of question, Blake. How about you? You fuck your wife regular?"

Stiles took two long strides forward. "Goddamn you, Ward."

"Not me, Blake Stiles. Goddamn you. *Gun.*"

At the barked word Ward had used by way of punctuation, Stiles reached for his hip by instinct, only to remember he wore no rig and the only gun he'd brought up the hill was the Winchester still lashed behind his mount's cantle. But Ward wasn't calling him out. He was only finishing what the rancher had unfortunately begun, something for which Jackson and A.J. had solemnly prepared and practiced ever since the reverend left their homestead all those weeks ago.

The door squeaked open as Ward turned at the waist, hands up to catch the Navy Colt A.J. tossed to him. He caught the heavy pistol with his right hand and palmed back the hammer with his left, training the barrel right at Blake's chest in the same fluid motion.

"Always did hear you was a hand with a gun," the rancher said sourly.

"Are you leaving or aren't you," Ward said.

"Oh, I'll leave, Ward. But I'll be back with the marshal soon as I can rouse him."

"I am sure sorry to hear that, Stiles."

Jackson squeezed the trigger and the Colt geysered flame, firing a single .36 round into the middle of Stiles's chest and knocking the rancher clean off his feet. The man was dead before he hit the ground, bleeding out into the untenable dust Ward had tried so hard to work. Doc squealed and jabbed his heels hard against the flanks of his horse, nearly bucked from the saddle as the beast galloped a wild half circle before thundering down the hill from whence they'd come. Ward sprinted after him, squeezing off another shot and still another, but the doc stayed hunched over the pommel, riding hell for leather as fast as he could.

By then the stars were out and the night a deep blue-black blanketing the endless sky so that Jackson Ward could only barely make out his wife's face as she came up beside him. He still held the Colt, its cracked butt gripped so tight in his hand that his knuckles ached, and not far behind them lay their neighbor's corpse. The horse Stiles had ridden, startled by the gunfire, had wandered off apiece, but now grazed idly at the sweetgrass on the westside of the soddy.

"We'll go," said Audrey Jo. "We'll run."

"That or hang."

She nodded once, and together they returned to their shanty home to see about packing whatever they needed most for the hard ride ahead of them.

IX.

The man, Emma learned, was a rancher of some repute and sizable holdings called Blake Stiles. He'd been the neighbor and sometime benefactor of a number of failed sodbusters occupying a hilltop spread above his property, the sprawling Bar-T, to which Stiles never laid any claim on account of its poor topography. Since his murder, however, the eldest of the Stiles sons took over the operation and annexed the erstwhile homestead, which he let go to seed. Any squatters who came sniffing around it got chased off with buckshot, or so the marshal—the second of that profession to whom she'd spoken about the matter—claimed with a chuckle when he told it to her.

"I am sorry, Mrs. Hanlon," the marshal said, composing himself. "I surely do not mean to make light of the thing."

"It's me who ought to be apologizing," she said. Her head was lowered, eyes on the edge of the marshal's desk. The proper posture of the deeply ashamed. "It's my kin who did the killing, as sick to my stomach I am to say the words aloud."

"Blake Stiles was a friend of mine. He surely was."

The lawman leaned back and worked his jaw a little, either remembering something or forgetting where he was going with this. After a short while, he pursed his mouth and swallowed noisily before turning his pale blue gaze back to Emma.

"I don't believe they ever did find the son of a—pardon me, Mrs. Hanlon—your brother. I'm pure-dee certain I'd have heard. Rangers got involved, you know. Pinkertons, too."

"He's dead," she said plainly.

"Dead!"

The marshal all but lunged forward in his surprise, gripping the desk as he leaned in.

"Yes," Emma said. "But as for Audrey Jo White, I can't say."

"I expect she's being looked for, too."

"That's what I am doing, Marshal. Or trying to do."

"I see."

"There's a claim to Jack's inheritance on account of her being his widow."

"Now that I can tell you is not true."

"No?"

"Nor possible."

"I've heard something about that."

"That right? And what is it you heard, if you don't mind my asking?"

"Only that there is some speculation and some confusion regarding the woman's actual sex."

The marshal nodded and, gradually, sat back in his chair.

"There's been investigation enough into that question to lay it to rest. That A.J. White is no woman at all, Mrs. Hanlon. Not as nature defines it, anyways."

"I have to confess," Emma said, finally bringing her eyes up to meet the lawman's, "it's still powerful hard for me to understand."

The marshal heaved a long, dramatic sigh and shifted in his chair, causing it to creak to the degree that Emma worried, if only for a moment, that it might collapse beneath the girth of him. He opened a drawer in the desk, withdrew a pipe from within, but after a moment of reconsideration he returned it and pushed the drawer shut. Stalling for time, he ultimately sighed again and cleared his throat to begin.

"All the towns along these trails, the cow towns you understand, are just about the vilest places you ever heard of outside Sodom and Gomorrah," he said. "Most of them, anyway, or at least they have been. There's some law coming in now—" He jabbed a thumb at the star pinned to his chest. "—and with it some small bit of order. Killings are down, but those boys—well, rough types. You know. Weeks and months driving cattle, their blood gets up. They challenge one another with stories and get to slavering for any kind of sin they might can find when they get into town and paid out their chits."

"Whores," Emma said.

The marshal nodded.

"Tolerated, of course, but corralled. Here, there's a time and place for it, and those boys aren't to go anyplace else or be armed at all. You just can't make it so they can't blow off any steam at all, or it'll all just blow to high heaven."

"Marshal, what has this to do with Audrey Jo White?"

"I hear tell of doxies like her from time to time. Didn't believe a word of it first time, of course. A girl who wasn't a girl. Couldn't get my mind around it, same as you right now, I expect." Emma remained still, listening. "But things can surely be a lot different out here, and further on West still, where there's like to be fifty men to every woman in a hundred square miles. Maybe that's it. And maybe some men is just different in ways I won't ever figure out. I just don't know. But the jasper told me about A.J. White—grub rider, thief, you know—that old boy told me she was all woman. And when I mentioned that piece of it that says she ain't, he only told me never to mind things I wouldn't ever understand."

"I guess I still don't, myself," Emma said.

The marshal laughed, a solitary honk that shook his entire frame.

"No, Mrs. Hanlon," she said, "I guess I still don't, either. But remembering the way that old jasper told tell, I guess there's something there and some girls are mighty different than you expect."

He shrugged and, at last, reached back for the pipe and set to packing the bowl.

"Yes, ma'am," he said, striking a match. "Some girls are just different than you expect."

More than once, she'd offered to live as a man. Cut her hair short, wear trousers and boots. They wouldn't be looking for two men; if nothing else, it might get them shut of Texas until they could reach the Territories, maybe California.

But Jackson would not hear of it.

"I won't have my wife disrespected," he said on the third occasion A.J. brought it up. "You are what you are."

They had made it as far as Del Rio, riding the north shore of the Rio Grande and making cold camps most nights, when Ward had given that final judgment on her offer. Disguise was one thing, but that was something else. Something that hurt her, and he knew it. You couldn't force a hog to be a heifer any better than you could force Audrey Jo to be what she wasn't, either. In a way, she looked disappointed, head hung low beneath the long-branched canopy of a bald cypress. More than that, though, she looked relieved. In spite of himself, he grinned at her, glad in heart that he'd made her understand how it was going to be. No turning back. Not to anything.

Black witch moths. *Before he was him and she was she.*

"I sure do love you, Jackson Ward," A.J. said.

He noticed a tear rolling its way down one apple-red cheek and he reached out to wipe it away with a blunt, calloused thumb.

"I love you right back, darlin'."

Audrey Jo smiled. Jackson leaned in close and kissed her.

The following night they came up a small border town, its name unknown to them, populated mostly by Mexicans but some whites, and elected to stay in a hotel with a proper bed and a bathtub for once. The manager, a round woman with steel-gray hair, hauled stove-heated water to the tub, bucket by bucket, while A.J. waited to bathe. In the meantime, Jackson went in search of some paper and a pencil.

Up the street from the hotel, he ducked into a general store, where he learned that there was no paper for sale, not exactly, but that the clerk would be happy to check the printer's office just around the corner, which Jackson bid him to do. When the young man returned, he carried with him a single sheet of foolscap, a pen, and a bottle of ink. He had to demonstrate how the pen and ink worked, as Jackson had never made use of one before. And, once he settled up, Jackson Ward returned to the room on the hotel's second floor where he flattened the paper on the floor and began to write.

When Audrey Jo returned from her bath—hair still damp, face and neck pink and soft—he motioned at the paper on the floor, ink slowly drying, and said, "I never told you, but my father has got a fair bit of money and land and such."

"You never talk about your family. Not so I'd notice."

"They haven't got much use for me. But I guess I'm still entitled to a share when the time comes."

"Where?"

"Back way we came."

A.J. tilted her head to one side.

"I know," Jackson said. "Not now. Not for a spell, most like. But someday. I just wanted to make it official-like. That it's yours, too. I mean, if there's anything left and I ain't been forgotten."

"Jack."

"I'd get it witnessed," he said, "except that's my name signed right there at the bottom and—well, you know."

"I know, Jack," A.J. said. "I know."

"Funny thing, too. You'd rightly expect I'd been a wanted man before, except I ain't."

He chuckled, then. A low, forced laugh. He'd tried so hard. So damn hard. But the world just never was an easy place to be. Harder still for her. It was almost enough to break a man, Jackson reckoned, but he hadn't seen his wife break yet so he figured on holding on as long as he could, too.

"I killed a man, A.J.," he said after a long, strained pause. "I killed Blake Stiles."

"I don't see how he left you a choice," she told him.

"Why couldn't he just leave us be?"

She closed the gap between them, five or six steps, and rested her warm head on his shoulder, her damp hair snaking coolly over his neck and chest.

"Why couldn't he just leave us be?" he said again.

"He was afraid," A.J. said softly, her voice muffled by his shirt.

"Afraid of what?"

"Everything. Men like that are always afraid."

That evening, A.J. and Jackson made love for the first time since they fled the soddy. Slow, unhurried. Like they always used to do, back before things started getting hard and the anxiety the reverend draped over them began settling heavily onto the spread. Ward dropped into a deep, dreamless sleep after that, having never gotten around to taking advantage of the bathtub, the weight of him and his worries sunken deep into the soft mattress and cotton blankets.

He awoke before dawn, sore but rested, his stomach rumbling for something hot until he came to realize that he was alone.

Audrey Jo was gone.

XI.

"This isn't any squat, ma'am—it's private property, matter of fact."

Emma turned slightly and narrowed her eyes against the afternoon sun to find a sweat-drenched man approaching her afoot. He'd come down from a bay mare some ten yards behind him, electing not to ride clear up to where she stood. To Emma's mind, this lessened the threat he posed, which she presumed was the point.

"I'm not looking to settle or farm," she told him, shielding her eyes with the flat of her right hand.

Already she'd spent the better part of an hour walking slow circles around the sod shanty, studying its every joist and crossbeam, the roof collapsed where it looked to have already been once repaired, a hint of frayed lace fluttering from beneath a table crushed underneath. His home, she imagined, though she could only barely imagine a man like Jackson Ward ever calling any place *home*.

"What might you be looking for, then?"

Shifting her stance in the knee-high grass and pigweed, she watched as the man came into focus, moving in front of the direct sun so that his rugged, squarish face appeared like from a dream.

"I spoke to the pastor in town," she said. "He told me my brother lived here for a time."

The man's face darkened, his eyes black slits.

"Jackson Ward," he said.

"Then he was here."

"Your brother killed my daddy."

"Oh," Emma Hanlon said, stepping back and covering her mouth. "Oh, my God. I—"

"I think you should get on out of here, now."

"I am so sorry."

"Go on."

She sniffed, her hand still covering her mouth, and nodded once. There was nothing more to say.

The younger Stiles walked resolutely away, back to where his bay browsed the tall grass, and with the experience of a life-long rider and the grace of the young, hefted himself up into the saddle in one fluid motion. By then, Emma had begun to cry.

Stiles wheeled the mare about, a light gig to the ribs to put her into motion, and rode her slow and easy back to where Emma stood weeping in the weeds.

"For what it's worth, they never did kill that doctor," he said. "Brandt was just drunk and fell off his horse. Everybody knew it, too, but they chalked that one up to your brother to ensure he got hisself hanged. Like my daddy wasn't enough."

With that, his heel met the bay mare's side once more, and he rode away from Emma Hanlon, through the swaying sea of green and yellow and down the slope of the hill to the sprawling Bar-T below. She watched him go, getting smaller and smaller until she could no longer see him at all in the orange glare of the late afternoon sun, and she kept on crying until the well went dry.

XII.

He never stopped looking. Right up to the day he died.

On that day, Jackson Ward was forty-six years of age and he had been riding most of the morning, more or less parallel to the Goodnight-Loving trail some fifty or sixty miles to the west. Around noon he stopped to take rest beneath the canopy of an oak grove's boughs, where he rolled a cigarette and stretched out his stiff legs. Halfway through the smoke, Ward got to thinking about having some pemmican and water to refresh him for the rest of the day's riding, but he never did have his victuals that day. Instead, his heart seized up in his chest, he dropped what remained of his cigarette the ground, and before another five minutes passed, he was dead against the trunk of a bur oak.

It was a stage that happened upon him three days later, the heat having done no favors to his earthly remains, whereupon the coachman strongly suggested lashing the body to the top of the stage for transport to Santa Rosa, the next town of any size. The passengers overruled the driver, and Ward stayed where he was. The next visitors to the grove buried him where they found him and took what sundries they dug from his pockets, Ward's will included. The document made its way to Fort Sumner, and from there to the home of Emma Hanlon. She did not know then that her brother had died of heartbreak, only that he'd died alone, and it was from her own share of the family coffers that she financed the disinterment and relocation of Jackson Ward's bones to the ancestral cemetery in East Texas.

The funeral was quiet and somber, sparsely attended. The pastor read over the open grave and closed coffin, the dirt was filled back in, and everybody went home in silence. It was another week gone before Emma began her search for Audrey Jo White.

And it was winter, some seven months later, when Emma finally found her.

XIII.

Colorado Springs was growing by leaps and bounds, and everywhere Emma Hanlon looked she found men scampering about scaffolding like so many ants, hammering and sawing and erecting buildings so fast it was a wonder to behold. She took a room at the Antlers Hotel, which was so new she could smell the pine sap from the floors and walls. The stage that brought her to town did not come through the area she intended to visit, nor would she have expected it to. The last thing any burgeoning town like Colorado Springs wanted was to advertise its vices and sins to every man, woman, and child who happened to pass through.

And, of course, Emma Hanlon was the last person anybody would have expected to go looking for them.

The bawdy houses and their adjacent cribs stood in the oldest part of town, away from the preponderance of the construction and more virtuous citizenry; a side street jutting out to the east that was surrounded on three sides by stark wilderness apart from the odd length of crumbling fence. Here Emma found drunks blacked out on the boardwalks, cowhands left behind weeks after claiming and spending their chits, all but nude women lounging on second story verandas and taunting red-nosed men wandering the muddy street below. She was accosted with crude propositions, harangued by doxies, ogled by hopheads from the windows and doorways of saloons that looked to Emma as though they might collapse to their foundations should anyone sneeze.

She found herself in a vile and frightening place, and inwardly she couldn't help but curse the name of her dead brother for having brought her there. All the same, she trudged on, through the ankle-deep mud, until she reached what she knew now was Jackson's destination when he died on the trail— The White Orchid, which was anything but a rare flower.

There, her muddy shoes drew no notice, but her face and figure did. Low voices muttered, eyes turned up from drink and cards. The bar man, husky and one-eyed, stomped to the end of the bar and said, "We're full up, sweet thing. Try Jake's joint up yonder."

He jabbed a thumb in the general direction of Jake's, but Emma ignored it. Instead, she went up to the bar, gently lay her hands on top, and said, "I am looking for Audrey Jo White."

The bar man stood still, his eyes meeting hers, and for several long seconds he said nothing at all. Most of the patrons dispersed around the room paid no mind, having gotten their eyeful of the newcomer and dismissed her; it was clear enough she was no whore. But one of the women hunched over the bar did look up, her brow crinkled and fingers tightening around a sweaty glass of gin on the bar top. The woman made a sound, deep in her throat, and with some apparently difficulty, she turned on her stool to meet Emma Hanlon's gaze. And in that moment, the two of them knew one another as plain as day, as well as one another's business there.

"He's gone, isn't he?" A.J. said.

Emma nodded, unable to speak the words. Audrey Jo nodded, too, just the once.

"Did he come looking for me?"

"He did."

"That damned fool."

"He always was," Emma said.

Something like a smile played at A.J.'s lips, but never fully formed. Instead, she gestured at her drink for the bar man to see. He got to work on replicating it as Emma walked hesitantly to where Audrey Jo sat and occupied the stool to her right. The bar man brought A.J. her drink, and also one just like it for Emma, who said, "Oh, my, no. I never drink."

"Then I'll have them both," A.J. said.

"I suppose one won't kill me."

"It would take a great many more than one to do that trick. I'm still here."

Cautiously, Emma raised the glass to her mouth and sipped. Her eyes popped, but more from pleasant surprise than loathing. A.J. chuckled softly, and after that, the two women sipped together in silence for a long time.

When she left the tumble-down saloon some forty minutes

later, Emma made sure to leave the envelope with the bar man instead of Audrey Jo herself, certain the other woman would otherwise have declined it. And when she returned to the Antlers Hotel, Emma was greatly relieved to divest herself of the single-shot Deringer she had secreted away beneath her skirts, where all afternoon it had scraped against her ankle, snug in her shoe. For a span of a few minutes she had considered asking her erstwhile sister-in-law whether or not she had truly loved Jackson, and that the woman's answer would determine her fate. But Emma never needed to ask.

People already asked too many damned questions of Audrey Jo White, questions that cut like knives.

She slept restfully in the soft hotel bed.

In the morning, she left the gun behind.

WEIRD WESTERNS

SOLO LA PISTOLA DI ANGEL SPARERÀ... E TU MORIRAI AMIGO!

Carol was counting out loud again.

"One, two, *three*, four," he said, emphasizing the odd syllable here and there. "Five, six, seven, eight, nine? Ten, *eleven*, twelve. Thirteen! Fourteen and fifteen!"

It was all perfectly ludicrous, of course. Only the greenhorns dared crack a smile; older hands at the game were so accustomed to it that they could almost imagine the dialogue that would be laid down in post. This was just the way they did business in Italy.

From beside the Arriflex, Nino Citti smoked a Gauloise and turned his sea-green eyes to Renato Savagnone, the actor on the other side of the bar from Carol. Like Carol, Renato used a pseudonym—it seemed practically everyone there did—and refused to acknowledge anybody on set who didn't call him John Wilde. Conversely, Carol could not have cared less if they called him Carol, his stage name Frank Cooper, or just plain *stronzo*. He only wanted to get the job done and move onto his next gig.

"John Wilde," barked Citti as he dropped the cigarette to the floor and stamped it out. He tore off the filters before he lit each one, with a separate pile of those near to the stamped out smokes.

Savagnone's eyes seemed to come alive for the first time, like an automaton just turning on. He said, "Uno, *due*, tre? Quattro!"

With that, Savagnone produced a revolver from beneath the bar and set it on the wet, worn wood between the two actors. Carol grimaced and dropped a hand to his own prop gun, sagging in its leather holster at his hip.

"Okay," Citti shouted. "*Bene. Bene.*"

The director clapped his hands twice and walked off the saloon set. His assistant director, a rat-faced guy no one could stand named Eugenio, stepped forward and called out, "*Pranzo!*"

Lunch time. The big shootout was going to have to wait until another day.

The picture was called *Solo la pistola di Angel sparerà... e tu morirai amigo!*—*Only Angel's Gun Will Shoot, and You Will Die, Amigo!*—or at least until it got changed a few times for a few different territories. And since Carol hadn't signed on to do his own dubbing, some other American would have the responsibility for turning Carol's counting into "Angel's" semi-coherent dialogue. With the babel of languages being spoken on any given production, it was typically the only way to do it. Producers wanted Americans in their films, but most of the parts went to Italians, Spaniards, and French actors, and hardly any three of them could understand one another. So they counted, just to get their mouths moving for some anonymous guys in recording booths back in Rome to fill in later.

"*Uno, due, tre, quattro,*" Savagnone grumbled, shaking two loose fists at the thick summer air. He left the gun on the bar and scratched at his week-old beard, grown out for the part. "This is acting, *giusto?*"

"Sure," Carol said, leaning over the bar. "Sure, Renato."

The Italian snorted and walked away, joining the small horde of crewmen jockeying to escape the bottleneck of the saloon set's doors for the catering table out in the middle of the dusty main street. The American lingered, eyeballing the bottles behind the bar and wishing they were filled with something a damn sight better than water and tea. Fake liquor, fake bar, fake cowboy. By that time the next day, he'd even get to have himself a fake death, because at least the Europeans weren't afraid to leave the audience on a bitter note once in a while. Carol figured it served audiences right. What had they ever done for him? He would have been back in L.A. drinking cocktails in an air-conditioned barroom instead of sweating buckets in the Andalusian desert if audiences hadn't already sealed his fate. The hell with audiences.

"*Vienes,* Frank?" The Spanish script girl stood in between the batwing doors. She wore a kerchief around her neck and smoked a long, thin cigarette. "Antipasto and spaghetti. Same as yesterday. Good espresso though, and somebody is bound to have some wine."

"Just call me Carol," he said. "I'll be there in a minute. Thanks, Elena."

"*Mangia, mangia,*" she said, letting the batwings slam together as she left Carol alone at the bar.

"Yeah, sure," said Carol to the empty room. "One, two, three, four, five…"

Somewhere outside a generator hummed. A cacophony of voices rose up from the lunch tables like the roar of ocean waves. Somebody started playing a concertina and the horses nickered and a woman laughed almost hysterically. Carol listened, but his mind gradually drowned them all out, the walls of his focus narrowing in on those dusty prop bottles and all the last shots and lost chances. Jack Grant's toothy smile when he promised to talk with his friend over at Paramount, and how anxious Carol got about it when he should have known what a Hollywood promise was worth. Watching the same people he came up with go on to bigger, better things while he rotted away in Rome, taking what he could get and wondering if anybody back home would ever see this crap or even remember who Carol Gildner—aka Frank Cooper—used to be. Purgatory was what it was, he decided. Frank was all but dead and Carol had to stick it out in the goddamn desert, paying for Frank's failures. Babbling numbers for lire. Losing himself a little more every day.

"Six, seven, eight, *nine…*"

His own stomach interrupted him, grumbling noisily. Carol made a face at it. He could hardly stand to eat spaghetti again, but he suspected it was preferable to starving to death, if only marginally. And if Elena was right about the wine…

He gave Renato's gun a little spin on the bar and pushed away, turning to the batwing doors, when the stark, dead silence overwhelmed him. It was thick and suffocating, worse than the desert air, like a wet canvas bag over his head. He stopped dead, facing the doors, and thought, *I've gone deaf*. Only that wasn't the case at all; he could still hear the mild breeze, the creak of the false front buildings lining the set's main thoroughfare, the drone of a fly somewhere in the saloon. Carol hadn't lost his hearing. Everybody else had just suddenly gone completely quiet.

"Funny," Carol said. "Real funny."

He snorted, cracked a smile. Pranking *l'americano*. It wouldn't be the first time. The one sword and sandal picture he did at Cinecitta in '61 was bad enough before somebody absconded with Carol's street clothes and he had to drive back to his flat in a faux tiger pelt and bare feet. He never did see those trousers again, and he never found out who played the joke, but just about everybody enjoyed the hot living hell out of it. Everyone apart from Carol Gildner, that was. *Ursus contro i mostri della luna*, indeed. It felt like Carol against himself then, and it still felt that way now.

"*Silencio, silencio*," he bellowed as he resumed his way to the doors. "*Uno, due, tre, quattro, cinque, sei...*" He couldn't remember the word for seven, but it didn't much matter one way or the other by the time he made his way through the batwings and onto the sandy boardwalk outside. There was nobody around to hear him.

No catering tables. No production equipment. No spaghetti. No concertina. No cast. No crew. Nothing. No one. *Niente.*

Carol said, "*Sette*." The word for seven was *sette*, wasn't it?

As though by way of response to that, a shot rang out and the wooden doorframe splintered just inches from his right ear. His entire body tensed when he felt the tiny fragments strike the side of his face and he realized that somebody had just fired a gun at him.

A *real* gun.

"Hey, what the *hell*," he croaked, touching his face where the splinters hit him. For that, he got another gunshot. This time, it went wide enough that Carol couldn't even tell where it hit. He didn't need to know to decide to get back inside the saloon. He didn't expect to get lucky a third time in a row.

He walked quickly back to the bar, where he spotted Renato's gun again, which reminded him of the one he had holstered at his hip. It was about as dangerous as a spoon or a pair of salad tongs, but it made him feel a small bit better to hold it in his hand all the same. Maybe whoever was taking those potshots at him would see it and think twice. With that in mind, Carol grabbed the gun on the bar, too. Now he had a fake gun in each hand. He wondered if he looked as ridiculous as he felt.

The silence fell over the set again, stifling and disorienting. Carol stood still by the bar, asking himself over and over whether he suspected who might be out there and why they were doing this. A lunatic? Or a terrorist? At least he understood why everybody else vanished so quickly—probably they scattered and hid where they could before Carol had the first clue what was happening. Which was typical, he thought. *Don't bother warning the American.* Like the whole goddamn Tonkin thing was his fault.

His hands tightened around the grips of the guns and he crouched slightly, peering under the batwings for signs of the gunman. On the one hand, if he couldn't see the shooter, then the shooter likely couldn't see him, either. Then again, Carol didn't exactly have a plan to escape, seeing as those swinging doors in front were the only way in and out of the saloon set. The joint was built with speed and expense in mind, not safety. It was all disposable. The films and the actors, too. And none of it really much mattered, not in the end. Not to Carol.

He heaved a sigh and went slowly back to the batwing doors, the prop guns swinging in his hands. "What?" he called out over the shuttered doors. "What's it all about, huh?"

"Either you come out," a voice roared back, "or we come an' get you."

Unmistakably American. Of course, Wes Donner finished all his scenes and caught the bus back to Rome the week before, which meant Carol was the last Yank standing on *Solo la pistola di Angel sparerà.* Until now, anyway. And whoever that was out there, it certainly wasn't little old Wes.

Carol said, "This some kind of a joke?"

"No joke," the voice same back. "Decide now."

"I don't think I'm who you want?" Carol winced at his weak, questioning tone. It was miles away from the gunslinger Angel he was supposed to be playing. But he wasn't Angel. He wasn't even Frank Cooper.

"Now," the man outside barked.

"Now," Carol said in a half-whisper. "My god."

One last time, he scanned the false fronts and the board-walk, squinting at windows and alleys for any sign of actors and staff crouching out of sight in service of the big laugh everyone was having on poor Carol Gildner. The sun was beginning to set behind the west side of the set, casting a harsh glow against the breakaway windows that forced him to narrow his eyes. He started to look away when he caught sight of a sparkle, a reflection of the red afternoon light from the rooftop of the faux bank building. The sunlight was glinting off something metal there, something that wasn't there before.

There you are, you bastard.

He had only just shot a scene the previous Tuesday in which a shooter was perched on the rooftop for the purpose of getting the drop on good old Angel. Naturally, Angel sensed this right away and picked the sniper off with a quick swivel of his hips and a single, effortless shot. Carol, on the other hand, only *seemed* to be armed. The ruse would only work until the shooter realized his quarry wasn't shooting back because he *couldn't* shoot back. And then what?

It was only at that moment that it dawned on him what the stranger on the roof had said. It wasn't that he was going to come after Carol—that wasn't what he said. He said *we. We* are coming for you. Carol wasn't just outgunned by one man, but possibly a whole group of men. A posse, he thought. But why? Stealing a guy's pants was one thing, but firing live ammunition at him?

"Insurance," he whispered to himself. That had to be it. The picture was in trouble. Somehow they got everyone away from the set so they could knock Carol off, claim it was an accident, and secure a nice insurance payout to finish the film. The publicity alone would draw out morbid thrill seekers far and wide to see the picture that killed Frank Cooper. Hell, for all Carol knew, somebody had the camera rolling to capture it all on 35mm. *When Angel dies, he* really *dies!*

But he wasn't about to just let these bastards kill him. Not Carol, Frank, or Angel. No matter the reason. His life and career might very well be in shambles, but that didn't begin to mean he was ready to call it quits. And when he was ready, it was going to be on Carol's own terms, not some marble-mouthed hillbilly on the roof of a fake bank in the middle of the God damned Spanish desert.

"What's it gonna be, Angel?"

Angel? Carol blanched. "Jesus jumped on Mary," he whispered to himself. "This really is some game to them, isn't it?"

He wasn't able to get a good look at the shooter, but it occurred to Carol that Nino had set down his viewfinder before leaving the set. He couldn't remember where, exactly, but he was certain it had to be there. *The camera—*

Except the camera wasn't there at all. Nobody had carried it out. It was just…gone. The tables, the food, the equipment, the cast and crew—nothing of the picture appeared to remain apart from Carol himself. Himself, and the two prop guns he carried at his hips.

He drew the one on his right side and hurled it as hard as he could at the dusty bottles lined up beneath the mirror behind the bar. They were breakaway bottles, sugar glass made to smash over a stuntman's noggin, which shattered easily when struck by the faux Colt. The mirror was real, but remained intact, unharmed by a harmless object meant only to look menacing. Carol caught his own reflection now, gruff and scraggly with the dark shadow of a beard creeping over his face and makeup to give him the appearance of rough living and little bathing. Even his own face was unreal.

"You're done, Angel!" the man outside hollered.

Carol cross-drew the prop gun from his left-side holster and pressed the barrel against his right temple, keeping his eyes trained hard on his reflection in the bar mirror.

"Go on and get him."

Somebody gave a war whoop. One of the man's accomplices, Carol figured. His index finger touched the trigger.

"Bang," Carol said. Something approaching a smile played on his lips. To his left, the batwing doors swung in and slammed on either side of the entrance. Carol pivoted at the hips like he'd been taught to do for the picture and brought the gun around as he eared back the hammer with his other hand. Again, he said, "Bang."

This time, he squeezed the trigger. And this time, the revolver in Carol Gildner's hand bucked with a loud blast, firing a .44 caliber lead bullet across the saloon and into the chest of a black-bearded man in the doorway. The bearded man grunted with shock, looked down at the hole in his chest, and dropped backward onto the boardwalk outside. He didn't move any more after that, on account of he was dead.

"Oh my God," Carol said. He moved his eyes from the boots of the dead man outside the saloon to the gun in his hand, its barrel still smoking. This, he knew, was not supposed to happen. The first time he ever handled a prop gun on a set, the property managed lectured him about an accident on the set of an old DeMille picture where live ammunition got confused with the blanks and an extra was killed. The lecture stuck with him, though he never worried much on productions where the guns weren't even designed for real bullets.

This was supposed to be one of those productions. And yet, there lay before him crystal clear evidence that it was not.

"Dead," Carol said. "Sweet Christ, he's dead."

"There he is!" the man on the roof screeched. "There's the Angel I know! I knew you was still you, boy!"

The man cackled like an old madwoman, unmoved by the untimely death of his supposed compatriot. Carol's stomach roiled. His day just kept getting stranger, and he wished it would stop. While he wished, he leathered his gun and got a hold of the dead man's boots in order to pull the corpse into the saloon. It seemed somehow wrong to leave him in the sun like that, and besides, Carol wanted his gun and ammunition. He'd learned at least a few things from working in the wild world of the *western all'italiana*.

Though the bushy beard gave the corpse a slightly older appearance, Carol could see now the fellow couldn't have been twenty-five yet. Just a kid—though a kid with a plenty mean-looking Colt Walker in his paw that Carol was willing to bet wasn't made at the studio property shop back in Rome. He took the gun, checked the cylinder, and satisfied with its five rounds, slid the weapon into his empty holster. Next he divested the dead man of the ammunition he had stored in his gun belt.

"Sorry, kid," said Carol.

And he was. He'd killed a hundred men or more just since he came over the Atlantic, but they always got right back up again when the director called cut. This was the first time nobody was capturing the moment, and the first time the moment itself was so grotesquely real. Carol had just killed a man, and there was no cutting away from that.

When he was done picking over the cadaver, he stood tall with a newly acquired gun in one holster, and a mysteriously real one that used to be fake in the other. The street outside was growing dark from the shadows of the buildings to the west, where the sun was beginning to set. Carol glanced around the room for candles or a lamp, but he couldn't recall ever having seen anything like that, at least not on this set. There were plenty of candles in the gambling room, but whereas on film that was going to look as though it was connected to the saloon, in reality it was across the street and down several false fronts, attached to the general store set. Then again…

He couldn't help but laugh at the thought. Something in his mind suggested he check behind the door next to the player piano anyway, knowing full well it was a false door that didn't lead anywhere. Still, if whatever the hell was happening to him happened to his gun, then perhaps it happened to the gambling room, too. The worst thing that could happen to him if he checked is he would feel ridiculous, and a little private embarrassment would be quite welcome for the brief moment it would overtake his cold terror. Carol decided to give it a look.

In the moment before he turned the knob and pulled the door open, the saloon was eerily quiet. That changed the instant the door cleared the jamb, whereupon a wild cacophony of raised voices, jangly piano music, clinking glasses, cranking roulette tables, rattling dice, and the clatter of clay and ivory poker chips rushed into his ears like water into a drain. And as the light faded in the street outside and the saloon grew darker by the minute, a warm tangerine glow spilled from the cracked door onto Carol like a blanket from what he momentarily saw were numerous low-hanging chandeliers repurposed from old wagon wheels. The gambling room was in full swing tonight—never mind that it wasn't where it was supposed to be, and none of the gamblers, dealers, or bartenders inside were recognizable to the stunned actor studying their faces from the entrance.

"Ain't that some shit," Carol said to himself.

The players at each of the tables wore better period costumes than all of the Western productions Carol had done combined. Every tiny detail was perfect, from the homespun shirts to the woolen trousers, and though he was almost completely sure why that was, he dreaded even thinking it. Thinking it made it real, and if it was real, Carol couldn't even begin to imagine how he was going to get out of this and back to where he belonged.

Where he belonged. He nearly laughed out loud. As though sweating through his significantly less-authentic clothes in Andalusia was where he belonged, rather than rushing through lunch at the Paramount commissary before heading back to the soundstage for a picture people might actually *see.* Maybe Carol didn't belong there, either. Maybe he didn't really belong any-place, and maybe that was why he ended up here—wherever *here* was.

"You just going to stand there catching flies, or you plan-ning on setting a spell?"

The voice, distinct from the rest of the noise, startled Carol into stumbling the rest of the way into the room and letting the door shut behind him. To his right stood a smirking woman with hair as red as fall apples. She carried three mugs of beer in each hand and had a sort of lacey red and white tiara perched on her head, just off-kilter. Carol laughed at himself and said, "Sorry, I thought the flies were for anyone who wanted some."

"Funny," said the woman. She nodded with appreciation and continued on her way to deliver the beer to her customers.

Carol watched her float across the floor and wondered if she was a ghost or a dream.

Or whether he was.

Across the room from him, on the other side of all the gaming tables with their green baize and separate ecosystems of cigar smoke, whiskey, and beer, stood the long oaken bar where a few men skipped the games of chance and stuck with what they knew. Carol decided to join them. He never had been much of a gambler, anyway.

But before he got within five feet of the bar, the mustachioed man who stood behind it started shaking his head. "No, no, no," he said. "Now come on, Angel. You know I can't serve you in here. Not tonight."

"Let's pretend I don't know," Carol said.

"I got a wife, Angel," pleaded the barman.

"What's that to do with me?"

The bartender seemed to deflate some, his eyes huge and watery. It was enough. Carol relented.

"Okay," he said. "Sorry."

He turned away from the bar, his guns slapping his hips as he spun. *I'm going to have to tie those down*, he thought. At least the *western all'italiana* hadn't left him completely high and dry. Carol *had* learned a thing or two along the way. He hoped it was enough to keep him alive.

"Leaving already?" Startled, he jumped as the redhead came back into his view, her hands now free and empty. "You just got here."

"Seems I'm trouble," he said.

"Seems like it," she agreed. "What're you going to do about it?"

Glancing about the room, Carol noted a separate entrance that led into the alley. He sucked in a deep breath and held it a moment before releasing it slowly. "Head out there and face the music, I suppose."

"You know Tom Kirby is still out there gunning for you, don't you?"

"That his name? Tom Kirby?"

"He ain't changed it, Angel."

"No," said Carol. "I expect not." He headed for the doorway to the alley.

"Hey Angel," the barmaid called after him, "good luck."

He said, "Can't see why it should start now." She laughed. He didn't.

Carol went outside.

———————

A bullet spanged off the side of the farrier's shop, right on the other side of the saloon with the alley between them. Carol Gildner was in the alley, and the bullet narrowly missed his skull by a matter of inches. It was the second time in the span of an hour that he'd nearly been killed, and the same person was responsible both times.

"Weren't very nice what you done to Bobby back there," Tom Kirby announced at the top of his lungs. "Weren't very nice a'tall."

Carol dropped into a crouch and flattened himself against the wall as best he could. What little light there was on the street at the mouth of the alley seemed to come from inside the saloon. A tremendous uproar of singing, shouting, and laughter came from inside, as well. Only minutes earlier it was dark, silent, and empty. Of course, back then it was only a film set. Now it was a real saloon.

If only that made me a real gunslinger.

Fact was, the bullet that slammed into poor old Bobby was the first real one Carol ever fired in his life. In the movies, he never had to aim; every "bullet" just found its way to the mark through the miracle of editing. Striking that kid in the chest was nothing more or less than plain luck. He didn't expect to get that lucky twice in a row.

Still, Carol drew each of his guns, the right and then the left, and spread his arms out to cover each end of the alley in which he crouched. No sooner had he assumed this position than a shadow appeared at the far end of the alley, away from the main street. Carol heard the distinctive click of a hammer being pulled back; he dropped flat on the ground as somebody's revolver spat fire. The bullet burned a path above Carol's head as he drew a bead on where the flash momentarily appeared in the darkness and returned fire—a bullet from each gun in rapid succession.

The only sound he heard in the immediate aftermath was that of somebody collapsing onto the dusty ground. Whoever it was, Carol killed him instantly.

"Jesus," he rasped. If it hadn't completely dawned on him that this was no game before, he was no longer in denial now. Two people were dead at his hands, and at least one more was still gunning for him. Gunning for *Angel*, whoever the hell he was supposed to be.

"Listen, Kirby," Carol called out before he knew what he was doing. "I don't know who in the Sam Hill this Angel is, but my name is Carol Gildner. I'm an actor from Meriden, Connecticut. I was in Spain before—well, before whatever the hell *this* is."

"*Carol?*" The mocking voice didn't sound like Tom Kirby. Carol realized the man still had at least one more subordinate, if not more. "He say his name was *Carol?*"

"Forget that," Kirby said. "He's actin' crazy, trying to get your guard down, you shit-for-brains."

Am I acting? Carol thought. He wasn't completely sure. Certainly he felt crazy, and more than once since the whole nightmare began he considered the very real possibility that he had, in fact, lost his mind. For all he knew, he was strapped to a gurney in the back of a white van right at that moment, hurrying along backroads to the nearest thing to a hospital the area had to offer. They'd have to finish the picture with a stand-in and do the best they could in the editing bay back in Rome. Would he get shipped back to the States? End up in some state-funded looney ward back in Connecticut, drooling out of both sides of his mouth while muttering to the orderlies about Angel and Bad Tom Kirby...?

If this is acting, he told himself, *then Paramount really doesn't know what they're missing.*

But acting wasn't exactly what Carol had been up to all this time in Italy and Spain. At least not the way he was trained to do it. American actors in these bottom-of-the-barrel productions weren't acting.

They were just counting.

So, Carol counted.

"One, two, *three*, four, FIVE," he announced.

The one who made fun of his name said, "What?"

"Six, seven, *eight*, Kirby. Nine. Ten. And *eleven*."

"The hell is he counting, Tom?"

In lieu of reply to his question, Carol leapt to his feet, swung into the street from the alley and fired his guns just as he had before, only this time he went by the sound of their voices rather than the flashes of their gun barrels.

Tom's remaining man caught lead in the left side of his neck, which went in and out of him with a sharp, wet noise. The man punctuated the noise with a panicked gurgle as he dropped his gun to the ground and threw both hands to the spouting wound. He was older than Bobby by a couple of decades, but that did little to assuage Carol's conscience. In another minute or two, the man would be the third he'd killed in under an hour.

He choked back the bile rising in his gullet and steeled himself for number four.

The one he missed completely, Tom Kirby.

In the windows of the saloon to Carol's left, a few heads popped up from the floor, jockeying with one another to get a look at the carnage. Most of the revelers seemed to have already run for cover, the piano player included.

One of the faces in the glass periodically raised a mug of beer to his lips. For a fraction of a second, Carol thought it was Renato Savagnone, the actor playing his antagonist in *Solo la pistola di Angel sparerà*. Carol looked twice. The second time around, the man didn't look a thing like Renato. For the first time since Kirby fired his first shot, Carol wondered who he would see if he happened to look into a mirror. Carol? Angel? Frank Cooper? Or someone else altogether?

Something to worry about later—if there was going to be a later.

Stepping forward into the light from the windows that spilled out into the street, Tom Kirby paused to tie his holster to his leg. All the while, he kept his cool gray eyes trained on Carol, a faint hint of a grin lifting the corners of his mouth. He was clean-shaven and his hat was pushed back far enough on his head to reveal a three-inch scar straight across his hairline. It looked to Carol like somebody had tried to scalp him.

"All right, old friend," Tom Kirby said as he straightened his posture and spread his arms out on either side of him. "Let's see what you got."

Carol said, "Why?"

Kirby's arms lowered a few inches. "What?"

"I said why?"

"I heard what you said," said Kirby. "I just don't understand what in hell you mean."

"I don't understand why we have to do this, to be honest," said Carol.

"You kilt three of my friends."

"They were going to kill me first."

"Makes a man sore, a little, no matter the cause."

"Then your mind is made up."

"That's right."

"And if I refuse to fight?" He was thinking of *High Noon.* If Gary Cooper could walk away from a fight, why couldn't Carol? Even if it was at night.

"Then I will shoot you in the back."

"Hardly fair."

"Choose now, Angel."

Carol heaved a sigh. From the corner of his eye, he could tell there were twice as many people crowding the saloon windows now. He wondered idly who they were rooting for, him or Kirby. It was like walking into a theater at the end of the movie, only he was the star of the film and still lacked the context to make sense of the situation he was in. It was somebody else's life he was living, somebody he doubted was the least bit real. A paint-by-numbers character from a dime-a-dozen Euro-western that would be forgotten by the time the next one came along. And yet every damned bit of it sure seemed real enough to the man Kirby kept calling Angel, including the blood he had drawn already by way of what were supposed to be play guns.

Choose now. "All right, fine," he said. "*Uno, due, tre, quattro…*"

Somebody said, "What's that, Mexican?"

Kirby's eyes shifted to look in the direction of the speaker for a fraction of a second. It was long enough.

Carol said, *"Cinque,"* but nobody heard it over the loud report from the Colt Walker in his hand. The flash from the barrel illumined Tom Kirby's face, allowing Carol to see the man's eyes flick back and widen. The flash briefly blinded Carol, who did not see the bullet strike Kirby at the bridge of his nose before disappearing into the gunman's skull. By the time his eyes began readjusting to the dimly lit nighttime street, Carol's opponent had already hit the ground.

"Sei, sette, otto, Kirby."

He slid the Colt back into its leather and stood still a moment, his vision clearing enough to focus in on the sparkle catching the light on the dead man's shirt. More bodies filled up the windows behind him, but they then flowed like a gorged creek through the batwing doors to gawk at the bloody aftermath in the street. As soon as the windows were again unobstructed, the inside light found that reflection on Tom Kirby's chest once more.

"Oh, Christ," Carol said. "Oh, no."

"Angel killed the marshal," somebody hollered. "Good God a'mighty, Angel has killed the marshal."

That can't be right. I'm the hero.

"I'm the hero," Carol wheezed.

The crowd from the saloon surged, all but exploding out into the street and fanning out around Carol in every direction. A few of them carried lamps from inside, while others snapped legs off chairs to make torches. Rifles appeared in the hands of a number of men—Henrys and Winchesters for the most part, along with the odd double-barreled coach gun here and there. The mob formed quickly, so quickly that Carol had no time to react, to think of a way out of this, to get to safety somehow. It was much too late for all of that.

"Goddammit, I'm the hero."

"Marshal Kirby was a good man," said a bear of a man with a chest-length, reddish-brown beard and a bartender's apron fixed snugly around his enormous torso. He brought up a sawed-off Parker shotgun and aimed it directly at Carol's face. "You're going to hang, son."

———————

Carol's trial was short.

Nearly forty people witnessed the shooting, and since he knew precisely nobody who could so much as say a kind word about him, it took the jury under an hour to find him guilty and sentence Carol to be hanged by the neck until he was dead. Just as the bartender foretold the night Marshal Tom Kirby was killed.

In his drafty, six-by-six cell, Carol sat silently at the edge of the tatty old Army cot provided to him, day in and day out. He refused all meals and remained completely silent. A minister appeared a week or so into his incarceration, but left after forty minutes of trying and failing to induce the prisoner to give himself up to the Lord. Every morning when the deputy rattled the bars to wake him, Carol quietly cried upon realizing he still hadn't broken free from his nightmare.

The night before they hanged Carol Gildner for the murder of Marshal Thomas Kirby and three of his duly appointed deputies, Carol dreamed about Roy Rogers. Specifically, he dreamed about the Saturday afternoon he and his brother Harry saw *Rough Riders' Round-Up* at the Bijou in New Haven two and a half times in 1939 and spent the following Sunday running rampant all over the neighborhood with their tin cap pistols and costume cowboy hats. The brothers only had the one toy badge between them, so they took turns being the lawman or the bad man.

He never admitted it to Harry or anybody else, but despite how much he admired Roy Rogers, Carol knew it was always more fun to play the bad man.

But there was no more time left for the bad man to play. Not anymore.

Now all Angel could do was count the days left until the hanging.

Uno...

Due...

Tre...

RED ANIMAL

"They were going to look at war,
the red animal—war, the blood-swollen god."
Stephen Crane, *The Red Badge of Courage*

A sharp kick to the ribs was what woke him up. He rolled out of the half-collapsed tent, unable to fully open his eye—the glare from the storm clouds blinded it and the graycoat with the hard boots glared harder still.

Get up, said he, and get you ready to muster.

The graycoat delivered a second, softer kick, from which the one-eyed man cowered. He'd endured many such kicks and punches, cigars extinguished on his flesh and snakes thrown into his tent. Yet still he cowered.

I won't fight, he told the officer, in no uncertain terms. Not for you.

We don't give prisoners guns, not traitors the likes of you, and there's no fighting to be done no more besides.

These words stunned the prisoner, who sat up in the mud and canted his head, awaiting more and afraid to press.

The captain'll have something to say to you horse turds, continued the graycoat, but the war's over and the nation lost and ruined. So get you up and muster, goddamnit.

———————

Despite the high, bright sun, the creek did not sparkle the way some creeks do. The water was brown and foamy, moving sluggishly over the angular rocks jutting up from the shallow bed.

Lee had dragged the coffin into a juniper's shade and squatted on it where the sun could not beat down on his bare head. He set to rolling a pinch of tobacco in a scrap of newspaper and watched the creek while his fingers did the work. It was one of the last few scraps left in his satchel, torn in more or less equal squares from an Arkansas Gazette front page bit about Arturo Ordonez. Lee could not read the article, but he had burned the accompanying illustration of Ordonez into his brain. Now that he no longer needed the paper, he used it for rolling cigarettes. For Arturo Ordonez was beneath him, inside the coffin.

The creek was fed by the Colorado River, which flowed from the Staked Plains of the Llano Estacado clear down to the Gulf, and which would provide Lee with a rough road down to Austin where he hoped to find the means to ship the corpse ahead of him to Little Rock. Traveling with the late Ordonez did not particularly bother him, but since his horse got snakebit north of San Angelo he had become more than Lee cared to drag across Texas afoot. Curious travelers stopped to inquire about the coffin now and then, but none of them were too interested in offering assistance to a man with no coin and a pine box smelling of week-dead human remains baking in the August heat. Lee could not blame them. He knew the sunken cavity where his left eye used to be played a part in their revulsion as well, and he did not begrudge them that, either. A plug-ugly stranger hauling a stinking corpse was bound to make the journey the hard way. As Lee's long-suffering Uncle Hershal was fond of putting it, *It be's that way sometimes.* Possibly these were the old man's last words before they hanged him. Lee could not know for sure.

Moving his eye from creek to sky, Lee decided it was about noon and much too hot to continue on. There was too little shade, mostly just scrub and cactus, and he had traded his hat to a Karankawa who had wandered up from the coast for a bladder of water after his sprang a leak. The Indian cut a hole in the top of it with his knife, "to let the wind in." Lee reckoned the lunatic had some wind that needed letting out too, but it weren't his business till the crazy Indian took a shot at Lee as he raised the skin to drink. How he missed at such close range.... All those preachers must be right that the Lord don't like savages. Lee left the Karankawa dead in the brush; with no reward promised for a dead Injun, the buzzards would have a feast.

He lay back lengthwise on the coffin, shading his eye with the flat of his hand, and thought about the girls the cadaver under him was supposed to have killed. The youngest was six years old, the eldest seventeen. Five in all, all of them the daughters of recently freed slaves. Their families and the community in which they toiled put half the bounty together, two hundred dollars cash money, and still nobody would take them up on the job until Lee came ambling down from Tennessee. The way things stood, the other two hundred might materialize and it might not, but Lee reckoned the half he got took him a fair distance. He had burned up most of the take in San Angelo on bad cards and worse women, but that was not something he was like to regret. In the moments before his light went out, his thoughts turned from the butchered girls to the high-stepping whores he enjoyed before his quarry showed his face at Dick Pritchard's place.

He must have dozed for next he knew the sun had passed behind the juniper and a fat man with a gnarled gray beard was looming over him. The man wore a slouch hat and deerskins; a necklace of thin white bones rattled over his broad, flabby chest. His nose was half eaten away by bright red papules. He flashed a toothless smile at Lee and rasped, "How do, One-Eye?"

"What d'you want, old man?" was Lee's reply. His fingers crept near the holstered Colt at his belt.

"Reckon I follered my nose," the man said, gesturing at his suppurating snout. "That corpse in there's raising a stink something terrible."

"I don't guess he smelled too sweet before he was dead."

Lee sat up, swung his legs over the side of the coffin, and squinted up at the stranger. On closer inspection, he decided that the bones comprising his necklace came from human fingers, probably Indians. Whether the old man found them or killed for them was impossible to say.

"You kill 'im?" the man inquired, canting his head and raising his eyebrows.

Lee nodded. "I did." A man should own up to his deeds.

"He need killin'?"

"Many do. This one did."

The man sucked at his gums and rolled his eyes back for a moment, then dipped a hand into his deerskin tunic and brought out a leather pouch. He bounced it in his palm twice, and it jingled.

"How much you want fer it?" he asked Lee.

"Want? For what?"

"The corpse, idjit. I'll be havin' a look afore I buy, but I'll pay a fair price."

"What in hell you want with a corpse?"

"Reckon that's my business, hoss. You sellin' or ain't you?"

The creek burbled behind the old man, dividing and reforming around the rocks. Lee surveyed the area from east to west, and it occurred to him that there was no horse, not even a burro, in view. Like himself, the old man had walked there.

Lee scratched his chin and remembered the freedman community back in Little Rock.

"I get three hundred for this old boy from the folks hired me to kill him," he lied.

"Three hunnert!" the man drawled, laughing. "Shoot, that's a pile. Yessir, that right there's a *good* price. What *they* gonna do with 'im?"

"Don't know. Bury him, maybe. He kilt some little girls. I 'spect they'll probably do bad by him and then bury him."

"Cut 'is balls off is what they'll do, I bet. Bury the boy with his own balls in his mouth—*ha!*"

Lee shrugged. It did not much matter to him what they did with the remains of Ordonez, so long as they took him off his hands and paid what they owed. Which, he recalled, they might not be able to. Or be of a mind to. It was a gamble, he had to admit, though he always had been weak for games of chance. Hope for the two hundred in Arkansas, or see what the old man had to offer? He stood up, rolled his shoulders, and stared down the length of the creek.

"What d'you 'spose you'd pay for him, anyhow?" he asked.

"We-ell," the man drawled, "I didn't know he was no child-killer..."

"That lower the price?"

"Shit, no. Raises it, matter of fact. Lookie here, son…"

He untied the string that held the pouch closed and dumped its contents into the palm of his other hand. A small shower of gold and silver coins formed a pile that gleamed the way the creek did not.

"That's *twenny-four* American federal dollars right there, hoss," he gloated.

Lee scoffed, planted his hands at the small of his back. "Hate to tell you, old-timer, but your arithmetic ain't so good. That's less'n a twelfth of what I'll get in Arkansas."

"That right?" he said, his voice going high. He frowned, dumped the coins back into the pouch, and jerked a knotted thumb at the coffin. "Give me a look at your corpse, and I'll see what I can't come up with to sweeten the pot."

Lee arched an eyebrow and angled to look back at the coffin. After he shot Ordonez—twice in the stomach and once right into his ear—he bought the box off an undertaker eager to get the outlaw in the ground. When the man asked Lee if he was the one responsible for burial costs, he was curtly informed to bring a rope instead of a shovel. For the journey down to San Angelo the coffin held up well, dragged in the dust behind his sorrel. The pine had begun to splinter since then, and through the tiny holes insects were making their way in for the big feast.

"Don't see why not," Lee said, and he dug the toe of his boot under the lid to kick it off.

Arturo Ordonez had never looked worse. The skin of his face was gray and tight, clinging to his cheekbones like wet cotton. His formerly thick lips had thinned and curled into a sneer, exposing the top row of yellow, spaced-apart teeth. The right ear was badly powder-burned from the shot Lee fired into it, and the blood that poured out of his nose like water from a spigot had dried and turned brown. The multitude of squirming maggots feeding on his face appeared to enjoy the flaking blood immensely.

The old man let out a whoop. With a throaty chuckle and a slap on his knee, he said, "Now that boy ain't pretty."

"Says the man with the rotted nose," Lee said.

The man frowned and took a step back. "Nothin' wrong with my nose."

"Well, what do you think?" Lee turned an open hand at the corpse like a medicine showman displaying a curiosity for a nickel.

"Not too old." The old man worked his jaw as he thought it over. "Looks like he's got good bones. How many you say he kilt?"

"Six. Little girls."

"Squaws?"

"Nigger kids."

"Hmn."

The man stroked his beard and squinted at the afternoon sun, hanging low and red on the prairie. A pair of shiny grackles lighted on the topmost branches of the juniper and squawked down at him while his face was turned that way. He licked his scabby lips and said, "Still. Six of 'em."

The grackles tittered and squawked some more, then one at a time they spread their wings and took back to the sky. The birds gone, the old man poked a finger into his coin pouch and stirred its contents, moving his lips but not uttering a word. He then removed the finger, kissed it on the tip, and touched it to the bones dangling from his neck. With a sharp nod he bent at the waist, farted loudly, and from the pouch he dumped a scattering of small, brittle bones on the ground. In the middle distance one of the grackles cawed shrilly; when Lee spun to see where they had gone, he spied one of them dropping from the purple horizon like a stone. Undeterred and focused, the man hurriedly rearranged the bones from one senseless configuration to another, crossing a pair here and forming a triangle there. When he was finished, he straightened up and regarded his work with an expression approaching pride.

To Lee he said, "Aw'ight. I'll take 'im off your hands."

Lee snorted. "Not for no twenty-four dollars you ain't."

He went back to the coffin, lifted the lid, and slid it back into place over Ordonez. The old man gathered up his bones and scooped them back into the pouch, which he returned beneath his deerskin. Lee watched him closely with his one eye, trying to see how he kept the bones inside when he wanted the coins out and the coins inside when he wanted the bones. He could not figure it.

"Oh, I got me a lot more'n that back the house."

"That a fact? How much is a lot more, you reckon?"

"A lot more'n *you* bargained for, sonny Jim."

"If it's more than three hundred, just say so, old timer."

By way of reply, the old man shrugged and started back the way he came. Lee glanced back at the coffin, and then the dipping sun. Behind him the creek burbled ever on, its brown froth moving determinately toward the river, where he himself planned to follow. Instead, he followed the old man, dragging Arturo Ordonez in his wake.

———————

Killing came easy to him, and killing was the order of the day. He shot men in the copses and drove his bayonet into their throats when close combat was called for. He enjoyed these moments, and during the interminable waiting hours between battles, he daydreamed about them—both killings past and those yet to come.

On an October evening, days after last he'd shot a ball into the fray, he found a man in the wood with red hands glimmering in the moonlight. The man muttered incomprehensibly, wheezed rather than breathed. He struggled to keep his guts inside, pressing hard at the yawning wound, but shiny ropes of intestine squeezed through his fingers like eels. The one-eyed private knelt by the dying man, touched his face, which was cool and clammy.

The man said, We ain't goin to win this war, son, no sir. And they ain't neither. Won't be none of us left to run what's left.

The private laughed and opened the man's throat with a razor from his pocket. While the man's life bubbled out through his neck, the private imagined a dead nation of women and children and cowards, all the men killed by one another, their bloated corpses filling the fallow fields until the sun bleached their bones.

This, he decided, seemed right. For war made animals of men, and animals were meant to be slaughtered.

_____

The night was the color of a day-old bruise when they crested a slight rise overlooking a gulch. The gulch ran jaggedly between the rise and its twin, a few hundred yards distant, and opened up on either side to flat prairie land spotted with brush and stunted mesquites. The old man pointed to the bottom of the gulch, where Lee could make out a small dwelling constructed haphazardly of branches and scavenged lumber. He could tell the lumber was scavenged because a length of it making up part of the roof had letters painted on it. He read enough to know it said Hotel.

"Home," the old man said, advancing to the edge of the rise.

"Fine." Lee looked down the sheer, scarred surface of the natural wall. "You want to jump down or can you fly?"

"Been meanin' to learn after the horse…. Well, these old bones ain't what they used to be, but duty calls a'plenty these days." He knelt by a tangle of whitethorn and pulled out a thick coil of rope from within. "Staked into the ground. It holds."

He tossed the coil over the edge and it yanked taut from the shrub. "Hope you ain't a'skeered of heights," he said as he went over.

"What about the coffin?" Lee shouted.

The man called back, "Lower it down ahead of ya."

Lee cussed and watched until the man made it safely to ground. He then pulled the rope up and set to securing it around the coffin. He felt a fool, following the loony coot out there in the gathering dark, but decided the worst that could happen was a delay in getting on to Arkansas. There would be no point in ambushing him down there; he had nothing of value to steal. Only the corpse was important to the old man, and only he and the freedman back in Little Rock would ever want it. As long as there was a chance he could get paid and not have to trek far for it, Lee figured it was worth the risk.

He lowered Ordonez in his pine box as the old man instructed, and when the rope was free again he made the way down himself.

Though he expected it to be cooler in the gulch than on the rise, Lee was nonetheless surprised by the chill in the air. The sweat on his neck dried and he shifted uncomfortably on his feet. The old man sat upon the coffin, a dozen or so feet in front of him, picking at his gums. Lee forgot all about the chill and went to meet him.

"This your land down here?" he asked.

"I live on it," the man said.

"Just you, in that...house?"

"Nobody dogs me here."

Lee rubbed his scratchy face and took in the dwelling. It was small, no bigger than a teepee, with an angled roof and animal skins serving as a front door. He found it difficult to believe any man who lived that way would have a store of cash in a hovel such as this, but there was no telling what a crazy old timer got up to in the loneliness of time.

"How come you ain't got no mount?"

"Had me one," said the old man. "Blood bay, it were. Runned off east a piece back. A blood bay sometimes can smell the gore what gives its color—and you boys washed the earth with it, didn't ye?"

Lee narrowed his eye and cocked his head to one side.

"How d'you reckon I'd anything to do with the war?"

The old man showed his gums, though Lee didn't know if that were grin or grimace. "Can smell it on you." the old man said. "A power was gave up to you to take peace from the earth, and that'n you ought to kill one another. That's what my bay knowed, and what I know. And I 'spect you know it your own self, hoss."

Crazy, thought Lee, regarding the man and, for the first time, wondering about his intent. *Crazier than a shithouse rat, this one.*

The back of Lee's head ached and the cool gully air sniped at him. He considered the old man's words, familiar like an old song his mama used to sing, lost to memory apart from its phantom.

War and blood.

Red animals.

"Let's see what you got, then," Lee said. "I don't guess I came down here for the fun of it."

"You best bring that inside," the man said matter-of-factly, gesturing at the coffin. "The coyotes'll smell yer friend 'fore long."

"Coyotes," Lee parroted with a deep sigh.

"Comanche think they're trickster gods, but they're just bastards."

His host disappeared behind the animal skins and presently an orange glow developed inside. The light leaked out through openings in the shoddy walls. Lee paused and held his breath, listening to the night to see if he could hear any coyotes crying. He heard nothing, but hustled for the dwelling all the same.

The interior was musty and cluttered with junk. A hand-made table stood in the middle of the single room, topped with dented tin cups and plates, the remains of a bird carcass, and a long, rusty knife. A fur covered a broad swath of the dirt floor, and a stove rested in one corner, cold, its black pipe rising up and through the slapdash roof. The old man squatted on a stump around which he appeared to have built the shack, and he gestured to a rickety stool when Lee came in, looking for space to stow the coffin.

"You can have some coffee," the man said, pointing to a pot on the stove, "but it's cold and stretched thin with grain."

"Thanks, no. I'll just be taking what you're offering and get along."

"What's your hurry?" The old man looked as if Lee had told a joke.

"No hurry," Lee lied, propping a boot up on the pine box. "I guess I'm just direct."

"Have a set and let's us talk about what we're gonna do with that there corpse."

"I done told you what I'm offered for him, which is three hundred dollars, and that's federal. You match that, you relieve me of having to travel on, and I'll be glad of it. Elsewise, I don't expect we can deal."

The old man spread his lips apart and displayed his jagged, infrequent teeth. A rattling cough rumbled up from deep inside of him, which was punctuated by a yellow glob that he spat on the hard-packed dirt floor.

"We can deal, son." He wiped his mouth. "We can deal."

In the Stockade, the war ceased to matter. Military prison was still prison, war or no. Only one side had guns, while the other had labor and abuse. He had seen a man pinned to the ground and treated as a woman, and he had seen men open their own veins, laboriously, with the edges of flat stones they hid in their tents. The Stockade was a special division of Hell, but Hell was where he believed himself to belong.

He did not shriek at night, as some of them did. But he did not sleep, either. Rather, he lay awake, sometimes in the reeking tent provided to him and sometimes in the warm South Carolina mud, where he recounted his victories and his failures and he despaired at the day to come when there would be no war.

For the private shone in war. He triumphed in death. He claimed no allegiance, not in his heart, but he could nearly feel himself lifted up into the air when he counted another coup, ended another enemy life.

When this business is done, he explained to a fellow Union private, his mouth dripping with the watery corn mush they were given in lieu of proper food, I'll keep on in this army. I figure the army ain't never going to stop. Never gonna stop lookin' for kills. I'll go to the plains and kill Indians if they want me to. So long as they give me a rifle and a mount, I'll do whatever they tell me to do.

The other private sneered at him, wary of the Hell the one-eyed soldier embraced, and in the night had his skull caved in for his trouble.

Lee balked when the old man set to kicking the dirt on the floor, covered his mouth and nose to keep from choking on the dust. He coughed once, which sent a pain echoing through his skull. When the cloud settled, he saw through narrowed eyes the trapdoor set into the floor, a black iron ring bolted into its center.

"I been hassled a piece," said the old man, bending down to grip the ring and heave the door open. "Comanche and land-grabbers and such. But I got me a place to hide out."

He grinned and touched his rotting nose, gave Lee a wink and slipped down into the hole in the earth. His clattering breath echoed in the darkness.

Lee rasped, "Damn."

He lowered his legs into the pit, found a step with his foot, and climbed down after the old man.

For the war against the Confederacy the government would take a man with only one eye, but come Reconstruction he was reclassified as crippled, in his way. A proper man needed two eyes to keep the conspirators in line. It seemed he was no longer a proper man.

There were five occupation districts and he would have gladly taken to any one of them—just give me a rifle, just give me a mount—but the private was mustered out with nothing but the clothes on his back. When he walked out of the Stockade that April afternoon, he hadn't even shoes on his feet.

Barefoot, he sniggered at the officers stripped of their now worthless ranks, to be sent home to burned farms with no one to rebuild them. For them, Hell was only just beginning. For him, it could never end, the fires could never be dowsed.

It did not particularly matter where a man like him wandered; there were always men who needed killing, wherever you went.

So the one-eyed private went.

"By the by, how'd you lose that eye?"

"Roan kicked me in the head when I was a boy."

"Still got it?"

"The roan?"

"The *eye.*"

"No…"

"Shame."

With a paper match the old man ignited a brass sconce that he raised up to illumine the cold, sandy cavern. The ceiling angled upward from where the ladder shaft let out, opening up into a broad, irregular rectangle of moss-strewn stone filled with bizarre knickknacks: a broken spinning wheel, a rusty scythe, a jagged pile of cutlery, a cracked oxen's yoke. Lee took it all in, considered it some manner of bounty, though for what he could not imagine.

"You built yonder shed on top of all this?" he asked the man at some length.

"Betcha I got me the biggest house in the county, all told."

Lee ambled to the assemblage of junk, picked up a candelabra and turned it one way and then the other. Its dull silver barely raised a glint from the torchlight.

"I don't want none of your loot, old man. Federal money, like I said, or I'm off to Arkansas."

"For money them niggers ain't even got? I don't think so." The man grinned and shook his head, and he crouched to squeeze through a fissure in the west wall. The light went with him, so Lee scrambled to keep up. He was broader at the shoulders than the old man by a fair piece, and for a panicked half-second he thought himself stuck, but with an earnest jerk to the side and down he freed himself and stumbled forward into the dank gloom.

The light was gone.

———————

In an abandoned West Tennessee farmhouse, he found—among other things—a dogeared bible. By the fire of the stove he looked over the book's thin pages, its tiny printed words meaningless to him, though he had an inkling as to their general meaning. He had heard enough preachers tell of brimstone and hellfire to catch the general drift of the thing.

He considered pitching the bible into the fire for kindling, but decided instead to make use of the pages' narrow margins to begin a sort of journal—marks like those made by the men in the Stockade to tally the days, only he intended to tally not time but men. Men who fell by his rifle, or his blade, or by the strength of his own two hands.

Every five were signified by four vertical slashes and a fifth crossed through, made by the sooty end of a sharpened stob. It was daybreak when he decided he could recall no more, and he had recalled twenty-three. It seemed nothing like a magical number, nothing of the sevens and tens and six-hundred-sixty-sixes filling the ramblings of the book in his hands. Just a number. He wondered how to imbue it with deviltry.

The following night, when a wanderer scuttled into the house and set to turning up the ruined kitchen in search of victuals, the former private concluded that the next thing to burn in the stove would be the man's heart. The organ did not release easily, nor did it burn well, fresh and wet as it was, but the one-eyed soldier opened the bible up and showed the sizzling red heart to the pages, and he thought then that he was making twenty-four into a number worth a thousand of any found in Holy Writ...

...and when the torch flared again, bathing the high cathedral walls of the chamber with sickly yellow light, Lee knew before he could count them that the corpses pinned to the stone on all sides of him numbered twenty-four.

He sucked a ragged breath into his lungs that came with sand and soot, and the old man turned to look upon the dry, gray bodies as though he was admiring old paintings in a city museum.

"The Mex don't count," he said in a matter-of-fact, off-handed manner. "Truth is, I can't really use him. But I'll take him off your hands all the same, if'n you don't much mind."

Lee beheld the soldier's yawning belly, the prisoner's fractured head, the itinerant's gaping ribcage. He saw the tattered remains of uniforms both gray and blue, shriveled strips of flesh both white and black. Somewhere in the recesses of his foggy memory he heard his mama tell him not to go war, not to pick up no guns. He hissed through his teeth at her to be quiet.

A power was gave up to me to take peace from the earth, Mama.

"This'un's heart smelled sweet, sonny Jim," crowed the old man, gesturing with his torch at the wanderer, whose shoulders were held fast to the chamber wall by thick, iron railroad spikes. He dropped his chin and picked at his nose, loosening a wet scab. "Four years, three weeks, and just shy a week," he went on. "Six hunnert twenny-five thousand kilt. You want you a magic number, boy? That's the one, right there."

"I'd have t' kill more n' four hundred a day," Lee mused, beaming at the notion of competing with a whole war.

"You always was good with numbers. Can't read worth goose shit, but a good head for numbers."

"The hell is all this, then? All these dead folk?"

"Your work, boy," said the man, stretching out his arms like bird's wings. "Your good work. A bone church to the Lord. Just so happens these days he's bloodthirsty."

Lee sniffed, dubious.

"Conquest and pestilence and death—they do a dandy job, I'll reckon, a right dandy job." The old man squashed one eye closed and jabbed a thumb in Lee's direction. "But yours and mine is war and war needs be done."

"Maybe you ain't heard," Lee snarled. "War's over."

The old man sniggered. "Not for you, hoss. It won't never be over for you. Or for me. Never known it to be over." He sighed like a contented man after a meal. "New land, new war, best one in ages."

Lee held his breath, reached up at one of the solders screwed into the rock and touched his hand. The skin flaked off like old paint.

"What 'bout Ordonez?"

"When that crazy Injun's ball spun right through your brains, I knowed you was the one," said the man, his eyes glistening, but if they were tears or gore, Lee didn't know. "That Mex can help, I 'spect. Pappy's bones'll see t' that."

He rattled the pouch, full of fingers or coin, or both. In Lee's ears, the bone rattling turned gracefully to the burbling of the brown, foamy creek, rolling always toward the Colorado, toward the Gulf, out into the great big ocean that wrapped round the world like a woman's funereal shawl. He could have floated the way down, warm and red in its embrace—a goddamn Karankawa's bullet rattling about the inside of his skull.

A quarter million rebels could not do him in, not in four long years, but a lone lunatic Indian with a hole in his hat only needed a minute and one ball to put him on this balmy red road to Hell. He seethed for a mad moment, the cavern going dark at his vision's periphery. But despite his best efforts, he could not hold onto the rage.

With tremulous hands, Lee touched the back of his head, naked for want of a hat, and snaked a finger into the spongy pit he found there. The old man was quick to slap his hand away.

"Don't fuss," he snarled.

"It's the war done this," Lee thought aloud. "War made this place."

"War made you, that's for sure and for certain."

"Hell's bells."

"Might as well be, hoss. Might as well be."

———————

The one-eyed soldier and the burn-faced Mex sat atop their mounts outside the cabin, quiet and patient. The night sky was charcoal with the coming storm, which terrified the distant beeves that mewled and shuffled in the dust. The Mex's black whinnied, too, stamped its hooves, and in a minute a lantern flared behind the grease-paper windows.

Él está aquí, breathed Ordonez.

Lee gave a sharp nod, his eye on the door that presently creaked open to reveal a stocky man with a bottlebrush mustache, wearing nothing apart from his nightshirt. He raised the lantern high above his bulbous head, grimaced into the night.

Whatchoo fellers want? asked he.

Tu corazón, replied Arturo Ordonez.

Got me a shotgun right here by my hand, lied the man. No law can put blame to a man for puttin' down rustlers.

Lee said: Cut him—I got the last one.

And while Lee made a mark in the margin beside Deuteronomy 32, Ordonez carved the man's heart from his chest with a bone-handled knife: a gift for Pappy from his red animals, the ghosts of war.

WRATH UPON HIM

The rains had stopped on the morning R was to be hanged, and the air was unseasonably hot even for August. Before that, it was more than a week since the last time a body could stand out of doors and not end up soaked through to the bone. The gallows hadn't been built yet on account of the weather, though all the timber had been brought in before R was even sentenced. That was how sure everybody was that, one way or another, he was going to swing. Now that the sky was clear, and in spite of the thickness of the humid morning air, half the able-bodied men in town came together at the bottom of the bald hill to the south of the livery to get all that lumber together into a shape adequate for the killing work to hand.

Even old Parson Bucksham, going on eighty to hear anyone tell it, and Miz Nadie Rose Shelling's daddy Ramrod Dick Rollins, who only had the one arm left to him after that business with the Kiowa at Antelope Hills, showed up to lend a hand to the construction. Anything to have a piece of it, hammering a nail or passing up the rope, whatever it took to know in their hearts that they helped to string up that devilish, sidewinding, no-account son-of-a-syphilitic-whore R and hang him by the neck until he was as dead as Santa Anna.

No one had seen this many people come together so eagerly for a common goal since the fiftieth anniversary celebration of Texas Independence Day, and whereas there wasn't a Mexican face to be seen on *that* joyous occasion, on the morning of R's execution even Raul Garcia and his boys, Chico and Juanca, showed up with a wagon full of scrap lumber and rusty old tools they wanted to donate to the cause.

Such was the power and depth of Hawk Nest's hatred of R.

The magistrate who handed down the sentence the previous afternoon, Judge Erasmus McNee, left Hawk Nest on the first available stage heading in any direction after the trial ended. The gray-headed old jurist grumbled something about having seen enough men meet their end at the end of a rope and shook his head as he ducked it to climb into the coach. Since McNee did not call Hawk Nest home—he was a circuit judge who had only been to the settlement twice before—he did not share the town's fierce, entrenched loathing for the condemned. He was doing his duty to the Great State of Texas and nothing more, meting out justice as required by God and law without any personal investment, emotional or otherwise. McNee took no joy in what he had done, and he felt no guilt. It was what it was, and he was more than happy to wash his hands of the whole incident and get it as far behind him as possible. Though, once the stage rumbled out of town, he was about the last person for miles to feel that way.

In the restaurant that occupied most of the ground-level floor of the Hawk Nest Hotel, women sat in clusters of four or five, sipping tea and coffee, nibbling dry biscuits with apricot preserves from the general store on Clipping Street, and whispered about the progress of the gallows. To a woman they were deeply anxious for the work to reach its fruition, eager for the event of the day—indeed, the event of the year—to get underway. None of them was keen to stand outside in the oppressive heat to oversee the job, but all of them agreed that if it was not complete by noontime, then it was surely taking much too long. Everybody wanted to witness the hanging of so hateful and malevolent a rogue as R, but nobody wanted to have to do it in the worst heat of the day. Miz Nadie Rose Shelling her own self flitted from table to table, asking after the ladies' needs and wants, mostly to gauge the moods of each group and hear a bit of the whispers. It was all of it just so exciting that she could hardly contain herself, and it was all she could do to keep herself from storming out into the cruel heat to see how the men were faring. Privately, Nadie Rose figured if she didn't hear anything soon, she would just have to go out there to the old bald hill and finish that gallows with her own two hands.

So, too, was the hostler at the livery stable at the foot of the bald hill growing impatient. Blue Jim Green, as he was regularly known on account of his affinity for denim duds, found himself overbrushing a chestnut pony in the first stall where he had a good line of vision to the worksite. It was not that Blue Jim was shirking his duties, nor that he disagreed with the general consensus that hanging R was, in point of fact, the most clearly righteous outcome the entire affair could have generated. Rather, the hostler was selected from among the pool of jurymen after the trial to serve as the official executioner, and as such, Blue Jim was exempted from participation in the building of the gallows. It was going to be up to him to drop the trapdoor beneath R's boots when the time came, thereby sending him down, down, down until his neck snapped or he choked to death, whichever came first. Jim would have preferred joining the other men with their hammers and saws and the sweat on their backs, but there was nothing for it. He was selected to send R to God for his final judgment, and that was how it had to be.

Blue Jim brushed the chestnut some more, despite her nickering protests, and kept his eyes trained hard on the men between the livery and the hill.

After ceremoniously hammering a single nail into a joist betwixt posts to heave the platform above the sandy earth, Parson Bucksham sat down in the shade of a juniper, his back against the trunk and hat on one knee, where he wiped the sweat from his brow with his shirtsleeve. He licked his lips for want of water, tasting the salty sweat there, and he thought about the avenger of blood in the Book of Deuteronomy—he to whom the elders of the ancient city sent the convicted man. Who in Hawk Nest, Bucksham wondered, fit that biblical bill? Was it Blue Jim Green, or Judge McNee who was the avenger? Or instead was it every man jack of them who poured out his sweat in that mean Texas sun to do what a simple, single bullet could do in an instant?

"Deliver him into the hand of the avenger of blood," the preacher rasped low to himself, his bone-white fingers worrying the brim of his hat, "that he may die."

"What's that, Parson?"

Bucksham started, dropping his hat between his legs, and shot a glance up to the man standing above him. With the sun to his back, the man was haloed by the bright August light and his face was hard to make out. The preacher squinted at him, mouth agape to show how few teeth remained in his head.

"Just speaking the word to myself, son," he said. "Just speaking the word."

"Right day for it, I expect," said the man, and Bucksham reckoned the fellow grinned after that.

The parson struggled against the juniper tree to get back up to his feet, and the stranger knelt with a hand extended to help. Bucksham took his hand, and the stranger hauled him up with a powerful jerk that nearly sent the elderly man stumbling off into the street.

"Thankee, son," the parson said, and he took a half-turn around the tall man to get the sun out of the equation as much as possible. Now he could make out the man's face in full, which was a big, clean-shaven, square face belonging to a man of about thirty-five. His eyes were ice-blue and hair magpie-black. He wore no hat, though his attire was unmistakably western, from his bolo tie to his cowhide boots. This was no Eastern dude, nor was he a familiar face to Parson Bucksham—and that meant he was a stranger to all of Hawk Nest, as well.

"Just a drummer, Parson," said the man, answering the unspoken question in Bucksham's rheumy eyes. "Came in on the ten o'clock stage from Darling, matter of fact. Hoped to find your fine little town's local medicine man to discuss some new patents out of St. Louis, but from the looks of things—"

"Busy day here in Hawk Nest, son," the parson cut him off. "Big doings."

"For the whole town, looks like," the drummer said. "And not just the avenger of blood."

"Ah, heard that one, did you?"

"Deuteronomy 19, if I recall my Sunday schooling."

"You recall," Bucksham said, nodding his approval. "You recall just fine."

The drummer nodded, too, evidently proud of his memory

and happy to be recognized for it. He smiled again as he knelt down to take up his brown leather case by the handle, which bumped against his canvas trousers when he turned to look fully upon Hawk Nest's big doings. The skeleton of the thing was in place, wanting only the platform to come together, along with the hanging frame on top and steps for R and Blue Jim to ascend. Parson Bucksham would climb those steps, as well, but up to that moment he had not yet chosen the scripture best suited for the occasion.

Remembering he was in the company of something of a scholar in the Lord's word now, he looked up to the big drummer beside him to ask his opinion on the matter, but the stranger spoke first.

"Tell me, Parson," he said without looking away from the gallows, "what was the crime that precipitated all of this? That is, if you don't mind my asking."

"Not at all, son," said the preacher. "Not at all. It was a killing, of course. Only thing that can get you sentenced to hang in this county, though there's more than one way to find yourself at the business end of a rope, if you catch my meaning."

"Oh, I do," said the drummer with a grave expression. No one was grinning anymore. "There's all sorts of different kinds of law, isn't there?"

"I reckon there is, my boy. All sorts between God and man. Only it was the circuit judge what ruled this case."

"And what case would that be?"

"Like I done told you, son. It was a killing, and R was the one what done it."

"Peculiar name," said the drummer.

"It's our way," the preacher said with a knowing wink. "You forfeit your proper name when you kill one of our own here."

"That right?"

"It's a fact, son. Whoever R used to be, that name won't never be spoke again and everyone what ever knew it will forget what it ever was."

"Like he never existed at all, I expect."

"Just like that," Bucksham said. "Not just dead, but dead, gone, and forgotten. Wiped from this earth like the flood of olden days. No name, no tombstone, not even any bones left behind."

"No bones?"

"After he's dead, they'll cut R down and carry him out into the wilderness on a wagon. Let the animals take him, and let me tell you, there ain't a thing left after a few weeks. No sign anything was ever there. An Indian tracker couldn't even tell, I reckon."

"Not even a tracker," the drummer said quietly, letting his voice trail off as he thought about all that the preacher had told him. His face fell and his shoulders sagged, his whole body reflecting what would have looked to anybody like despair at the notion of a man's utter annihilation. Annihilation from the world, from memory. From ever having been. "That's got to be just about the biggest punishment I've ever heard tell of."

"Ought to be," said Bucksham. "Big crimes call for big penalties. That's always been the Lord's way, and so it's our way, too, right here in Hawk Nest."

The old man looked the drummer over, studying him close like he was trying to read his thoughts from his face. If the parson had been a touch intimidated by the stranger when first he arrived, Bucksham betrayed nothing like it now. Instead, he stood as tall as his bent back permitted, one hand holding his hat over his heart and the other tugging idly at the braces keeping his night-black breeches up.

"Makes a kind of sense, come to think of it," the drummer said at some length. "I wonder how much things might be different if none of us ever heard of the likes of Billy Bonney or Jesse James."

"Names worth forgetting," said the parson, his voice taking on an ecumenical fervor he usually reserved for the pulpit. "Wiped from this earth."

"Big penalties," said the drummer.

"Big penalties."

Just beneath the platform floor of the gallows, Ramrod Dick and Raul Garcia conferred about whether to nail down the floor before cutting out the opening for the trapdoor, or the other way around. Dick was for the former, while Raul preferred the latter, and it was ultimately left up to Hawk Nest's mayor, the Hon. Samuel Keller, Esq., to make the decision. Keller figured that since the platform was already in place, they might as well go on ahead and nail it down, and then proceed with cutting out the trapdoor.

"It doesn't need to be a great work of art, men," the mayor said, one hand on Raul's shoulder and the other on Dick's. "As long it drops R and he ends up dead at the end of that rope, that's all anyone could ask."

The men agreed and shook hands, which pleased all involved. After that, Raul instructed his sons to fetch their saws from the wagon and to get cutting as soon as Micah Warbeck, the proprietor of the Clipping General Store, secured the platform. At the same time, to the left of the platform, the Everett cousins, barbers and undertakers both, sawed planks into steps and built a staircase of four stairs to affix to the side of the gallows. On the other side, blacksmith Bill Sharpe, farmer Duke Clark, and Little Steve Neemins, lately of no known occupation, put the hanging frame together. Everyone present would have a hand in it, no matter how small a hand. Though none of them would speak of it after that day, all of them would know they'd taken their part and contributed their labor.

"It is the way," Bucksham said to no one in particular, watching the last components come together as the drummer wandered across the way to the hotel. "It is our way, and it is a good way."

If the stranger to town had wondered where the women of Hawk Nest had gone to while their men set about the business of the gallows, he questioned no more when he walked through the front door of the Hawk Nest Hotel and saw the hen party in the hotel restaurant. For a moment, he froze up there in the doorway, more than a dozen pairs of eyes locked upon him as every hushed voice, clink of chinaware, and creaking chair fell dead silent. He only found the blood in his veins again when the clerk, Jasper Washburn, appeared behind the front desk and let slip a small chuckle at the drummer's predicament.

"Don't you worry, mister," said Jasper. "They don't bite."

The drummer's cheeks pinked and he offered an embarrassed

smile, to both the clerk and the ladies in the restaurant.

"My apologies," he said to one and all.

"Needing a room, then?"

"No, I'm afraid not. I'm just waiting on the next stage back to Darling and wanted to get on out of the sun for a spell."

"Wise man," Jasper said. "But I got some bad news for you on that stage. Next one's ten o'clock tomorrow morning."

The drummer's mouth opened, then closed. He swallowed, rubbed the back of his neck, and cursed his luck for having chosen Hawk Nest to sell his wares on that of all days.

Jasper continued: "Most times, there's three every day— morning, noon, and evening. But on account of the occasion…"

"Like a town holiday," said the drummer.

"Like that."

"In that case," he said, bellying up to the front desk like one would the bar in a saloon, "I suppose I'll be needing that room, after all."

As disappointed as he was to have to spend a fruitless night in town, the drummer couldn't help but be amused at the renewal of noise in the dining room the second he disappeared up the stairs. It was as abrupt as the silence was when he came in, and he wondered if the topic of conversation hadn't switched, at least in part, to the stranger in room 7. This amused him some, as well, and he smiled to himself when he found the correct door at the end of the hall on the second floor, turned the key in the lock, and entered the small, slightly musty room.

He heard the shouts, hammering, and dragging of lumber against the ground before he threw open the curtains on the first of the room's two windows, which offered the drummer an unencumbered view of the men at the end of the main street, at the foot of the bald hill. It seemed in the short time it took him to pay for the room and take his case up the stairs, the men had gotten their own stairs completed and attached, and they were now in the process of heaving the hanging frame up, hand over hand, to the platform. It wouldn't be long, now. And though the drummer had doubts that the presence of a total stranger would be tolerated at so intensely personal an event for the town of Hawk Nest, he practically had a bird's eye view right where he stood.

In fact, the drummer had never witnessed a hanging or any other method of execution. To hear the Eastern dime novelists and big city newspapermen tell it, men were strung up by the dozens day after day in just about every square mile of the frontier, from Nogales to Laramie and clear to the California coast, and it mattered to no one who was behind the hanging, be it lawmen or vigilantes. That much, he knew, was hardly the truth. There weren't hangings from every tree branch any more than there were gunfights in every street and corral. None-the-less, they did happen, and when they did, it tended to be an affair of great interest to the general public. Families even brought baskets for luncheons on the grass to observe the grim proceedings, women and children included.

People were morbid, thought the drummer, but he didn't move from the window, nor did he take his eyes away from the finishing touches to the gallows. The Garcia boys nailed in the ratchet and hinges to the trapdoor while simultaneously, Sharpe and Clarke held the frame in place and Neemins nailed it to the platform. Now the only thing missing was a rope.

"And R," the drummer reminded himself aloud.

In short order, a rope was produced. Raul Garcia fetched it from his wagon and handed it to Duke Clarke, who sat down on the brand-new steps—thereby demonstrating their sturdiness—and worked the rope into a noose at one end. From the other side of the Hawk Nest Hotel, the Everett cousins came loping up the main strip, each of them hauling what looked like three sacks of flour apiece. The younger of the pair stumbled just in front of the hotel, dropping one of his flour sacks. The burlap flew open and spilled sand at his feet. The older man laughed at his kin's small misfortune, and together they continued on to the gallows, leaving the fallen sack behind for the time being.

As Clarke completed his noose, the Everett boys took up the far end of the line and ran it through the loops in the sacks of sand they'd carried over there, providing the needed counter-weight to sustain the tautness of a hanging rope. When that was done, the younger Everett bolted back to the hotel, scooped as much of the sand as he could back into the sack he dropped, and ran it back to complete the weight.

The noose went over the top of the frame and the weights were tied off, and every man at the site threw up his arms and let loose a shout, whoop, or rebel yell for a job well done.

The gallows was finished. It was time to hang R.

The drummer opened the window to let in some air, and pulled back the curtains on the second window in order to do the same. It was at the other window that he caught sight of the sheriff for the first time, a moon-faced, white-headed man of about sixty with a round belly and bandy legs. He wore a tin star on his cowhide vest and a gunfighter's rig around his waist that carried a sizable six-gun in the holster. The lawman was coming around the corner from the adjoining street when Ramrod Dick came tramping up, hollering, "It's done, Jack. It's time."

The drummer checked his watch. It was ten to eleven and getting hotter by the minute. Beneath him on the street, Sheriff Jack "Boy" Berry motioned for Dick Rollins to follow him, and together the two men walked back around the corner, vanishing from the drummer's view. Almost as soon as they disappeared, a gaggle of bonneted women emerged from the hotel's front door, pouring into the street with parasols and fans to ward off the brightness and the heat of the sun. The assembly was led by the hotel's owner-by-default, Miz Nadie Rose Shelling, whose skirts swayed in the otherwise stagnant summer air as she marched at a brisk pace to finally see the new gallows.

No sooner had the women from the hotel reached their destination, a chorus of voices seemed to rise up from every other direction in town. The drummer craned his neck to look out over the northside of the settlement, and in seconds he found group after group, family after family, coming out of the buildings, from alleys and side streets, or riding in on horses, wagons, and buckboards from outlying farms and ranches. The whole of Hawk Nest was coming together, filling the main thoroughfare until there was hardly any room to move at all, and pressing forth to get the best views left to them as they chattered and laughed, shouted and sang. What had looked for all the world like a sleepy little town of no importance and little populace when first he arrived on the morning stage now appeared to the drummer a bustling and cacophonous metropolis in miniature, hidden in open sight on the northwestern Texas plains.

He doubted there was a single soul left in all of Hawk Nest or its immediate environs who hadn't showed up to catch a glimpse of R's last minutes on this earth. People shook hands, hugged, sang hymns, and called out happy greetings to those they might not have seen in ages. Old Parson Bucksham was making the rounds down there, too, taking hands in his and muttering words of spirit and grace to everyone he saw. Soon, Ramrod Dick Rollins reappeared from wherever he had gone with Sheriff Berry, this time alone. He walked directly to the livery, or as directly as he could weave through the crowd, where he fetched Blue Jim Green. From there, Rollins and Green went side by side through a crowd of two hundred people or more who parted like the Red Sea before old Moses himself when they saw it was the elected executioner who needed to get by. Blue Jim looked grim, but nearly everyone on both sides of the street smiled and nodded encouragingly to him.

"Good luck, Jim," called Harry Bloom's widow, Hettie, still in her weeds.

"You'll do fine, son," said Pete Daughtry, come into town from his farm for the first since early spring. He had his hands on his only son's shoulders, Little Pete, just five years old last June.

"Thank you," Blue Jim muttered, hands touching his arms and back and hands, falling away only to be replaced by more. "Thank you, thank you."

Parson Bucksham fell in step with Jim when he came within spitting distance of the gallows, and they walked the last few yards to the steps together. Blue Jim was beginning to feel like the condemned man himself, his heart heavy and vision swirling as he looked up at the rough lumber contraption looming above him.

"It's easy as pie, Jimmy Boy," the parson whispered in the hostler's ear. He'd known Green since the man was knee-high to a locust and felt the right to call him such. "All you got to do is put the loop over his head, tighten the knot at the back of his neck, and when I give you the signal, kick out the ratchet to that old trapdoor. Then it's done."

"Easy as pie," Blue Jim repeated. "Easy as pie."

"Maybe Miz Nadie Rose can whip you up some pie when this is all said and done," Bucksham added. "Rhubarb—with fresh cream! That would sure be the thing."

"It surely would, Parson."

The drummer stayed by the window, his shirt just about sweated through, and watched Blue Jim climb up to the platform, step by step, with that wizened old preacher right behind him. There was nothing so much as approaching a breeze in the still, muggy air, but the noose swung and twisted all the same, Jim's eyes focused hard and unblinking on it as he came up behind it. Everybody else stared at the noose, as well, for what seemed to the drummer like a long, eerily quiet moment, which was only broken when Eustace Dee Thacker, one of the women who followed Miz Nadie Rose from the Hawk Nest Hotel, cried out, "Here they come!"

And because the drummer was where he was, nestled between two windows on the second story of the hotel where the main drag met the side street down which Sheriff Berry had previously gone, the stranger was the first one in town to get a clear, close look at the lawman come back around. This time, Berry walked alongside another man, a deputy in a wide-brimmed hat with a Henry repeating rifle cradled in his hands. In front of the sheriff and his deputy, shuffling in the dusty street with his shaggy head down and wrists tied together with a braided lariat, was a small boy.

The boy's hair hung over his dirty, cherubic face, a curtain of sandy blond that did a poor job of work masking the kid's tears and terror. He couldn't have been a day older than eight, even if he was small for his age, and he had obvious trouble maintaining the pace the two grown men behind him wanted him to keep up. When he stumbled, the deputy kicked him in the rear end, sending the boy flying forward into the dirt, face first. He moaned pitifully, eliciting a loud groan from Sheriff

Berry, who picked the boy up from the ground by the back of his shirt and set him back on his feet.

"God damn you, R," Jack Berry said, "don't go making this any harder than it needs to be."

"R," the drummer gasped, half-hanging out of the window and staring agape at the scene beneath him at the corner of the hotel. "No—no, it can't be."

R wiped his face with the back of one hand, trembled slightly, and continued around the corner to face the jeering throng.

"Dearly beloved, avenge not yourselves, but rather give place unto wrath," Bucksham bellowed from the gallows, his scratchy voice carrying out over the crowd. "For it is written: vengeance is mine! I will repay, saith the Lord."

Some of the townsfolk murmured their agreement with the apostle's words, whether they understood them or not, while others kept their attention on R's steady approach down the middle of the street. It was one of these latter, Mary Bullen, who waited patiently until the boy was within range to hurl the tightly packed clump of mud she held in her hand. The mud smacked R hard in the face, splattering him and knocking him back. Unable to do much about it with his hands tied in front of him, the lad landed smack on his back, the mud dripping down into his ears and his open, gasping mouth. He rolled over to one side, spitting and gagging, blinking the filth from his eyes, while most of the onlookers had a good laugh at his expense.

"All right, now," Sheriff Berry boomed in a paternal tone. "That's enough of that. Hang it, Mary, I know you got plenty of cause to hate R, but don't you think he's already getting what's coming to him?"

"Maybe he is," she spat, wiping her hand on her skirts and staring down with cold eyes at the boy on the ground between her and Berry. "But won't nothing ever be enough. Won't nothing ever bring my Pearl back, will it?"

"No, Mary," Berry said. "No, I don't expect anything can do that."

He touched her arm and gave a lingering, sympathetic look. Deputy Esposito heaved R up by his arms and gave him a shove past the sheriff and the grieving woman, whose tear-filled eyes followed the boy as he continued by. There were plenty of furious gazes for the rest of the walk to the gallows steps, but nobody else threw anything or said a single word to R along the way. The assembly settled into such a complete silence that they could hear the steps lightly creak under R's fifty-five-pound weight. He took them one at a time, stepping up until he had both feet on a stair, and then advancing to the next.

"For he is the minister of God to thee for good," the parson thundered in front of the noose. "But if thou do that which is evil, be afraid; for he beareth not the sword in vain. For he is the minister of God, a *revenger* to execute wrath upon him that doeth evil."

At the last possible minute, Bucksham had found his voice; the verses he needed came to him the moment he found himself standing on the platform, looking out over the faces of his flock, every man, woman, and child—or well near to it—in the town of Hawk Nest, Texas. While every one of them knew how the Jehovah of the Old Testament thought on the topic to hand, it was good old Paul's letter to the Romans that spoke to the elderly minister's heart that August morning. Hawk Nest's God was indeed a fair and loving God, but no one could deny that vengeance must come where vengeance was due.

No one, it appeared, apart from the sole stranger in their midst.

"Stop," the drummer screamed, barreling out of the hotel's front door and into the street. "For God's sake, stop it!"

The big man went scampering into the middle of the thoroughfare in his sweat-soaked shirtsleeves, his blue eyes wide and wild, his broad chest heaving. On the other side of the crowd, Deputy Esposito goaded R the rest of the way up to the gallows platform, but on the drummer's side, Jack Berry went quickly in a direct line to where the drummer stood gawping.

"Now, listen here, mister," Berry said, his left hand out in front of him and right floating near to the big iron at his hip. "Hawk Nest tends to be a right peaceable and welcoming town to damn near anybody wants to visit, but we don't cotton to strangers disrupting the rule of law and order in the middle of a dad-blasted hanging, you hear?"

"But he's just a boy!" the drummer shouted. "He can't be any older than eight or nine!"

"He's seven and a half," said the sheriff, "not that it's any of your business or makes one speck of difference. A killing is a killing, and we treat one the same as another."

"That's the craziest thing I've ever heard, Sheriff. Who's the boy supposed to have killed?"

"He killed my Pearl, that's who," said Mary Bullen. She stormed out from the dense horde of her neighbors and friends, her dress stained brown with the mud she'd thrown at R, and stomped at the drummer until Berry threw out one beefy arm to block her way. "He done killed my Pearl, Sheriff."

"I know it, Mary," Berry said. "We all of us know it."

"It had to have been some kind of accident, then," the drummer protested. "It couldn't have been on purpose. A seven-year-old boy?"

"Seven and a half," Sheriff Berry reminded him.

"It weren't no accident, damn your eyes," Mary growled. "As sure as I'm looking at you, that boy drew a bead down on my Pearl with his daddy's Burnside and shot her dead. It was in cold blood and I seen him do it."

"That's enough, Mary," Berry said, pushing her back even as she surged against his arm. "R was tried by a judge and convicted by a fair jury. You ain't got to prove your case."

"A fair jury?" the drummer said. "Was it made up of children, too?"

"And that's enough from you, too, mister. One more word out of your smart mouth and I'll lock you up until this thing is finished, and maybe clear through to the morning, if I feel like it. None of us is happy to see a thing like this through, but it's got to be done, and it's *going* to be done without any fool medicine show drummer from who-knows-where coming 'round to pass judgment on a lot of hard-working, hard-grieving folks. Now get on back to your room in yonder hotel and stay put until the morning stage comes to take you the hell out of here, am I clear?"

"Hasn't he got a father?" asked the stranger. "A mother?"

Mary Bullen laughed bitterly and her eyes filled again,

spilling anew down her sweat-speckled face. "You ignorant, prying jackass," she said. "I *am* his mother."

Unable to speak, the drummer stared at Mary for most of a minute before he saw what was happening behind her, past the mass of tightly packed people, on the gallows. Deputy Esposito moved R into position atop the trapdoor, and behind him, Blue Jim Green slipped the noose over the boy's head.

"Christ," the drummer rasped. "Jesus Christ, you can't."

He shouldered past Mary Bullen and Jack "Boy" Berry, sprinted into the crowd, and pushed people out of his way with as much force as he could muster on his mad dash for the gallows. Hands grasped at him in an effort to get ahold of the stranger, to keep him from getting any further than he already had, but he twisted free, slapped them away, ducked and bobbed through the mob as Green moved out from behind R to where he could reach the ratchet with the toe of his boot.

"Somebody get that man," shouted Pete Daughtry.

"Stop him, stop him," Hettie Brown cried out. "He's crazy, he is."

Diving at the steps, the drummer narrowly missed a fist to the side of his head, the only one left to Ramrod Dick Rollins but still more than powerful enough. Instead of caving in the stranger's skull as he'd hoped, Ramrod Dick spun in a circle, leading with his clenched hand, until he grew dizzy and fell against one of the gallows posts to steady himself. The drummer pushed out his hands to brace himself on the stairs, catching a few splinters when he landed on his palms, and rolled off into the mud. Men at the front of the crowd pressed forward, pushing at one another to try and grab the stranger. Esposito pointed his rifle but couldn't get a shot with so many people milling around the target.

"God damn it, you men," he barked. "Get out of the way!"

The drummer scrabbled on his hands and knees, kicking at clutching hands, and made his way up the side of the bald hill. One of the men seized him by the ankle, but he pulled his foot and it came free of the boot. With one bare foot, he continued up to the top of the hill, covered in mud from head to toe, and stood looking down at the outraged multitude.

"Listen to me," he called down to the red, angry faces beneath him. "Whatever it is this boy is said to have done, there can't be any malice or forethought in it. He's only a child, for Jesus' sake! I know you got your ways, but please—*please*, people, don't do this thing."

Deputy Esposito, no longer blocked by the men in the mud, aimed his repeater up at the stranger's chest and breathed out through his nose. He held his breath and sighted down the barrel, but Parson Bucksham gently pushed the barrel down, looking up in the deputy's eyes and shaking his head.

"Son," he said loudly, turning and making his way for the steps. "I know you know the Good Lord demands this of us, that you know all the scriptures on it as good as I do and maybe even better."

The preacher tottered down the steps, people backing away to give him room, and he started up the hill.

"Why, Parson?" the drummer asked, his eyes shimmering wetly in the bright midday light.

"Simple, friend," said Bucksham, and for the second time that morning, he accepted the stranger's outstretched hand, which pulled him the rest of the way up the hill. "He killed Pearl, just as sure as God made little green apples."

"Who was she?"

"Pearl? Why, she was Miz Mary's best milk cow. R had no call to do what he done except for pure-dee meanness."

"A cow?" the drummer said. His voice shook slightly, his eyes widening. "A *cow*?"

"A good milking cow," the parson said.

The drummer stared, then let out a hoarse laugh before snatching Bucksham by his lapels and shaking the old man. Bucksham sputtered and ogled the much larger man, helpless in his grasp.

"You're *mad*, you old fool," the big man spat in the old man's face. "You're crazier than a shit-house mouse—all of you are!"

"Why, you can't—you can't..."

Parson Bucksham gasped and trailed off, his pale face going whiter still as he seized up and gazed in mute horror at the drummer.

"He's going to kill Parson Bucksham," someone shouted.

The drummer looked in the direction of the voice, unable to tell who had said it, and at the same time he let go of the preacher's coat. Bucksham let out a small moan, dropped to the ground like a stone, and then rolled feebly down the hill. He came to a stop in the mud by the gallows steps, where the same men who had tried to get the drummer rushed to help their preacher. It was Little Steve Neemins, kneeling in the muck beside the old man, who was the first to say what everyone could soon see for themselves.

"He's dead," said Little Steve. "My God, he killed the parson."

"He killed Bucksham," Ramrod Dick said, his face a mask of disbelief. "The stranger murdered Parson Bucksham!"

"No," the drummer shouted down at him. "No, that's that true—I didn't kill him. I didn't kill anybody."

Sheriff Berry bulled his way through the crowd, sidearm drawn. His deputy prepared to get the shot, but Berry hollered, "Don't end him, son—we've got the gallows now, and by God, we'll use it again."

Hearing this, the drummer dashed down the opposite side of the hill. In an instant, he was gone.

"Some of you men get mounted and after him," the sheriff commanded.

Pandemonium reigned, the whole writhing throng of people screaming, shouting, crying, and pushing to get either after the stranger afoot or toward the livery and hitching rails to saddle up. Though unable to help much, Dick Rollins oversaw the job of lifting Bucksham out of the sludge and carrying him to a patch of yellow grass where he could lie with more dignity than offered by the mud.

The drummer made it a few dozen yards onto the Staked Plains beyond the limits of Hawk Nest before it occurred to him that he should take his one boot off and just run barefoot the rest of the way. The one foot was cut to ribbons already from the rocks and the low-crawling cacti hidden in the scrub and short grass, but there wasn't anything for it; nobody could make it far in just one boot. He abandoned the boot in a copse of stubby hackberry trees and continued on, avoiding anything in his path that would further tear up his feet as much as he could.

Close behind came a dozen men and some women first, running after him with shouts and curses, and then came the mounted posse. Five men on barrel-chested horses thundered past their neighbors, gigging their mounts with the heels of their boots and riding like prairie fire after the stranger who killed Parson Bucksham. A few shots were fired, but none of them had been aimed directly at the drummer. They meant only to frighten him, the rounds slamming harmlessly into the ground or flying far overhead. To a man, they conceded with the sheriff's position that the stranger's end would not come by way of a rifle cartridge, but at the end of a rope. Just like R.

Luke Woods, who happened to be the ramrod that succeeded Dick Rollins out at Matt Shank's spread, led the charge. He rode a white-and-red paint that stood fourteen hands high and galloped like its hindquarters were aflame. In Luke's left hand was his bridle, and in his left the Colt Peacemaker Mister Shank gave him after his first three years on the job. Not too far behind him rode Esposito, content to let a superior horseman take point, along with Duke Clark, the eldest Everett cousin, and Cash Bowman, the teller at Hawk Nest's sole bank. Only Everett and Bowman were unarmed, having not come to the hanging heeled.

In the end, it didn't much matter who did or didn't carry a shooting iron—the drummer petered out a little over a mile from the bald hill, stumbling from a run to a staggering walk and, eventually, coming to a halt. He bent at the waist with his hands on his knees and gasped for air, his feet a mess of ragged skin, blood, and dust. The riders circled him like a Kiowa raiding party, cutting off any avenue of escape, and stared the drummer down. Those who had guns kept them pointed at the stranger, and the two who didn't looked ready to spring from their saddles the moment he made a move.

"I didn't," the drummer rasped, spittle foaming on his lips. "I didn't kill him. I didn't."

"Reckon that's up to the judge and jury, son," said Jack Berry, loping up on a pinto gelding. "What's your name, anyways?"

The drummer rose back up to his full height and told him.

"Well," said the sheriff, "I expect it's D, now. Let's walk him back, boys. Nobody made him do that fool run, so he can stay on his feet a little longer."

Though he was afforded a small window, D could not see the gallows from the cell Berry and Esposito locked him in. Even if he could have, however, he wouldn't have watched. Once D was in custody and out of sight, Mayor Keller pleaded from the platform for the crowd to come to order and show a little respect for the grim doings that still needed doing. Neither Blue Jim Green nor R had left the gallows throughout the whole ordeal with D, and now that it was over, Keller handed the business back over to the hostler, who returned to his position at the small, metal ratchet holding the trapdoor in place.

From his cell, D heard the slam of the trapdoor and the dull thud of the body dropping through and pulling the rope taut, and he cursed himself for not having thought to cover his ears with his hands so that he wouldn't have. But even when he did cover them, he could still hear the great, joyous roar from the town of Hawk Nest, a deafening chorus of relief that it was all finally done. That the criminal, R the killer, was dead at last.

"Hurrah," said D. He moved his hands from his ears to his face and cried into them, only vaguely wondering how long it was going to take for the circuit judge to come back to Hawk Nest to give its people just a little more value in the gallows they came together to build on a hot August morning at the bottom of the old bald hill after the rains had stopped. "Hurrah."

LAY LOW

The first shot that splintered the air didn't startle Charlie one whit. The bullet slammed into the outcropping just above his head, sending down a shower of rocks and dust that covered his hat and shoulders, and all Charlie could do was wait for the detritus to stop falling on him so he could look up to see what happened. The second shot came from an altogether different direction, further up the narrow mule trail that snaked through the low mesas and jagged hills like teeth, where Charlie's claim lay hidden. This time around, the lead fried the air by the prospector's left ear, close enough to have found purchase in his brain had he turned his head a couple inches either way. Finally, he realized that someone was down there shooting up at him. More than one somebodies, in point of fact. And that didn't make a lick of sense, since anybody who knew anything about Charlie Lee Landry or the Lay Low mine he formally owned by the law and decree of the Territory of Arizona knew that Landry had put his chips on the wrong card. In twelve weeks of digging, panning, and praying, all Charlie ever pulled out of the ground was less than forty dollars' worth of ore, far less than he'd paid Hutch Russell for the claim.

Lay Low was worthless.

"Which maybe means it's me they after," Charlie said to himself.

"Hello, the mine," one of the shooters called up to him. The voice echoed eerily through the hills, making it hard for Charlie to determine where exactly the shooter was hiding. "You hear us, Charlie?"

"I hear you," Charlie hollered back. "Who the devil do ye be, by God?"

"I am Dan Jessups and my brother Finn Jessups is here, too, Charlie," the shooter said. "We have come to kill you."

Charlie's mouth dried up at hearing the names of the men shooting at him. Now he knew it had nothing to do with his claim, but rather his past, far from Arizona. Though it was true he had enjoyed a dalliance or two with Beulah, one of the handsomer Jessups sisters, Charlie was fairly certain it hadn't been him who put her in the family way. The timing was all off, as he understood the nature of the thing, and the only reason the Jessups had to lay it at Charlie's doorstep was he was an easier target than some of the rougher sorts Beulah kept company with. All they really wanted was a corpse they could haul back to Arkansas so they could prove they killed the son of a bitch what knocked up their sister, and in their enfeebled minds, their honor would be restored.

"Dan and Finn," Charlie yelled, "I done told you back at Fort Smith it weren't me, damn you. Ain't nobody ever hear of a woman gone big with child going on a whole year, and you know it."

"It weren't no year," Finn bellowed from the stubby trees in the foothills.

"Damned near was," Charlie corrected him. "Eleven months, leastways."

"Beulah always was slow about things," Dan said.

"Don't work that way," Charlie said. "Slow or not."

"We ain't come to argue, Charlie," Finn said. "We come to kill you and that is the way it is."

Charlie ducked his head and wished to God he never met Beulah Mayflower Jessups, or that he leastways might have had the personal fortitude to resist her sundry charms. *Two things that will almost always go bad for you,* his Peepaw told him once, *is gold and women.* That was why, when he decided to try his luck out west in some diggings, Charlie opted to look for silver rather than gold. Peepaw never said a word about silver. But he had warned the boy off Beulah, in a way, and Charlie had failed to heed the warning. Now, regardless of what he tried to pull up from the earth, he was paying the price.

Another shot pinged off the rocks close to where Charlie squatted, and he glanced over to where Esty, his pack mule, stood nosing at some chuparosa. The only gun he ever owned was in one of the bags draped over the swaybacked old mule, the same Allen & Wheelock revolver he was assigned back in the War and kept ever since. Trouble was, there was more than enough open ground between Charlie and Esty for Dan and Finn to get a good shot, and what was worse was that Charlie never kept the old gun loaded. As a matter of fact, he hadn't loaded it once in all the years since Appomattox, and he wasn't wholly certain he remembered how. He only killed back then because the State of Arkansas told him he had to. Charlie had fervently hoped in all the years since that he'd never have to do so again.

He was not likely to start now, either. More shots were fired in sporadic bursts, which Charlie figured only quietened when the Jessups brothers were forced to reload. The notion occurred to him that he might to try to suss out a pattern, run for Esty and his gun at the lull, but there was no pattern he could discern. To go for his gun, Charlie ultimately reckoned, would mean near to certain death. His only option was to head into the mine, try to hide in the slim tunnels he'd hollowed out over the months, and wait the brothers out.

Charlie ran for the mouth of the mine, shored up with lengths of mesquite and ironwood he'd chopped down his own self, and slipped into the darkness. From outside, he heard more shots, and then more shots after that. He heard Esty give a great, despairing haw and knew she had been shot, which hurt Charlie's heart and let him know the Jessups were getting closer. A lot closer. So Charlie Lee Landry got down to his hands and knees, and he went deeper into Lay Low.

"Poor old Esty," he wheezed, and he tried to make himself smaller as the shaft got narrower.

Had he been paying closer attention, he might have gotten a decent idea of how much farther it went until he reached the end of his work thus far. As things stood, his attention was held firmly elsewhere, so that Charlie was astonished when it dawned on him that he'd been bellying his way along for what seemed like a lot longer than he ever had before. He never dug this deep. He never aimed to. By the time the Jessups showed up, Charlie Lee was just about through with prospecting, and figured on finding some other sucker to buy the claim off him in Ash Grove or Camp Lewis. Where he was now was something else than his own skinny, worthless little tunnel. Where he was now was something else altogether.

Oh, dad-blast it, Charlie thought. *Them Jessups ain't gonna kill me. I gone and killed my own dumb self.*

Charlie was like to suffocate, that far into the toothy hills and beneath the earth where the Good Lord never intended men to crawl. He wasn't any gopher or mole or prairie dog or wiggly worm, meant to traverse the layers of rock and dirt and silver and gold God filled the world up with, and acting like one just to get his hands on forty dollars seemed more foolish now than ever. His only hope was that the Jessups brothers would crawl in after him, get wedged up the same, and choke to death on the same dirt Charlie was eating.

"The devil with them, anyhow," he rasped.

"And Beulah, too?" asked a voice in the dark, small and reedy like a poorly played flute.

If there had been any room for Charlie to move, he would have jumped. All he could do was gasp, which only served to fill his mouth up with more dirt. He coughed and sputtered, spitting out the same gravel and sand he'd been shoveling, picking, and sifting for most of a year.

"Who's there?" Charlie said. He felt slightly crazy, talking to the dark like that, when he knew perfectly well there couldn't possibly have been anyone else in there. There wasn't room enough for a deerfly, never mind another person.

"It is not fair," said the reedy voice, somehow both close and distant, the same way sounds got all around a man in the canyons and gulches and all the ragged, jagged places in Arizona. "Not fair, not fair."

"What ain't fair?"

"Forty dollars, Charlie. Forty dollars and no more silver, no more silver. No more silver and two boys with their big guns, big guns."

As impossible and upsetting as the voice was, Charlie could not argue with the logic. It was true: it *wasn't* fair, the way things had turned out for him. Sure, mayhap he ought to have married Beulah before ducking into the barn with her, but it wasn't anything illegal they'd done in there, leastways as far as Charlie knew. And he *did* know it wasn't him who put her up the stick, anyhow. A man didn't need schoolhouse learning to know that, nor did he have to be some marvel at ciphering to know forty dollars dug out of a hundred-dollar claim was a bust.

"Big guns," Charlie said. He listened carefully, holding his breath so that there was nothing but his own heartbeat in his ears. No more shots.

Or I'm too far in to hear.

"They are out there," said the voice, going absurdly high in the last few syllables. "They are waiting."

"Can you see 'em?" Charlie wondered aloud.

But the voice only repeated itself. "They are waiting."

"You said that."

He pushed a sigh past his lips and, thinking that the less air there was in his lungs, the more room he had in the tunnel, he kept on exhaling until he felt deflated. It didn't much help. He was still pressed in on all sides except for his feet, which felt like they were sticking up out of a barrel. His shoulders were squeezed so that they folded in on his chest, thus he couldn't move his arms any to propel himself forward. If, for nothing else, to see if there *was* any way forward, or if Charlie was just faced up against pure-dee rock. Rock that would become his tombstone if he didn't think of something fast.

The pointed tip of his left boot scratched at the tunnel floor, and Charlie tried to get some kind of a hold that he could maybe pull himself back.

"I wouldn't go that way if I were you," said the voice. "That way and the Jessupses kill you, Charlie."

"Ain't no other way," Charlie said.

"Keep going," it said. "Down, down, down, down..."

"Down? Down where?"

"Down," said the voice, "to me, Charlie."

Past the teeth, thought Charlie, remembering the fangs of the hills, *and down the throat.*

"Down, down, down. Come to me, Charlie. Come to me."

I can't, Charlie thought, *even if I wanted to.*

Nevertheless, he attempted to push with his feet, and to his immense surprise, his body skidded an additional inch forward. No, not forward—*down.* The rock was still there, unmoved and unmovable, but there was something else, another way. He pushed again, gained another inch, and with still another push, still another inch. His head was dropping down in the darkness, first at a slight angle, but gradually the decline grew sharper. With a little more effort and a great deal of patience, Charlie was rewarded by attaining an angle where gravity took half the work from him, drawing him down through the scree like a sled down a hill.

"Good, Charlie, good."

Charlie elected not to reply just yet, afraid of opening his mouth and ending up with another taste of dirt and pebbles. Instead he just kept on, wriggling his way down the subterranean channel bit by bit, mouth and eyes shut but nose full of dust. The voice never got closer or farther away; when it spoke to him, it was always right there, in both ears, like the whispers of a secret lover in the barn loft. Like Beulah Jessups.

"Almost there, Charlie," she said.

"Beulah?"

"Almost there."

Almost where?

He found out soon enough, as the descent sped up so that he no longer needed to wriggle or kick, and he slid down the passage into open air before crashing down to solid ground. Charlie landed on his chest and skidded, his chin torn across the hard ground for a foot and a half. He let out a long, anguished moan, the wound burning, and rolled onto his back. For several minutes, he blinked his eyes at the tar-black dark and listened to the slow, steady drip, drip, drip of water somewhere close. Then, he blinked again and when he opened his eyes, it wasn't dark anymore.

The chamber in which Charlie found himself wasn't exactly

brightly lit, but in an instant he could make it out fairly clearly. He could see the shaft through which he'd come, and he could see the limits of the chamber itself, with a high, vaulted ceiling and enough room to fit the cabin he grew up in five times over. There were no other tunnels or openings immediately apparent to him, but there were several crooked columns of stone that went from floor to ceiling, probably keeping it all from caving in on him. The damp walls seeped brackish water, and in places it sweated into the droplets he'd heard pattering the ground.

And on a huge limestone boulder across the chamber from him, there squatted an oily, gray thing with hair like Spanish moss and skin like a dead fish. Its perfectly round eyes were bulging, colorless orbs with no irises or pupils, its wide, blubbery mouth hanging open to reveal two rows of narrow, gray teeth. As unknowably otherworldly as the creature looked to Charlie, it had the same number of limbs as he did, the same number of fingers and toes. It had ears and a nose, though neither was much to speak of, and it breathed the same air Charlie breathed. It surely wasn't human, but if pressed, he would have had to admit it was a bit *like* one.

"Hello, Charlie," the thing said. It spoke with Beulah's voice.

"Oh, God," Charlie said. He struggled to sit up, while at the same time scuttle a little further away from the creature on the rock. *It is the devil*, he thought. *Them Jessups done kilt me and I have gone to hell.*

"No heaven, no heaven," the gray thing said. "No hell, no hell."

Its voice was getting reedy again, dropping back into the same voice Charlie first heard in the mine above. *How far above?*

"No hell?" Charlie said.

"No gods, no devils. Just Charlie. Just Charlie and me. Hello, Charlie."

"What—who are you?"

"You are Charlie," it said, "and I am me."

With that, the being's broad mouth seemed to curl up into a kind of drooling, open-mouthed grin.

"I am Charlie…"

"And I am *me*."

It stared—or leastways, Charlie thought it stared, but it was hard to tell if it saw anything at all with those milky marbles it had for eyes. In any case, its face stayed facing his, and Charlie was quick losing faith that the creature was ever going to answer a question sensibly. It clearly liked to talk, but it didn't say much that wasn't just talking in circles. Preachers, in Charlie's experience, were like that. Now he knew cave creatures were like that, too.

"Sure," he said. "You're you, I'm me, but where in tarnation am I, by God?"

He looked to the mouth of the shaft and wondered whether he'd be able to climb back out again. It didn't seem likely. There was hardly room to move and he only managed to get down thanks to gravity. To get back up, he'd need space enough to crawl and claw and such, and the channel was much too tight for that. He'd gone in and kept going out of fear of being shot to death, but now a new fear crept over him like a cold, damp wind.

Charlie was trapped.

The gray thing tittered.

"Ain't funny," Charlie complained.

"It is better they shoot you?"

"No. I don't know. Maybe."

"I will not shoot you, Charlie."

"You ain't even got no gun," Charlie said. "Jeezum Crow, you ain't even got no clothes on."

The creature had nothing specifically obscene on display that he could see, but the state of undress alone was sufficient to bother him. He hadn't even seen Beulah *that* naked, on account of how dark it was in the barn loft that night. Now he was surely going to die down in that cool, damp chamber, and that awful, leathery thing on the rock the most nude he'd ever see somebody. He wasn't completely sure why, but it was just as sad as the dying itself, somehow.

"I *like* you, Charlie," said the gray thing, but Charlie ignored it this time.

He rose and haltingly returned to the opening in the cavern wall, where he probed the edges with his fingers and peered inside. There was a muted, hollow sort of sound emanating from within; it reminded Charlie of times as a boy when he'd jump into the swimming hole and listen to the water in his ears when he was completely under. To him, it sounded like darkness looked. Like nothing, yet still there.

"I *love* you, Charlie," the monster said in Beulah's voice.

Charlie swung toward it and scowled.

"You best quit that mess," he warned. "And tell me how to get out of here."

"You can get out of here," it said in its own voice, "but you cannot go up. You cannot go up, but you can go down, Charlie. Down, down, down, down."

"How does that help me any?" Charlie said, his voice cracking. "It ain't down I want to be at! I want to go up!"

"No up, no up. Oh, poor Charlie. Poor, poor Charlie did not get shot. Poor, poor Charlie is so ungrateful."

The creature hunched over further than it already was and buried its oily face in its hands. Its shoulders trembled and its long, wormy fingers curled over its skull as it appeared to weep from the pain of Charlie's lack of gratitude. Charlie heaved a sigh and looked again up the dark, steep shaft. It was so narrow that he wasn't even sure he could get back into it, never mind crawl up. The prospect was hopeless, and now all he had left to him was this curiously lit chamber in the deep underground and the horrendous, sobbing obscenity that lived in it.

"I should of let them Jessups shoot me," Charlie muttered. "Dad-blast it, I should of gone for that cotton-pickin' gun."

He remembered poor old Esty, surely dead in the dust by now, the ancient Allen & Wheelock rusting in her packs, and his eyes welled up with tears. If only he'd never met Beulah Mayflower Jessups or bought that worthless claim from Hutch Russell. There wasn't one aspect of Charlie Lee Landry's life that hadn't gone to hell in a handbasket, from the trouble with the brothers to the lousy forty dollars already come and gone from Lay Low, and there wasn't one thing he could do about any of it thanks to—

"You," Charlie said. "This is all your fault. You done this to me."

The thing's shoulders still shook, but when it brought its hands away from its face, Charlie could see it wasn't weeping at all. It was laughing at him.

And though the creature retained its cloudy, sightless eyes and suety mouth, there was enough subtly changed about its nasty face that Charlie slowly realized he recognized the deformed thing. He wasn't the same as he'd been that night in the Long Branch Saloon when he talked Charlie into ponying up for the claim, but there was little doubt in Charlie's mind that he was looking at old Hutch Russell his own self.

"Down, Charlie," Hutch said. "Down, down, down."

He chortled and pointed to the tunnel. Charlie looked, and his breath hitched in his chest when he saw that it no longer led up at all. The channel now angled sharply down, further into the rocky earth beneath the fanged hills around Lay Low. There never was any way he was going to get back up to the mine shaft, not really, but even the most insignificantly puny chance of ascent was now erased completely. Now there was only the chamber, and there was *down*. Charlie swallowed dry, wanting for water but afraid to lick the moisture in the walls for fear of being poisoned by something. Nothing he needed or wanted was in Hutch's terrible chamber, not even the most basic needs, and Hutch himself just grinned that awful, thin-toothed grin at him while the fear spilled over his heart like molten lead.

Down, Charlie thought, *can't be worse than here.*

Hutch Russell quivered all over, pointing his entire body toward the hole in the wall that dropped into the unknown darkness below, huffing and groaning with unpleasant anticipation. Charlie gazed into the blackness, and he wondered if whatever was down there was what made Hutch Russell into what he was now, or if that was what Hutch always was. Mayhap there was water down there. Might could be another way up. Then again, Charlie knew it may very well be his own tomb awaiting him at the bottom of that tunnel. He looked back from the hole to the Hutch-thing and suppressed a shudder at the way the creature convulsed like raw animal fat.

"Down, Charlie," Hutch said.

"Yeah, I know," Charlie said. "Down."

He gingerly touched the underside of his chin and winced at the tenderness there. This time, he'd be more careful about the landing. With a long, deep breath in through his nostrils, he pushed it back out of his lungs through his mouth and stuck his head into the hole in the wall. It was as tight a fit as before, but he was a rawboned man and managed to wriggle his way in until only his feet kicked out into the chamber. He found that if he rotated his shoulders, he was able to pull himself slowly forward, and after a few minutes of that, he propelled himself far enough to begin the descent in earnest. Charlie slid through the scree again, lifting his chin as far as he could to keep it from further injury, and he went down inch by inch, foot by foot. The tunnel narrowed—imperceptibly at first, but enough so that he had to use the shoulder trick again—and the soil loosened until it piled into his nose and mouth and ears as he went along.

Charlie swallowed the dirt and breathed it into his lungs and kept going.

"Come, Charlie," Beulah said softly, right in his ear. "Come to me."

"I'm coming, darlin'," said Charlie before taking on another mouthful of his grave. "I'm a-coming."

WE GO THE UNKNOWN WAYS

May 17, 1857

Only three days out of St. Louis, a mere 42 miles, and we have an axle broken. Jim says it could be worse for us, as the Overturfs still have not met back up with the train since putting down one of their oxen yesterday. The poor, stupid beast found the only prairie dog hole in the entire roadway, stepped right into it, and snapped its foreleg in half. Mr. Tucker would not stop—Mr. Tucker can never be convinced of any-thing—and thus we left the Danes behind in their Conestoga wagon and only the one left ox to pull it. I heard the shot from Esben Overturf's flintlock before we were half a mile down the trail from them, and Jim scolded me for flinching at the echoing blast. I have to learn to be more resilient or else this journey will be much too hard for me to bear. Such is my husband's opinion, in any event, and I suppose I must respect it.

In truth, it was the opinions of James Dowdall that first drew me to him, and it was his opinion that if Oregon was to be a free state, then it would be "a d—n sight better than Missouri," to quote the man directly. It would be safer also, though this was not spoken by him, at least not to me. Free Soilers are no more welcome in Missouri than freedmen, and with Enos Parker's house and barn burnt to the ground in the dead of winter, there is little choice left to us lest we be next. One need only listen to the dread winds blowing through the idle talk of the wagon train to know war is inevitable, and Missourians shall be called upon to fight for the preservation of slavery, not to abol-ish it. Thus shall we transform ourselves from Missourians to

Oregonians—if indeed Jim and Tom Flood, the boy he hired for the journey, can repair the axle in time to rejoin the train.

Tom Flood is an odd duck. He was not known to us before signing up with Mr. Tucker, who strongly recommended that Jim find a young man to help. The lad's chief quality, as near as I can determine, is that he asked for less pay than others Jim interviewed, and though Flood is by no means idle or lazy, he has a staggering gait and nervous look about him that puts me at unease. Jim never thinks twice about leaving me alone with the young man, but when he does I will usually find someplace else to be. If Flood is offended by this, he has not made it known to me. In fact, he has barely ever spoken more than a word or two since making my acquaintance. More often than that, I get only a nod or a grunt. I find this agreeable enough, for I would not like to listen to the thoughts that float behind eyes like his.

For the last few hours, however, I have sat alone with my diary, dividing my attention between this diary, watching the men work and curse as though I cannot hear them, and looking out over the sparkling surface of the Missouri River. I doubt I shall ever see it again.

May 28, 1857

We are two weeks on the trail and yet still in Missouri. On the day our axle broke, the repair was not done until nightfall, forcing us to wait for morning before continuing on. Because of this, we traveled alone for two more days before catching sight of our train in the middle distance, and it was not until the day after that when we finally rejoined them. Mr. Tucker gruffly advised Jim to be more attentive to the condition of his wagon and stock, for the further west we travel, the higher the chance of a lone wagon on the prairie will fall under Indian attack. Though this was hardly the first I'd heard of such a thing, for whatever reason Mr. Tucker's dismal warning kept me awake all that night in fear for my life. Jim remarked that I looked a fright come morning, but I said nothing about the terrors that plagued me. Just as when I was a girl, I maintain a silly concern that voicing my fears might somehow realize them.

The trail was strangely crowded on the first week out, and it started to thin out slightly over the course of the second week. I suspect this will be a trend that continues until at some point along the way we may see no sign of white people other than ourselves. Already I have spied abandoned chests, chairs, a Davenport desk, a refectory table, and even an ornate bureau of mahogany that must have cost a small fortune, all dumped in the grass like so much refuse by pilgrims who needed to lighten their loads. Thus far, it is not at all uncommon to find people picking through these artifacts and taking whatever they can carry or cart away, pieces of some family's life left behind so that might forge on to a new one. I find it queerly sad.

The Overturfs never reappeared or rejoined our train. I pray they turned back to try again with another trail master.

June 5, 1857

Jim and Tom Flood had an argument over whether Flood should be paid half his wages when we reach the South Pass, or if the full sum should be remitted at once in Oregon. To my embarrassment, the argument turned to blows, though I could hardly determine who threw the first punch, and the fight could only be brought to an end after several men rushed to separate my husband from our hired boy. Thereafter, Tom Flood was taken in by another family, Phillip Tippet and his brood, until such a time that he might be reconciled with Jim, who has not uttered a single word to me since the incident. I am aghast.

But I say nothing.

June 29, 1857

43 days out of St. Louis. According to Mr. Tucker's estimation, this means in one week's time we should be halfway to our objective. Naturally this is based upon Tucker's original estimate of 100 days travel, which must now be amended to account for the uncommon sluggishness of our outfit. Rather than nearing the South Pass, we have only barely begun plodding along the Platte River from the Little Blue. Every day our wagon master's mood

grows darker for the ruination of his intended pace, which he takes out on whomever happens to cross him. The plain fact is that Mr. Tucker is one of only a very few men amongst us with any experience on the trail, or even with the beasts and conveyances we must all master to traverse it. Still, there have been many delays from further accidents causing damage to wheels and axles to lamed oxen, in addition to which there is much disagreement about whether some travelers must divest themselves of weight that slows the passage for everyone. Tempers are high and friendships few. These are challenging days.

We shall soon reach Fort Kearny—which indeed we should have left more than a week ago—where we will replenish possibles earlier than intended with the sutler there. Jim has not tasted coffee for several days and I pray the resupply will brighten his disposition, if only a little.

He and Tom Flood never reconciled.

July 5, 1857

Mr. Tucker killed a man today.

I had no inkling of any kind of disagreement until the moment I saw Tucker come riding back from the front of the train, whipping his dun into a gallop and then suddenly pulling the reins to halt beside the slow-moving Button wagon. Roy Button had been meandering alongside, walking stick in hand and his wide-brimmed hat shading his downturned face when the trail master drew up to him and pointed a Dragoon pistol at the startled farmer.

Button said something to the effect of, "What is this for, Tucker?" whereupon Mr. Tucker said, "We hang thieves where I come from, only there are no trees to hang you from." Both men spat vile oaths at one another after that, and when Button raised his walking staff as to strike Tucker with it, Tucker shot him in the eye. Ola Button tumbled out of the back of their wagon, having been resting out of the sun due to her delicate condition, and she fell bodily upon the still remains of her husband, weeping widow's tears for the first time.

My Jim was the first to ask what Button had done, and for

an instant I felt horribly certain Tucker would murder him next. The man's eyes belied the fact that he considered it. But instead, Mr. Tucker announced in a loud voice to no one in particular that thievery will not be tolerated under his watch and leadership of this outfit, and he commanded two of his adjutants, cowboys I have only heard called Hook and Swan, to bury the body.

They have carried Roy Button away from us, toward Chimney Rock. The corpse was draped over a mule and the men carried their own shovels for the job of work assigned to them. Ola was not permitted to join them, so Reverend Rothbart stays with her for the evening, reading quietly from his bible and praying with her.

Tucker paces the line, his hand ever near to the Dragoon in his belt, eyes dark and watchful. I know I am not the only one who has grown afraid of him.

July 8, 1857

What once was one outfit of fifteen wagons and some 46 weary travelers has been divided into two. One column stays with Mr. Tucker, though I doubt out of any loyalty or admiration for the man, but rather due to his knowledge and experience with what lay ahead. This detachment numbers nine wagons with their attendant 28 men, women, and children. Mr. Swan remains also with his boss, though Mr. Hook has detached from the main body of the train to lead the rebels who have determined Tucker both mad and dangerous, and that they shall be in better stead without him. It is to this latter column that Jim and I have thrown our lot.

Extraordinarily, Mrs. Button has stayed with the main train—and with the rogue who murdered her husband.

Jim did not ask my thoughts on the subject, though if he had I believe I would have agreed to join Mr. Hook and depart from Tucker as soon as possible. I am terrified of forging ahead without the benefit of Mr. Tucker's experience, but I fear the man himself still more. Hook's acumen has yet to be tested, though tested it shall be.

We all shall be tested in the days and weeks to come, I think.

July 31, 1857

Jonas Tenler, the sole Roman Catholic among us, is sick. He is a quiet man who never asks for help though is always first to offer it, and generally well-liked by his fellow travelers. Even now, forced to hurry away into the grass every so often to be ill, the fellow refuses help from anyone but his own hired hand, a tall and lanky man of some forty years named Peter Keen. Jim has heard it said that Mr. Keen is half Sioux and as such will be called upon should we have any difficulties with those people on the plains. To me, he simply looks like an undertaker, or perhaps the expired spirit of one. If anyone among us is quieter even than Mr. Tenler, it is Peter Keen, whose voice I have never heard at all.

In any event, Tenler's man must now help him on his regular visits to the long grass to evacuate himself, and the longer this goes on, the more I hear worried whispers about contagion. Few of us are utter strangers to the signs of cholera, nor would many of us be surprised to know how often the dread disease strikes on the road we walk. Most keep their distance from poor Jonas Tenler for reason of these anxieties, though all keep a close eye on his condition. I hope the dear man improves.

August 1, 1857

Jonas Tenler died in the night.

August 17, 1857

It is my belief, and the belief of several others, that we are lost. We should have crossed the South Pass ages ago, but we have not so much as seen the Devil's Gate supposed to precede it. The last we felt assured as a assembly that we were on the correct path was Fort Laramie, where once more we resupplied and several of us traded for fresh oxen or horses. Paul Kegg, his young bride Angela, and their three small children stayed behind at the fort when we decamped, deciding they had gone far enough and opting to search for land to settle upon in that region instead. We are now only 12, and I doubt any of us believes Mr. Hook has the slightest idea where we are.

"Somebody must speak up," Jim grumbled to me over supper tonight. He says the way we now go is hardly a road at all, and it is clear that few if any at all have come this way in some time. That alone is proof that we are no longer on the Oregon Trail, and there is no question in my mind that my husband is working up the backbone to confront Mr. Hook about it. "The fool will lead up right into a Sioux war party if he isn't spoken to."

Three months out from St. Louis and we have not reached the halfway point. Now we are lost in the wilderness. I will wait for Jim to go to sleep before I cry, but cry I will.

August 20, 1857

I saw a man on the hill and Jim does not believe me. It is not that he thinks me a liar, only that I must have mistaken something else for what I thought was a man—a rock or a tree trunk, perhaps. I protested that neither a rock or tree walks like a man walks, which this figure most certainly did. He was only in silhouette against the low light of dusk, but I am sure I made no mistake about what I was seeing. A man, only much taller than any man I have ever seen, maybe eight or even nine feet in height. He appeared from behind the hill, gliding easily to the top where he stood for a moment before walking several paces to the south, his arms swinging like strands of Spanish moss in the breeze. Thereafter he turned back and vanished whence he came.

Reverend Rothbart allows that I might very well have seen a man, though he could not have been as tall as I claim. The reverend proposed it could have been Peter Keen, who is indeed quite tall, but I saw Keen within moments of returning to the encampment to tell Jim. "An Indian, no doubt," Rothbart believes. "And there is never just the one Indian. I shall speak to Mr. Hook. We must be alert."

A lot of good Hook will do about it. We are no less lost than before, no closer to finding the correct trail again. Yet still we move on in a generally western direction until we near whatever mountains loom in the distance ahead of us. Then we will have to either locate a pass or take the long passage around the range, if such a passage exists. I no longer feel the need to cry. I want only to scream.

And I know perfectly well the man I saw on the hill was no Indian.

August 29, 1857

All of the men and some of the women have carried rifles, muskets, and pistols everywhere they go since word of the "Indian" spread throughout the train. Nobody goes anywhere alone, not even to make privy. Worse than this, a distrust of Peter Keen has been sown owing to his suspected Sioux blood, which he now vehemently denies to be the case. Should anything happen to Mr. Keen, the fault will lay squarely at my own feet, for there would be no talk of skulking Indians had I not spoken up about the man on the hill. I told Jim I must have been dreaming it, that he must tell the others that there never was anyone on that hill, Indian or otherwise, but he says the damage is done. I cannot tell if he is annoyed about it, or instead determined to believe in an unseen band of red men stalking us on our wayward journey toward the nearing mountains.

It is the mountains upon which I keep my eyes trained, for more often than not I am afraid to look elsewhere, lest I see another strange, tall man—or something still worse.

September 2, 1857

Someone cut Peter Keen's throat while he slept. The horrid scene was not discovered until it was time to move out and it appeared as though Mr. Keen had not yet risen. When Reverend Rothbart looked into the wagon to rouse him, he said there was so much blood that the murder could be properly called a butchery. And while none among us will confess to the heinous crime, few seem terribly affronted by it, either. Jim assures me that the body was buried, but I am afraid I can hardly believe there was time enough to do it when the rest of us got under-way so quickly following the gruesome discovery. The oxen formerly belonging to Jonas Tenler were unhitched and div-vied up, as were a number of items removed from the bloody wagon including flour, coffee, tobacco, saleratus, a Dutch oven, an axe, and the late Mr. Tenler's Kentucky long rifle. I witnessed men wiping blood from several of these things, but I never saw any of them heft a trowel or spade for the purpose of a proper Christian burial.

I can scarcely understand why anybody here should fret over savages in the trees and hills, when one need look no fur-ther for savages than his neighbor or himself.

September 7, 1857

It seems to me that no matter how far we go, the mountains ahead of us never get any closer, almost as though the road lengthens beneath our feet and wheels, or the range moves imperceptibly faster than we do. I say as much to Jim, who scoffs and explains how it is an illusion, as he might to a small child. What little patience he managed to muster before has been whittled down to a nub. Practically everything irritates him now, and he has the harried, haunted look about him of a man who hasn't slept in days. He may not have; I would be the last to know. Jim has taken to sleeping outside of the wagon for the last six nights, claiming the air within is too stifling.

I suspect the departure of Steven and May Hammatt has much to do with his temper. The Hammatts turned back soon after the initial Indian panic, Steven having convinced him-self we are only driving deeper into danger. Mr. Hook curtly insisted they remain with the train, for if indeed there was any danger from the Sioux, a lone wagon would be an irresist-ible target, but Mr. Hammatt would not hear of it. We are now reduced to just 10 persons, two of whom are mere children, and Hook has publicly declared the Hammatts as good as dead, to the tremendous consternation of all, Jim very much included.

Those left to our little rebel band are myself and Jim; Mr. Hook; the Reverend Rothbart; Rand and Mary Quist, and their boy Douglas; and Henry and Fay Penny, with their infant daughter, Bonnie. For the large part, each family sticks to their own, though the reverend visits each of us in turn from time to time—in spite of Jim's grumbling protests. To me, privately, Rothbart has twice recommended I pray whenever possible, something he says with the gravest heft as a physician would prescribe medicine to a dying man. The third time he came to me, this midmorning, the reverend did not speak of prayer. He said only, "Those mountains frighten me, Mrs. Dowdall."

I could not bear to tell him that they frighten me, too.

September 12, 1857

The man I saw on the hill walks freely among us. He is every bit as tall as first I imagined, if not taller, and where before I ascribed his duskiness to the low light, I can plainly see he is black as a shadow in any light. The man—if indeed he is a man— moves dreamily, like smoke, weaving in between the wagons and people and beasts, pausing now and again to bend low so that he might examine something or someone closely with cold, pale eyes. Should he have any further qualities to define anything resembling a face, I have yet to notice them. Only the eyes, which are hardly any kind of eyes at all, but rather deep, hollow pits of the sort of low light one sees in the sky just before a storm breaks. I fear one may be about to break now.

There is no panic this time, because this time I have told no one of the man's presence. I believed at first there was no need. I believed the others could surely see what I saw, but they did not. Even when the tall man stoops to bring his face within inches of another's, whomever he studies will not react one whit. The sole exception I can find to this comes when the man visits the children, Douglas and Bonnie, to whom he appears to whisper indistinctly, close to their ears. In these moments, the children will smile, or laugh, as one might upon hearing a joke. Yet still, the young ones do not appear to see the towering figure floating up and down the train, hour after hour, day after day.

Indeed, what is noticed is not who or what is here, but quite the opposite—weeks have passed since last any of us saw another human being or even sign of one, assuming one excludes the "Indian" Jim imagines I invented to allay the tedium. I do not think anyone is much worried about Sioux attacks anymore due to this utter dearth of human sign, and although I expect everybody has already thought it, Rand Quist is the first to speak aloud the idea that even the Indians will not enter this endless wild country. Only us.

Us and my shadow man, of course.

September 18, 1857

I was awakened last night by the sound of a wretched scream. Everyone convened together within the circle of wagons Mr. Hook has insisted upon for some days now, and it was no great matter of deduction to identify Fay Penny as the screamer, for she was gone. Henry Penny was frantic, and it was he who hurriedly collected most of the men to storm the woods with lanterns and guns to search for his wife. Only Reverend Rothbart stayed behind with the women and children, and as I am the only woman among us with no child of my own to mind, I volunteered to look after little Bonnie while Mr. Penny, Mr. Quist, Mr. Hook, and Jim scour the darkness for the missing woman.

The shadow man stayed outside of the circle, occasionally appearing between wagons to look in on us. At one juncture, he paused between our wagon and the Quists', and he merely stared at me. I stared back at him, and this must have gone on for some time for I was startled badly when Rothbart touched my shoulder. I jumped, woke Bonnie, and upon looking back to where our frequent visitor was, he was gone.

"My apologies, Mrs. Dowdall," the reverend said. "I did not mean to frighten you."

I turned to face him, and I was immediately struck dumb by the frightful state of him. Reverend Rothbart looked as haggard as any of the men, from his shaggy beard and sunken cheeks to the rat's nest of sand-colored hair on his head for which he had no helpmate to cut. Yet it was his swollen, red right eye that most stunned me. The skin surrounding the eye was puffed out and riddled with bumps, and the eye itself red as carnations. More alarming was the fact that, while his left eye was fixed on my face, the right one rolled and wandered in its socket, flitting here and there like an anxious insect.

"Reverend," said I, "your eye."

Rothbart seemed somewhat taken aback, though he quickly recovered himself even and smiled while he touched the eye with his fingers. "Oh, it is nothing," he assured me. "I am sure I can come up with a poultice to treat it, if it does not go away on its own. Too many biting and stinging things out here, you know."

I did not know, since in addition to the conspicuous absence of people on our errant road, I cannot recall the last time I saw any of God's creatures apart from those we brought to this place. If anything was biting or stinging Reverend Rothbart, then he alone could see them, much as I alone saw the shadow man of the wood.

Yet where has he gone? With the men, to search for Fay? Or perhaps he is with Fay herself? I cannot help but wonder if he was the cause of her scream and subsequent disappearance. I wonder too if Mrs. Penny shall be the last to vanish.

September 19, 1857

The men did not return to the circle until daybreak. I was up most of the night, only slipping away for small snatches of sleep, whilst watching over Bonnie first by the fire, then inside our wagon. Mrs. Quist was the one who spotted them, straggling in from the misty trees, and it was I who realized that Fay Penny was not with them.

It was I who noticed first that my husband was not with them, either.

"Tell us what happened," Rothbart breathlessly demanded. His infected eye had by then swollen almost completely shut.

Henry Penny would only babble and shake his head, making no sense. Rand Quist fought back tears and with some difficulty, explained to the reverend that Mrs. Penny attacked my

Jim as might some wild animal of the wood—"Teeth and all" was the phrase Mr. Quist used in particular. To this, Mr. Penny commenced shouting, "That was not my wife, that was not my Fay!" Mr. Hook needed to restrain the man whilst Quist took his rifle away, for Mr. Penny wanted to bolt back into the forest.

"Please," I pleaded, "tell me, what has become of Jim Dowdall?"

Reverend Rothbart laid his hands on my shoulder as the tears spilled from my eyes, the men tending to Penny looking to me with the utmost pity. None of them had the courage to tell me my husband was killed, and none of them needed to.

I am now more than merely lost and afraid. I am now alone, as well.

September 21, 57

New developments. The shadow man is returned, and he has brought more like him. The towering figures drift among us, one poking his head into Mr. Penny's wagon, another chattering incomprehensibly to the infant Bonnie on Mrs. Quist's lap, still another closely studying Hook with its head canted sharply to one side. For the large part, these creatures appear to ignore me outright, as though bored of the sole grown person who is able to see them. They prefer their hiddenness, their tricky ways. And if any or all of them are in any way responsible for the horror that occurred in the woods, they are none-the-less as startled as any of us when the hoarse, throat-shredding screams sound from the trees behind us, where last Fay Penny was seen.

Walking beside me, Reverent Rothbart dropped his chin and muttered a prayer when she last screamed, about noon today. I cannot say why I thought it prudent, but I told him, "Fay is something else, now."

I quite nearly apologized for the remark, but the reverend spoke before I could. He said, "It is this place, of course. It will change us all." He uttered a bitter sort of laugh, still looking down with his one good eye, and when he at length raised his face to mine, I could see plainly that the infection surrounding his swollen, knobbly eye was spreading in all directions. It was a dreadful sight to see and the unfortunate man was beginning to smell terribly sour, but for politeness's sake I smiled and said, "I suppose it must be."

"The worst about it," Rothbart continued, "is that we shan't escape through death. I have long supposed every Christian must secretly long for death, as I have, but no more. Now I fear it as much as anyone, knowing what I know."

"What do you know?" I asked him.

"Why, Mrs. Dowdall, you do not suppose this wilderness is quite finished with our dead, do you?"

Rothbart's good eye spilled a tear. The bad one seemed to quiver some. And somewhere, to the front of our sad, slow column, a sound like thunder rumbled ominously. I thought I heard someone, perhaps Mr. Hook, exclaim that it was the mountains to the west of us—ever to the west and never any nearer. The reverend said, "I will go and see," and he walked briskly to the head of the train, swatting at invisible insects with his hands as he went. So, too, did the shadow men gradually cease their silent investigations and make their way, one by one, past the wagons and oxen and tired, frightened pilgrims to the head of the column. Something was happening.

Something is happening.

September 22

The mountains are shaking themselves apart. We are none too closer to them than ever we have been since first they were spied by Mr. Hook, but all the same, the great, noisy quakes have frozen my heart with fear. The shadow men have left us, as though called to the mountains by the very horror that terrorizes us, and as such they have accomplished what our sorry column cannot—namely, they speed toward the crumbling peaks to the west...

Only they are not west at all, or at least not any longer. I am sure they once were, but the sun sets and rises in an entirely different pair of horizons now, so either the mountains have shaken themselves and our meager road like the hands of a clock, or the sun now rises in the south and sets in the north.

Should either astonish me? Should I be astonished that the oxen are dying, or that the whole of Reverend Rothbart's face is now riddled with swollen, red pustules that have closed his remaining eye and make it nigh impossible for the man to breathe? Must I tremble at the continued screams that fill the air to the rear of us, though none of us can see so much as one solitary tree anymore? Perhaps.

Or, perhaps my late husband was correct when once he argued for an emotional economy, that one must choose carefully what one invests care into, lest one becomes overwhelmed and drives herself mad. If this is to be my method, then I choose to fear the violently disintegrating mountains and I shall save the rest for such time that take precedence. I ignore Mrs. Penny's ghostly shrieking, and I stanch the flow of widow's tears. One waking nightmare at a time, I can all but hear Jim tell me.

In the meantime, I expect we have circled our wagons for the last time, for there is not one beast of burden amongst our holdings that could possibly carry us or our paltry property and supplies another quarter mile. Half the oxen are already dead, the other half lowing horribly in their death throes, and Mr. Hook has just shot his own horse in the brain to end the wretched creature's misery. There is no plain reason for the animals to have taken ill, gone off their feed, and die, but each one of us fears we shall be next.

We are now but eight pitiful pilgrims, and we are afoot.

September 28 or 27

Henry Penny refuses to go on, and there is no one of us who can or will argue with him about it. Instead, I have again taken charge of little Bonnie Penny, whom I carry in my arms as the remaining seven of us make our dreary way along the path without the benefit of our wagons and very little victuals to sustain us. Bonnie sobs against my neck, screaming for her Papa, and I daren't look back at the man, seated on a trunk inside the circle of wagons with a rifle across his lap. He has pledged to take care of the remaining animals, and though I promised myself I would not, I could not help but count the number of shots I hear over the course of the ten or fifteen minutes it takes Mr. Penny to fire, reload, and refire until the job is done. There were eleven animals still living when we walked away from the circle and Henry Penny. Eleven animals, and twelve shots. It is too much to bear.

A small mercy, the screaming has stopped. So, too, has most of the mountains' frightful shaking, though there comes the odd rumble now and again. In the distance, in whichever direction they now lay, the nameless peaks have been reduced to mesas surrounded by massive boulders in the foothills, the ruins of their once imperious summits. I almost wish to ask Mr. Hook whether that is our objective, knowing as well as I do that Oregonians we shall never be. It may as well be, since there is nothing else to mark on the landscape; there are no more trees, no rivers or streams, no birds in the sky or crawling things on the earth. There is not even a path, though truth to tell there has been no path to speak of since first we unwittingly diverged from the Oregon Trail. There is only us, the vast, black lands that surround us, and the impossibly distant, broken mountains toward which we seem never to gain an inch.

I might mourn that we are all alone in the world now, but I know better. Alone we may be, but we are not in the world.

October Today

We sleep on the cold, black ground, and whenever any of us awakes, the sun remains where it is now always, hidden behind the decapitated mountains, only giving the weakest, grayest light with which to find our way. We, too, have grown gray. Gray and sunken and thin, wraiths that once were pilgrims, once were people.

Rothbart's dying words were, "Water—I need water. These infernal insects." He died hardly a man at all, but rather a lumpy, pink mass of irritated flesh and seeping wounds. Mr. Quist made to retrieve the reverend's bible, that he might read something over the corpse, but the pages are thoroughly ruined by the fluids that leaked from him, crown to toe. Without tools of any kind to dig a grave, we guilty survivors move away from

Rothbart's horrid remains, leaving him to rot on the ground.

I have not prayed for him. I wonder if anybody will.

Now

Two items of interest: the children are missing and the mesas are closer.

I fell asleep with Bonnie in my arms, and I awoke to find her gone. The boy is also gone. I cannot recall his name. Only Bonnie, my poor Bonnie. Mama misses you so.

Reverend Hook cares not a whit for the children. He says if we do not tarry, we might make the mesas before exhaustion demands we rest. The mesas were the mountains and the mountains were so far away. The earth is black and the low clouds gray, and on the far, far horizons walk immense beasts with legs like stalks and heads subsumed by the great mists. It is so gratifying to see these creatures, larger than the mountains ever were, and I cannot wait to tell Jim that things are at last looking up.

Behind me walk two men and a woman, ragged, haggard, and glum. I try not to laugh at their long faces, but I find it difficult to resist. The giant beasts on the black plains roar and stomp their spindly legs, yet somehow this cheers no one but me. The woman weeps. One of the two men collapses to the ground; Jonas Tenler, I think. Reverend Mr. Hook breaks into a run for the mesas, hollering something nobody understands. This time, when I hear the rumbling, I believe it really is thunder. A storm. A storm.

Komme, says Esben Overturf, beckoning to me from the driver's box of his Conestoga wagon. The prairie schooner is tugged along on wobbling wheels with broken axles by a team of dead, skeletal oxen. *Kom, fru Dowdall, kom.*

He will not get far on those axles, not with dead oxen, for goodness' sake, but I take the Dane's hand if only to get out of the rain. To sleep where it is warm and dry, and perhaps, when I awake, to find those mountains on our back trail and our new, wonderful life on the bright horizon before us.

Won't that be wonderful, Jim, darling?

Won't that be grand?

ABOUT THE AUTHOR

Ed Kurtz is the author of The Rib from Which I Remake the World, Bleed, and other novels. His short fiction has appeared in numerous magazines and anthologies, including Best American Mystery Stories and Best Gay Stories. Ed lives in Connecticut.

BIBLIOGRAPHY

Boon
Vengeance of Boon
A Requiem for Boon
Angel of the Abyss
At the Mercy of Beasts
Bleed
Blood They Brought and Other Stories
Control
Dead Trash
The Forty-Two
Freight
Horseblood: Frontier and Weird Western Stories
Nausea
Nothing You Can Do: Stories
The Rib from Which I Remake the World
Sawbones
A Wind of Knives

Curious about other Crossroad Press books?
Stop by our site:
http://store.crossroadpress.com
We offer quality writing
in digital, audio, and print formats.